TRACKER HACKER

CODENAME: WINGER #1

JEFF ADAMS

TRACKER HACKER

CODENAME: WINGER #1

JEFF ADAMS

ALSO INCLUDES:
A VERY WINGER CHRISTMAS

"An unforgettable thrill ride! Equal parts smart and suspenseful, *Tracker Hacker* is filled with dangerous twists, nerdy fun, and a sweet romance bound to capture readers' hearts. A brilliant start to a can't-miss series."

JULIAN WINTERS, AWARD-WINNING
AUTHOR OF *RUNNING WITH LIONS*

"Jeff Adams is a genius—and *Tracker Hacker* is proof. Think Adam Silvera meets Anthony Horowitz: a YA technothriller that'll have you rooting for Theo as he faces down the bad guys and cheering as he builds a happy relationship with his boyfriend, Eddie."

GREGORY ASHE, AUTHOR OF THE
HOLLOW FOLK SERIES

PROLOGUE

I guess most people probably think their life isn't much different from their friends', and it's probably not. But mine very much is.

My name's Theo, and I'm a sixteen-year-old junior at McKinley High, where I'm a damn good, high-scoring winger for Tigers hockey.

I suck at science and literature, but I can do anything with a computer. I've been taking afternoon classes at MIT since last year.

Eddie's my awesome boyfriend. He's a science nerd who makes me swoon. All he has to do is look at me over the top of his geeky black glasses and I'll pretty much do whatever he wants. It was murder having him as my chemistry tutor last year, because all I wanted to do was make out with his cuteness.

Here's where my life gets weird.

Five years ago I used my mad computer skills to figure out why my parents often left for long periods of time.

I wanted to know why they weren't like other parents.

Usually if one parent's gone, the other is around. Not so

for me. They traveled together a lot, leaving me at home with Uncle John.

When I asked what they did for work, all they said was that they helped people for an international relief agency. I told them I was doing a report for school. They answered all my questions. But it'd seemed like I wasn't getting the whole story.

So I hacked their phones.

I discovered they were agents for something called Tactical Operational Support. They traveled around the world solving problems, though I didn't understand what kind.

Oh, and Uncle John. He's not related. He works for TOS with my parents. One of his jobs is watching out for me when Mom and Dad are away.

Mom and Dad grounded me for the phone hack.

I'd impressed TOS. They signed me on as a contractor to work with their tech teams on software and technology. Mom and Dad weren't keen on that but decided since I already knew their secret, it was okay if I helped out.

I make some serious bank on the job. It's more than enough to keep me on the cutting edge of technology, have a sweet bike, and save for college and beyond.

I work on missions sometimes, especially ones my parents handle.

My first was when I was fourteen. Uncle John woke me up in the middle of the night to break my parents out of a confinement cell. The agency techs couldn't do it, and John was certain I could. It was easy—I triangulated on the building TOS knew they were in, looked for the cell phones the bad guys were using, found the ones on the LAN, and....

I suppose I shouldn't talk about that. Ultimately I broke

my parents out and disabled the baddies by locking the doors around them.

These days I'm teaching the agency guys how to be more agile and more confident with on-the-fly coding to solve problems.

As strange as this gig is, I love it. It's a blast working through complex problems to get the job done, whether it's an emergency like saving my parents, or helping keep the agency's tech up-to-date.

It sucks not being able to tell anyone, though, especially Eddie. Mom and Dad say telling anyone could be dangerous. That's why they didn't want me to know about them.

My friends think I do consulting work through my MIT connections, which would also be awesome.

Want to know what's super cool about working for TOS?

To them I'm not Theodore Reese, or even Theo.

They call me by my codename—Winger.

ONE

"Defender, Winger here," I said once the call connected.

"Winger, thanks for getting back to me. Are you secure?"

"I'm secure enough. What's the situation?"

I was in Coach's office at the rink. Practice had ended a few minutes ago, and when I got to my locker, I found an urgent text from Dad. Officially it was from Defender, but I always translated that in my head to *Dad*. He was out on a mission, and he needed something, which was why I had to be somewhere private to talk.

This wasn't the first time I'd had to take a call here. Luckily the coaching staff let me use their offices when I needed to. They thought I sometimes took client calls and just wanted to be away from the noise of the rink. They didn't know I did secret agent stuff in here.

"Intel I have on this mission says the door I need to go through has a keypad," Dad said. "However, I found an upgraded biometric fingerprint screen. I was in touch with Doctor Possible to see if he had anything I could use to get past it, because I brought tech to deal with a keypad. Anyway he referred me to you. Seems you've got a prototype app you've been testing."

"That I do. Still working on it. It's only about 70 percent accurate. You wanna give it a try?"

"Might as well. Not much to lose and I'd rather get what I came for."

I was glad I'd grabbed my backpack when I decided to take the call, so I had my computer with me. I wished I had time to shower before calling. Sitting in a desk chair while still in my hockey gear wasn't comfortable, and it was gross having the sweat drying on me.

"Do you have a tablet with you?" I asked.

"Yup. ID three-five-seven-one-two."

"Got it. Stand by."

I logged in to the rink's Wi-Fi and scrambled my signal using TOS encryption. Then I quickly got onto the TOS network and into the program I'd been working on. Connecting to Dad's tablet was easy, and I was able to see his face looking through its camera.

"Perfect. I see you. Place the tablet against the interface. Make sure it covers all the touch points."

"Like this?" he asked.

When the tablet's camera focused, I saw blue circles where users put their fingers.

"Exactly. Hold it steady."

I put the program to work separating out the fingerprints. The great thing about these panels, at least from a break-in point of view, was they weren't often cleaned. It was easy to lift prints, and using the same forensics software police used, piece the prints together. Then, using a system of my own design, the program projected the prints back to the touch pad.

"The prints are built." The program had worked for less than a minute.

Time for the real test. When the app failed, it was usually a problem with projecting the prints strong enough for the reader to capture. Time to see if I'd fixed that problem.

The panel flashed green, and I heard the success tone through Dad's phone.

"Yes!" I was louder than I meant to be.

"Well done, Winger. That did it. I gotta move. Thanks."

"Great. Let me know if you need anything else."

He cut the connection and that was that. There was no time for pleasantries when he was working.

I hustled back to the locker room because I was late to meet Eddie. I got showered and stowed my gear in record time. As I headed for one of the rink's exits, I looked around for Eddie but didn't see him where he usually waited. I didn't see his Jeep in the parking lot either, which was weird because I thought he was picking me up.

I pulled out my phone and found nothing from him.

Instead I discovered I had more than fifty unread emails from TOS. There'd been nothing when I'd gone into practice two hours earlier. It'd been quiet for weeks with just the usual chatter between me and Lorenzo Davenport, my main TOS contact. He was the Doctor Possible Dad had referenced. I tended to call him Doc P.

Besides the fingerprint scanner, Lorenzo and I were working on a new authentication system for agents accessing the TOS network. I'd suggested the upgrade because I'd found some security holes one day while I was helping Dad.

According to the emails, something was up with tracker chips. I didn't even know what those were, and I thought I knew all the agency's tech. It sounded serious. I picked the most recent message and scrolled through the long chain. Something about the system going off-line for a few minutes, followed by a handful of agents not showing up in the system anymore. TOS declared a Code 1-2B alert, which was one step down from the highest possible.

I dialed Lorenzo to see what was up and if I could help. He picked up before it even rang on my end.

"Doctor Possible, Winger here."

There was never a hello with these guys. Protocol was to give the name of who you were expecting to talk to, followed by your own codename. I'd found out the hard way how much they enforced that, when I called Lorenzo once and said something like "Hey, Doc P, what's goin' on?" He'd instantly fried my phone to make a point about following directions.

"Winger. Were you able to help Defender?"

"Yeah. We can mark down one field test. It worked like a charm."

"Awesome," he said excitedly. Despite being a stickler for procedures, Lorenzo was always excited when new tech worked right. "So you saw the emails?"

"Yeah. What are these tracker chips anyway?"

"Really?" He sounded exasperated. "One second?"

I heard him typing lightning fast. The clicking of his keys was one of my favorite things about talking to him. The *clickity-clack* was soothing to me for some weird reason.

"Sorry, Winger. I gotta go. Red Hat's calling an emergency meeting."

"Understood. Let me know if I can help out."

"Will do."

He hung up.

Where are you?

The screen lit up with a message from Eddie before I could pocket my phone.

I typed and sent my reply: *What do you mean where am I? Where are you? Thought we were meeting at the rink.*

Um. Yeah. I'm waiting at the pizza place.

Oops. Totally forgot we were eating there.

Be right there.

I sprinted through the rink—the six-rink facility—so I had to dodge around people. I finally came up behind Eddie, kissed his fuzzy head, and wrapped my arms around his shoulders.

"I'm so sorry," I said. "I thought we were headed straight to your place."

He put his hands on mine and tilted his head back just enough so I could kiss his forehead.

"Did you end up with a head injury? We decided to eat first since it's Cheap Pizza Tuesday."

"Right." Oops. Totally forgot the plan. "I ran suicides right at the end of practice and then talked to a client for a few minutes. I guess I got flustered because I knew I was late."

The suicides were true, but I hated lying about the rest.

"Not a problem. When I saw Tommy and Mitch leave but I hadn't seen you yet, I sent the text." He craned his head back farther, and I leaned over so I could kiss his full lips. "You're here now, so let's eat and then we can go."

I put my backpack on the table next to his, and we got in the pizza line to fill up on two-for-one slices. We'd discovered this a couple of weeks ago and decided we'd milk it for all it was worth because the rink pizza was good.

Eddie Cochrane had transferred to my school at the start of sophomore year. I'd seen him around before he became my tutor, but I was too intimidated to introduce myself. He was way too cute with his bushy afro and inquisitive brown eyes, which were always darting around behind his nerdy black-framed glasses. He swam and had the tall, lean physique you'd expect. He didn't join the school team until this year, but last year he'd practiced every morning as if he had.

It only took one tutoring session at his house for me to get up the courage to ask him out. I thought I was getting a vibe from him, and I didn't have much to lose. Even if I misread his interest—at the time I didn't know if he was gay or not—I didn't expect him to go off on me or anything.

Turned out he wanted to ask me but he'd been too shy, even though he knew I was out. We laughed later about how skittish we'd been about asking each other.

He taught me chemistry. I helped him in courses where logic was key, because I used that kind of thinking with my computer work.

We each learned about the other's sport too. He ragged on me because I was so covered up when I played, whereas I got to drink in his sleek, sexy body anytime I watched him practice. Eddie in those tight swim shorts was a sight to behold. I was already looking forward to December when his season would start.

Honestly I loved how heads turned when we were together. He was a half foot taller than me and his dark skin was such a contrast to my pale, freckled complexion. Add my flaming-red hair and you couldn't help but notice us.

"Look at you," Eddie said after I'd ordered six slices.

"Long practice plus cheap food means I'm trying one of every pie they've got out."

"So you'll have plenty of energy to, oh, I don't know, make out for a while?"

Yes!

"There's always energy for that." I collected my food, and waited for him to get his paltry two slices.

As soon as we sat down, I tore into a slice of hawaiian. As Eddie only got two slices, I needed to eat fast. I didn't want to lose out on any more make-out time than I already had.

"So I was wondering." He sounded unsure and paused. That was odd, because he usually had no trouble saying what was on his mind. "Um. Do you think we could go to the fall dance in a couple weeks?"

Interesting. Usually going out meant movies, food, maybe a party at someone's house. We'd never gone to a school thing. Did he even know how to dance? I sure didn't.

"It'd be something different," he continued. "See if we like it. Maybe it's a dry run for prom in the spring? Something to think about since we're juniors now."

School'd only been back for a few weeks, and he was already thinking about spring. That was cool.

I nodded while I chewed. "Sure," I said finally able to talk. "Why not? Do you know how to dance or are we going to look silly?"

"I've got no idea. I tap my foot to music. I've never really tried to do more."

"Okay, so it'll be a couple of firsts, I guess."

Eddie smiled big. I wondered if the dance was on our anniversary. It'd be right around then, so we should be doing something special for that anyway.

My phone vibrated in my jacket pocket—four pulses, a pause, and four more. It was TOS, most likely Lorenzo. I had to answer, which sucked because I wanted to give Eddie my full attention.

"Sorry." I pulled the phone out and checked the screen. "It's the client I was talking to earlier."

Eddie gave me an annoyed look but kept eating. He hated it when I had to take work calls when we were together. Most of our friends, if they worked, had a job with very clear-cut hours. Mine could be all over the place, and sometimes involved emergencies.

I couldn't ignore the call, so I said nothing and answered.

"Winger. Doctor Possible here."

"Doctor. What's up?"

"Can you talk?"

"Nope."

"Okay, just listen. I've got to get you access to the actual system, but here's the basic scoop."

I listened closely. Because I was in public, I couldn't take notes like I would in a secure location. At least I'd tricked out my phone with encryption and a special speaker to ensure the TOS-side of conversations couldn't be overheard.

"Some background first. All TOS agents have an implant tucked just behind their left ear that allows us to track them."

This was news to me. Did my parents have them? Did they know they had them? Did I have one? Technically I'm an agent, even though I'm not traveling around the world. I felt around my left ear, which made Eddie raise an eyebrow at me. I didn't feel anything out of the ordinary.

"The trackers work unless the agent is somewhere that the signal can't penetrate," Lorenzo continued. "With Wi-Fi and cell towers everywhere, that doesn't happen very often. Anyway someone has hacked the system. A dozen or so agents are off the tracking grid, and we can't get in touch with some of them. A couple of others have had their IDs switched inside our system."

I had to choose my question carefully so I wouldn't reveal sensitive information. "Why do you think it's a hack and not a failure?"

"Logs show traffic that's not ours making requests through what should've been secure nodes. It started a few days ago. We thought we had it plugged, but today things got worse."

"What can I do?"

Lorenzo sighed, which was unusual for him. "Right now, nothing. I'm working to get the system available to you so you can have a look. Mission Ops denied the initial request, so I've escalated it to Raptor, because I think your skill can be very useful."

Whoa. If he took it all the way to Raptor, this was serious. Raptor was *the* head guy and for him to be involved in a question of clearance was abnormal. Usually Joanna Bristow, aka Red Hat, aka Lorenzo's boss, could take care of anything access related. I'd only talked to Raptor once, and that was when I first started working with TOS. He wanted to meet the kid who hacked their phone system.

The other question I had, that I couldn't ask while I was in public: why was it such a problem to clear me? I thought I had access to everything.

"Okay. Let me know."

"Will do. Thanks, Winger."

I hung up and set my phone on the table. "Sorry about that."

Eddie shrugged, but the roll of his eyes told me he was less than happy. He wouldn't talk about it.

"Everything okay?" he finally asked.

"Yeah." I took a bite of my pizza before I continued. "Client thinks someone's hacked their system. I'll probably have to do some work on it later."

I talked as I ate. It was something we both did, even though our parents hated it.

Eddie took the veggie slice off my plate and chomped into it. "I'll help you eat faster. That way we can get outta here." He grinned before taking another bite.

"You've got a one-track mind today, and I like the track."

At least Eddie's mood cleared quickly. I leaned over and we kissed. Eddie and I hadn't had much alone time lately, so part of me hoped Raptor wasn't going to make a decision for a couple of hours.

Yes, I wanted to dig into the problem. But I hated the frustrated look Eddie had while I was on the phone. It was a difficult split. I loved Eddie, but I loved my job too. There were only so many hours in the day.

We scarfed the pizza and then headed to the parking lot. Once we got to the bike rack, I unlocked my bike, and rode to Eddie's Jeep.

"I'll see you in a few minutes," I said. "Maybe I'll beat you this time."

"That's only happened once and only because of traffic."

I scooted up to him as he unlocked the door and gave him a kiss. Then I sped away to race him to his house.

I HATED LEAVING Eddie's house. A couple of hours tangled around each other under the covers was difficult to walk away from. But we both had homework. Plus it would look really bad if his parents caught us undressed when they got home, which would be soon.

I'm pretty sure our parents knew we messed around, but they all made it clear they expected us to behave most of the time. When I was at Eddie's house, there was a door-open policy—of course that only happened when his parents were actually there.

We never could've gotten away with what we'd just done at my house. When my parents were gone, Uncle John, aka Shotgun, was there. He's Mom and Dad's primary support for missions. For a while that included babysitting me. Now it's more about appearances—making sure an adult is around when they're gone for long stretches—because I'm old enough to take care of myself.

It still sucked never to have the house to myself. At least Eddie has that fairly often.

It was an exhilarating ride home. Eddie lived about five

miles away, and on crisp fall evenings, I loved the trip. I zipped all over the place on my road bike. I was speedy. No one understood my obsession with the riding as I had a perfectly good driver's license. But on the bike, I was never stuck in traffic, and I got to enjoy the outdoors.

Mom and John were both home. They must be strategizing something if John was here. Maybe they were working on the tracker issue too. I hadn't heard back from Lorenzo yet, which was strange. If it'd become such a high-profile issue, I didn't understand why my access was still a problem. The emails were still flying around. I hadn't caught up on them, but several had come in while I was with Eddie.

I parked my bike in the garage, putting it up onto its rack to help remind myself to pump up the front tire in the morning. I could tell it was a bit flat because of how the bike handled on the way home. I had a corner of the garage for my bike work. I liked to try out new hardware from time to time, like swapping out the derailleur, to make sure it was lean and fast.

In the house the kitchen was empty, as was the living room. Mom and John were in the office she and Dad shared. You'd think a house where two operatives lived would have an office tricked out with gadgets, but it didn't. Mom and Dad each had a laptop and a couple of monitors. It looked like a basic home-office setup with an antique oak partners desk, which allowed them to face each other. John had a separate desk along the wall with a similar setup. The office looked nothing like a high-tech base of operations. The three of them might as well have been accountants.

Mom and John huddled around her computer.

"Hey, Mom." I went over and gave her a quick hug.

"Hey, John." He and I did our usual fist bump with an explosion.

I didn't put myself in a position to look at the screens. I knew better. They respected my workspace upstairs and I respected theirs. We were each cleared for different things. Many of the projects I worked on in the tech world were things they weren't allowed to see. Missions that Mom, Dad, and John worked on were often outside my clearance unless I was their assigned tech support.

"How was school?" Mom asked.

"S'okay. American Literature is going to make my head explode. It's so boring."

John clutched his chest like I'd just stabbed him. "Ouch."

Mom and I both turned to him, surprised.

"What? I minored in American Lit. If I wasn't doing this, I might've been a teacher."

Mom raised an eyebrow and went back to her screen. I looked at John like he'd just grown an extra head.

"Wait. You were a cop before you joined the agency." I dropped my backpack and sat down in a nearby chair.

"I was. I graduated with a major in English and the lit minor, but after graduation I went on to the police academy. Who knows, I may still teach one day."

"Maybe you can tell me why I should read about the early 1900s in some book called *Ragtime*. It seems irrelevant."

"Oh, Theo, there's so much in that book that's important today," he said with more enthusiasm than I thought possible. "I can help you. We'll talk later."

"I'm glad you like a challenge. So, I've got a question." I changed the topic. "Do I have one of those tracker chips in me?"

Mom and John traded a glance that gave me the answer before they said a word. Did they really think I'd miss that? I rubbed behind my left ear again and didn't feel anything unusual. Of course if it was always there, it wouldn't feel unusual.

"You do," Mom said.

The look of irritation I gave her probably would've gotten me in trouble with most parents, but things were different here. "How could you not tell me?" The irritation went right into my voice too.

"Everyone has them," she said. She closed the laptop and focused on me. "Remember when you had your tonsils out right before your twelfth birthday?"

Of course. If I had thought about it long enough, I'd have figured that out. It was the only surgery I'd ever had. I'd had broken bones and sprains from hockey, but those hadn't provided a moment where something could be implanted without my knowing about it—unless it was some groovy nanotech. As far as I knew, TOS didn't have that kind of capability yet.

"Why didn't you tell me?" I returned to the issue. "That's not exactly fair."

John backed away from the desk and leaned on the credenza. He wasn't going to get involved in this.

"You were twelve," Mom said. "We thought it best we didn't try to explain that there was something in you that would track your every move. Even now you don't like the idea."

She was right. I didn't have anything to hide—well, okay, I did. It wasn't like I wanted people to know I spent hours unsupervised in Eddie's bedroom. And knowing how TOS designs tech, I was sure it could capture that specific detail.

"It's standard issue," she continued. "Anyone who works for TOS has one whether they're in the field or not. The only reason you didn't get one as soon as you started is because we were trying to keep you out of that until you were older. But when that surgery came up, they insisted."

I shook my head. "I work on some of the most complex and sensitive aspects of TOS's tech and I don't get to find out I've got a chip that tracks my location?" My voice got louder.

Mom nodded, looking sympathetic. "We made a bad choice. Especially to keep it a secret so long. You're right. You carry a significant responsibility, and you should've been aware. We made a mistake. TOS left it to us to tell you. You wouldn't have been exempt from having the implant, but you should've been aware."

As usual she knew how to defuse me with her apologetic tone. It was easy to see why she was so good at what she did. She could be so diplomatic it was impossible to stay mad and not see her point of view.

"So who's watching me?"

"I would guess no one. Protocol is that we only actively track agents on missions. We don't look at day-to-day behavior unless there are special circumstances. Unless Lorenzo or Joanna have motives that we wouldn't know about, you wouldn't be tracked."

My phone buzzed in my pocket. It was a TOS call, most likely Lorenzo.

"Sorry," I said to Mom as I answered.

Lorenzo gave the usual opening.

"Hey, Doc. What's the latest?"

"Red Hat got in touch with Raptor, and you're cleared for the tech. Are you home? Can I walk you through the basics?"

"Sure. Hold on." I put him on mute. "I need to go. One last question. Do you and Dad track me?"

"No. Absolutely not," she said, and her tone left no doubt it was the truth. "Understand that the only way we could access your info would be for a mission. We've never done that. Besides, I would hope you know that we trust you."

I nodded and came around the desk to hug her again. "Thanks, Mom."

I picked up my backpack and headed out.

"Don't forget your homework," Mom called as I headed up the stairs.

"I won't."

At my door I gripped the knob and waited for it to vibrate. It was a special bit of tech I'd worked on with Lorenzo to secure a door without something like a keypad or a visible fingerprint reader. In this case, the reader was in the doorknob. It only opened for me, my parents, or John. If anyone else tried it, it would simply stay locked. There was no audible alarm, although my phone got a message anytime someone other than me touched the knob, and I knew if the door opened or not. Plus TOS got a record of it since there were sensitive things in my room.

It was bonus security on top of the tech in the computers. I had a standard laptop I used for school and personal stuff. I'd added security measures to it so I could use it away from home, like helping Dad earlier. Three other computers on my desk connected to TOS and were used for the work I did for them. I could also do a lot on my phone because it was souped up and very secure. I also had a computer specifically for gaming.

Was it over the top? No.

I constantly worked with Lorenzo to increase the security of the network and the things we did on it. Not to mention trying to come up with new, useful features that could integrate with the agents' phones. TOS probably had the smartest smartphones anywhere.

My room was unlike any of my friends'. Half of it was pretty unremarkable—dark-gray walls, a bed, dresser, closet, and bookshelf. The gray had been my choice, because it gave the room a sleek look. There were posters of my favorite hockey players—Crosby, Zetterberg, Crawford—and that was it.

The other side was tech heaven. The desk was U-shaped, and the computers and monitors arranged for optimal work, whether I was working for TOS, doing home-work, or playing games. Steel rack shelves held spare computer parts as well as various routers and processors, which were a mix of functional and for show. I liked the flashing lights, so I have some equipment that's decorative—if anyone paid attention when music was playing, they'd see some of the lights pulse to the rhythm. To finish it off, I had a couple of chairs I could pull closer to the monitors when it was time for hardcore game sessions.

Basically my room was perfect.

I tossed my pack on the bed and then took Lorenzo off mute as I closed the door.

"Okay, I'm secure. What's the update?"

"It's bad. We've been over the logs for the past several days, and we can't find the breach. We've tested several different methods and haven't been able to hack the system ourselves."

I dropped into my very comfy, leather, high-backed chair, which I could sit in for hours. I fired up the screens and logged in to TOS with my password, retina scan, and fingerprint, and I saw what Lorenzo was sharing to my screen: Screenshots of logs, schematics on the chip, and details on the missing agents and the ones who had their IDs changed.

"Are you sure it's a breach and not that the agents have been individually targeted somehow or, a less fatal option, that chips have failed?"

Lorenzo hesitated. I wished I had him on video so I could see why he paused.

"We've been in touch with some of the agents who have disappeared from tracking. Of the ones we can talk to, they say there's nothing out of the ordinary going on. Six of seven aren't even deployed. The others we can't locate at all, deployed or not. Two have missed check-ins."

This was bad. Even under the most difficult of circumstances, protocols and tech were in place to ensure a check-in could always take place.

"Okay. How do these things work anyway?"

Lorenzo launched into a half hour of technical specs as different images flashed across my screens. The gist of it was, the chips used the existing network, much like a phone uses Wi-Fi, cell networks, and whatever else it can, for GPS location. It wasn't just the civilian network TOS used—military and government networks also provided data. From what Lorenzo said, it seemed the chips could ping off practically anything. To mask the chip's real function, it would mimic an array of phones, allowing it to ping the available networks as a different device every time. The list of possible phones was massive, so the odds of it showing up as the same phone in the same place was statistically unlikely. To top it off, layers of encryption and security were in place to prevent the chip's ping from being identified and traced. There was even more security to keep the locator system itself from unauthorized access. Admin access needed one of the highest clearances possible, which is why Raptor approved my credentials.

"I don't suppose you see anything obvious in all this information?"

"I'd love to say yes."

"I was really hoping you'd give one of your snarky 'why didn't you look at that' comments."

"Sorry, Doc. Let me spend some time with this. Can you send me a chip? It'd help a lot if I had one here to work with."

"I'll messenger you one tonight."

"Thanks. I'll keep you posted. Even if it's just a random idea."

"We'll do the same. Thanks, Winger."

I disconnected the call and dropped the phone onto my desk.

The system seemed sound, both in terms of how it functioned but also the security. Of course anything on a network can be hacked. You just have to hope you design well enough—or change it so often—the flaws aren't exploitable.

I reviewed everything Lorenzo had gone over to see if I'd missed anything. After that, I turned to my homework. I worked best on problems if I did something else while another part of my brain churned on it. So I decided to kill two birds with one stone and get ready for tomorrow's classes.

"Theo, man, we kicked ass today," said Mitch, our team captain and one of my best friends. "If we can keep that up in Friday's game, we're gonna beat Cullman and knock them off that number one perch."

We bumped fists as we entered the locker room.

"Yeah!" Practice had me pumped. "Those patterns Coach has us doing are working now that we're doing them right."

I've been tight with Mitch since we met on a team when we were six. We've played together as linemates, whether on teams or in pickup games, ever since. It was a huge score when he moved into McKinley's district as a freshman. Coach saw our chemistry immediately and our partnership continued uninterrupted.

My locker was a jumble because I'd just tossed everything in when I got changed. I hit some nasty traffic coming from MIT. I was on the sidewalk walking my bike for a few blocks. I hated being late for practice, even though Coach knew I cut it close on Mondays and Wednesdays. He was cool with it. I was not.

I needed my phone, which meant getting my sweaty hockey hands all over everything, because my clothes weren't hanging up in an organized fashion.

Ick.

I'd had an idea during practice about how the chip hack might've happened and I wanted to give Lorenzo the info now, because I was still an hour or so away from being home. I opened up my TOS inbox and scanned the incident email thread to see if there was relevant new info.

Around me the guys went about their postgame routines. I sat on the bench, intent on my screen.

"Everything okay?" Mitch asked. "Not like you to not head straight for the shower."

"Had some ideas about a problem I'm working on for a client. Wanted to send it off while it was fresh in my head."

"I'm glad they pay you well. You work at some of the strangest times."

I wrote: *Is it possible for the security protocols to malfunction in a chip? Maybe change how it's identified? Are there diagnostics or anything that run to ensure chips work correctly?*

I sent it off.

I'd either see some response in the thread or from Lorenzo directly. I got out of my gear and left it on the floor outside my locker. With my clothes in a jumble, I couldn't put things away, so I'd deal with it after I was clean.

Even though I ended up being last into the shower, we all had our spots, so I took my place in a stall between Mitch and Tommy.

"You and Eddie want to hit a movie with Iris and me this weekend?" Mitch asked. "Maybe do some laser tag after?"

"Iris wants to play laser tag? That's random. Usually

she just shoots up a video game like the rest of us." I looked at Mitch over the three-quarter wall to see if he was joking. He looked serious, and I didn't know what to make of it.

"Right?" He half looked at me as he shampooed his short brown hair. "Her debate team has been challenged by Lancaster's to a paintball game. I'm not sure how debate turns into paintball, but she figures laser tag is good practice while being less messy."

"Hard to fault that logic. I'm in. Let me ask Eddie. I'm not sure where he stands on the whole laser tag thing."

"Fair enough," Mitch said. "It'll certainly be a different kind of date."

"That's for sure. Laser tag doesn't even cross my mind."

Despite getting in last, I was still one of the first out of the shower, following right behind Mitch. I wanted to get home and poke around some more on the tracker problem before Eddie came over. We had an eight o'clock date that involved watching the Bruins game while doing homework.

"I'll text you later about this weekend," I told Mitch while I straightened out my locker and got dressed.

"Cool," he said. "I'm already thinking it's me and Iris versus you and Eddie. It'll be fun to take you guys down."

"You think that's how it'll play out?" I asked, slightly annoyed he would discount hundreds, if not thousands, of hours of video-game play. "You know Eddie and I are a solid CoD team. As soon as we take one of you out, we'll double-team the other. Game over."

Mitch got quiet and I knew I had him. Finally he just rolled his eyes and stepped over so we could bump fists.

"Later, man." He grinned as he spoke, another game of who can trash-talk better ended with a win for me.

"Later."

I quickly stored my gear in its usual way so it had a chance of drying out before tomorrow's practice.

Leaving the locker room, I had to make a hard stop so I wouldn't run into a guy who stood just outside. It wasn't a smart place to stand.

"Whoa. Sorry," I said as I moved to get around him.

"You're Theo Reese, right?"

I stopped and turned to face him. I recognized him from school, but I didn't know him.

"Yeah," I said hesitantly.

"I hear you're good with computers. That true?" This kid, who was maybe a freshman, sounded terrified.

"Depends," I said, hedging my bets. My skills were widely known among my friends and through much of the junior class. The fact this kid wasn't sure gave me pause.

"My mom's in trouble. Someone's trying to take me away from her and put me with my dad. She's got the signed papers. But everything in the court computer says I should be with Dad, and he's got papers I know can't be real. Mom's lawyer can't seem to do anything because the judge says the computer has to be right. They think my mom forged her papers since the judge that signed them is dead and none of his staff can clearly remember a case from two years ago." He paused and it looked like he might cry. Thankfully he managed to keep himself together. "I can't end up with my dad."

Shit. My friends also knew better than to ask me something like this. I'd made it clear a long time ago that I wouldn't do anything illegal. But how do I ignore the look this kid is giving me?

"I'm sorry. It'd be against the law for me to even try to find traces of someone changing the information in the court's computer without permission."

"But someone already got in and messed it up, you'd just be—"

"I'm sorry." I cut him off because he was getting loud and a couple of my teammates stared at us as they left the locker room. Maybe the school could help. "Have you talked to the principal? It must be in your file who your legal guardian is. It isn't likely the school's computer is directly connected to the court. And if your father's hurting you, they can certainly get you help." My phone pulsed the TOS ring. "Look, I'm sorry, I have to answer this."

I turned from the kid and moved a couple of paces away to answer. Since I'd just emailed Lorenzo a few minutes ago, the call was a surprise.

"What's new?" I asked after Lorenzo ID'd himself.

"I got your email. Interesting idea. Are you going to investigate?"

"Yeah." I considered my words carefully. "I wanted to share it since I'm not sure I can create a malfunction."

"I'll have someone here work on it too. There's a theory we're working on that the trackers might be breaking down in the body, which could play into the idea you had of a malfunction. The agents whose trackers went off the grid have had them more than six years."

That was an interesting idea.

"What about the people with the changed IDs who haven't checked in?" I asked.

"That's why this is only a theory. One of the agents who hadn't checked in has surfaced and we verified the reason behind the lack of check-in. We still haven't heard from one. The IDs—I'm with you. That's still fishy. Have you had any luck with the chip we sent?"

"Haven't had much time with it yet, but working on it more tonight."

"Understood. We'll talk later."

We disconnected. I turned back, and the kid was gone. I'd dodged that—at least for the moment.

In the parking lot, I took my pack off so I could put my U-lock away after I unlocked my bike. There was an envelope jammed into one of the smaller pockets.

"Damn," I said softly, opening it.

Cullen Watson was his name. He left me copies of the information he'd said changed. I didn't want this stuff. I also couldn't shake the look he gave me when I said I couldn't help. I was more about stopping hackers, not getting in and hacking myself. I didn't even have proof he was telling the truth.

I'd try to find him tomorrow and talk some more. Maybe there was someone I could send him to who could help legally.

I stuffed the lock in my pack, slung it over my shoulders, and headed for home. The ride wasn't very relaxing today, since my brain crunched on two issues at once. I looked forward to Eddie showing up. He'd make for a great distraction while I worked these things out.

FOUR

Eddie had me pressed up against my locker while he laid kisses on me. I had more bulk than he did, but he knew how to use his tall, lean frame—not to mention his lips—to make me do exactly what he wanted. It wasn't fair, because I needed to take off for my Friday MIT class, but I wasn't going to complain.

Classmates hurrying to get out of school filled the halls. We weren't the only ones taking a moment for ourselves at the end of the day, though. We were definitely the best-looking couple—at least as far as I was concerned.

"Do I need to separate you two?" It was Mitch.

I opened my eyes to find Eddie had extended a hand with the middle finger raised. He intensified the kiss, which forced me to close my eyes. I was weak in the knees when he pulled away.

"No need, man. I'm done with him now." Eddie wiggled his eyebrows at me and we both laughed, which made Mitch give one of his signature eye rolls.

"I hear you're in for the date tomorrow night," Mitch said to Eddie as we all walked toward the parking lot.

"Oh yeah," Eddie said. "Looking forward to taking you guys out."

"I gotta go." I checked my watch and saw I had just enough time to make the trip. I leaned in for one more kiss with Eddie. "I love you." Turning to Mitch, I said, "See you for the game in a few hours." We fist-bumped as I left.

Eddie'd kissed me a little too long, but I was pretty sure I'd be able to make up the time.

I waved when Eddie passed me in his Jeep as he pulled out of the parking lot and turned left. As I watched him go, I saw a gray van parked on the curb that bordered the school. The tinted windows were so dark I could barely see the outline of the driver through the windshield. If this were the elementary school, I'd wonder if they were planning to snatch a kid.

I snickered quietly. I clearly watched too much TV growing up. I sped out of the parking lot, going right, and settled into the bike lane. My legs pumped as I cranked up the speed. It was a chilly day, and the wind was bracing against my face, but I loved it. Traffic was good as far as I could see, so I pushed to get to my max speed because I'd wanted to get to campus with time enough to get coffee before class.

It was a perfect fall day. The sun was out, allowing the leaves to show off their bright colors. The next few days were likely to be perfect riding weather. Maybe I could snag Eddie for a picnic this weekend. The sun should make it warm enough to sit outside for a while.

At a stop sign a couple of blocks from the school, the gray van pulled alongside me. There was no doubt it was the same van because of the windows. Who tints that dark? It made the van creepy. After it pulled away from the stop sign, it spent a few moments matching my speed. I shot the driver an inquisitive look. With no cars in front, the driver shouldn't want to go my speed. Either my gaze, or the cars behind, snapped the driver back to reality because it sped up.

Weird.

After going over the Chelsea River, I turned onto my favorite street—it was a mix of businesses, houses, and scattered trees. The traffic also wasn't insane. Suddenly the van was back and parallel to me again. What the hell? Had I pissed the driver off with the look I'd given him? I didn't spook easily, but this felt weird.

I could've called John, but he'd think I was being foolish. I triggered a call to Eddie on my watch as I kept pedaling down the street.

"Are you biking and calling?" Eddie asked as he answered.

"Yeah, but I'm on the watch, so it's okay," I said, louder than I wanted to, but I had to make sure he heard me.

"I should've figured that, since I hear the wind. What's up?"

"Did you see that creepy-looking van when you left school?"

"The one with the major tint job? Yeah. Why?"

"I think it's following me."

"And why would it do that?"

"I dunno. But it's here just in front of me, and it's the second time it's turned up."

"Where are you?"

"Williams Street, almost to Dunkin Donuts." The van sped up and made a left turn. Maybe I was paranoid.

"I'll catch up to you. I'm just leaving school again, because I forgot to get the books I needed from the library."

"Thanks. It's probably nothing."

"Yeah, you just want to see me again."

"Only always."

"See you in a few. I'm leaving the parking lot now."

"You're the best."

"Yes, I am," he said and disconnected.

I kept going, and the van was nowhere in sight. I'm gonna owe Eddie for taking him out of his way. I cruised down the street and almost stopped because the donuts smelled so good. They must've just made a fresh batch. If I wasn't already late, I'd have a break for sure. As I passed and the sweet aroma faded, I was sad I couldn't go back.

Suddenly the van passed me. It must have come back onto the street at the intersection.

The van pulled ahead, jerked into the bike lane, and stopped. I crushed the levers to engage the front and back brakes.

There wasn't enough room and the front tire slammed into the van's bumper. The rear wheel lifted up, and for a moment, I thought I was going to be thrown into the doors. Instead the wheel dropped back to the ground, and me and the bike fell over because I couldn't get my feet planted.

Two guys jumped out of the back. I was sluggish from the impact as I worked to untangle from my bike, but I noticed they were wearing masks. It was cold but not that cold.

I struggled to get up, but the bike wasn't cooperating. I heard traffic going by. Why wasn't anyone stopping?

One dude gripped my shoulders and pulled me up. The other yanked the bike out from between my legs and tossed it toward the sidewalk.

"Hey? What the hell? I—"

The guy who threw the bike stuffed a cloth in my mouth, so I spoke muffled gibberish.

A horn sounded frantically. Someone was really laying into their horn, and it sounded like it was coming toward us.

Struggling against the guy holding me was futile. He was like the Hulk. The other guy grabbed my legs, and they threw me into the van. I landed with a thud and a grunt. I quickly stood despite the pain radiating through me. Hulk shoved me back down as the other guy closed the door, and the van took off.

This was bad.

I looked to the front of the van but couldn't see the driver because of the blacked-out window. The horn was close, though, right behind us maybe. Eddie. It had to be. Maybe he saw what happened.

Fuck. I thought fast about my options. I couldn't see where they were taking me. Between Eddie being outside, and it had to be him, and the TOS chip in my neck, they'd find me. I could also make like they were a defensive pair, try to fake them out, open the doors, and jump.

I scrambled to my feet. I'd get out and Eddie'd pick me up. We'd get the plate number and call the police.

Bad choice.

Hulk pulled a gun. I froze.

"Sit down." He spoke softly, but he made up for the lack of volume with a menacing tone. I complied.

The honking stopped. What happened? Eddie had to be out there. What if he'd stopped at a light, though? Would he let me get out of sight?

The van's brakes screeched under us as it came to a hard stop. We hurtled toward the front of the van, slamming into the steel bulkhead. Hulk lost his gun as he tumbled.

It was time to go.

Pain be damned, I was up and smashing through the door. Luckily I'd been in enough vans because of travel hockey that I didn't have to guess how the door release worked.

I jumped out and got rid of the cloth in my mouth. I heard sirens in the distance. Had Eddie called? Or maybe someone who saw me get knocked off my bike?

I limped around the side of the van and caught sight of the driver poking his head out of the window. He wore a cap and sunglasses. It was gonna be hard to give a description of him.

Then I saw what we hit.

No. No. No.

The van had hit Eddie's Jeep.

I turned at the noise behind me. Hulk emerged from the van.

I can't leave Eddie.

I can't stay here.

Hulk was on me in my moment of indecision. Instincts kicked in and I dodged his grab, moving back and out of his reach, as if I were avoiding a defenseman. He came at me again and this time I landed a punch against his jaw and sent him backward. He fixed a steely glare on me as he charged forward.

"Leave him," the driver called out. "We gotta go. The cops are coming."

Hulk grabbed for my wrist and ended up with nothing but shirt. The fabric gave out as he pulled, and I lowered my center of gravity to resist. I fell against the van while he stumbled backward.

"Leave him, or I'm leaving you," the driver said, already backing up the van.

Hulk bolted to the rear doors and got in. The other guy must've been hurt because he didn't help Hulk recapture me. I was thankful for that. The van sounded rough, but it kept going, and I saw Hulk close the doors as it passed.

What the hell was happening?

A groan from Eddie focused me. His head moved to the side. The van's impact had crushed the Jeep's door.

I pulled my phone and dialed John in secure mode.

Traffic slowly went around Eddie's car. People looked, but no one stopped. The sirens were getting closer.

"Shotgun," I said when he answered. "Winger here."

"Really? Shouldn't you be in class?"

"I...." I had no idea what the protocol was. I'd never had to call for help before.

"Winger?"

"I need help. Someone just tried to...."

"Okay." John's voice was soothing. "Calm down. Where are you?"

"Um...." I looked around for street signs. "Williams Street. Near Cherry. Someone grabbed me. I was in a van. Eddie...." I ran up to the Jeep. His eyes fluttered like he couldn't focus. "Eddie cut them off. He's hurt."

"Stand by." I heard John typing. "Are you hurt?" he finally asked.

"Maybe. Probably just bruises."

"I've got an ambulance and police coming. They'll address you by codename first for confirmation and then by your regular name."

"I already hear sirens."

"I had those diverted. We need agents at your scene just in case."

"Theo?" It was Eddie. I stopped listening to John.

"I'm here." The window was on the pavement, so I leaned through the empty frame. His face was peppered with cuts, some large enough for blood to flow. I pulled a glove out of my jacket pocket and used it to get some of the blood off him.

"I can't move," he struggled to say.

"Stand by," I said into the phone before I jammed it in my jeans pocket.

The door gouged into his side, no doubt causing him breathing trouble. A bloody spot on his shirt slowly got larger. I took off my backpack so I could get out of my sweatshirt. I balled it up and put it against Eddie's side. He hissed as I applied pressure.

"I've called for help."

I ran my hand through his hair, trying to be soothing.

"Are you okay? I saw them...."

His eyes fluttered closed.

"*Eddie?*" I pulled my phone out and screamed into it as I tried to keep pressure on the sweatshirt. "You gotta get someone here now!"

"Are you guys okay?" I jumped at the woman's voice. She was in a plaid shirt, jeans, and an apron. I couldn't tell where she came from. "I heard the crash from the back of the shop. I called the cops."

"Winger, they'll be there in a couple of minutes." John used the same voice he'd used on me when I was six and thought there was a monster under the bed. He tried to calm me down. "Who's there with you? That didn't sound like Eddie. Is he conscious?"

"Oh man," the woman said as she looked closer at Eddie.

It was too much to process with this woman I didn't know plus Eddie's injuries and John on the phone.

"He was," I said into the phone, ignoring the question about the stranger. "He keeps looking like he's trying to wake up."

"Can you get the door open?"

"Let me see."

I left the sweatshirt and tried to secure it in place with the seat belt to keep some pressure. I tried the door. It was stuck.

"Help me!" I yelled at the stranger. More people gathered on the sidewalk.

She didn't hesitate to step up as I again pocketed the phone. We put our hands on the handle and pulled. We gave it all we had and ended up falling backward when the handle came free of the crumpled metal. I lost my balance and fell to the pavement while she stayed upright. She offered me a hand up as I let go a string of curse words Mom wouldn't have been happy about.

I snatched the phone from my pocket as I heard sirens in the distance.

"We can't get it!" My voice cracked on every word.

Police and ambulance careened onto the street and pulled up a few feet from me.

"They're here," I said.

"Work with them. Leave the phone connected and I'll be here if you need me. I'm gonna get in touch with Snowbird and let her know what's happening."

"Winger?" the police officer asked quietly as two paramedics from the ambulance went to the car. Another officer went to the woman who'd tried to help me with the door.

"Yes, sir," I said. I was shaking now. It was cold out, but the temperature had nothing to do with it.

"I'm Iceman. You can call me Officer Clark." He pointed to the nametag on his uniform.

I nodded and shuddered.

"Let's get you to the other medic," Clark said.

"I'm okay. We gotta get Eddie...."

My legs gave out, and if it hadn't been for Officer Clark, I would've been on the ground again.

"We'll take care of him. I promise. Let's get you taken care of too."

He walked me over to the other medic, who was in the back of the ambulance. "Theo, this is Flurry."

Agents surrounded me. It didn't help me calm down.

"You can call me Jenny," she said. "Let's lay you back so you can relax."

I lay on the bench she indicated. "Can you find out how Eddie is?" I looked back at Clark. "Please?"

"Sure thing."

He nodded at Jenny as she took my pulse. She nodded back. I noticed she had a gun under her jacket. I was pretty sure that wasn't standard paramedic issue. The sounds of metal ripping echoed outside. They must be tearing the door off.

Officer Clark reappeared as Jenny felt around my chest, which made me flinch and sometimes gasp depending on where she hit.

"He'll be out of the Jeep in just a few minutes. He's conscious now. They want to take him to the hospital for stitches, X-rays, and to monitor for concussion."

I shook uncontrollably and nodded. I had to keep my shit together. These were agents. I couldn't break down like a little kid.

Clark put his hand on my shoulder, and the sympathy in that nearly broke my efforts not to cry.

"You're both going to be okay," Clark said. "Let Jenny take care of you. We'll take care of Eddie. He'll be in here with you in a few minutes."

As he said that, one of the medics came and pulled the stretcher from the ambulance.

"A TOS doc will see you at the hospital, and we'll keep you secure there. Your mom—"

"My game. Tonight. John's got to...."

Shit, I'd said his name. But these guys were okay. They were TOS. But dammit. Clark and Jenny looked at each other. I wiggled around to free my phone. It was still connected.

"Jo—" I caught myself. I wasn't thinking straight. "Shotgun, you've got to get hold of my coach and tell him what's happened. I don't think...."

The shakes became uncontrollable and I dropped the phone. As I reached over the side of the bench to get it, dizziness overtook me and—

FIVE

"Eddie!"

I sat upright and looked around. Mom and John had been talking softly by the window and rushed to the bed. I was shirtless and hooked up to a heart monitor and an IV. I was in the hospital. Suddenly pains shot through me. It felt like a huge defenseman had mowed me down while I was on a full-speed breakaway.

"Oh, Theo. I'm so glad you're awake," Mom said.

Mom gently laid me back down and pulled the sheet over me. Taking inventory of my body, I quickly realized everything hurt, sometimes sharply. Someone had taken my jeans off, but I was still in boxers and socks. I seemed to be able to move okay, though.

I found the controls on the side of the bed and raised myself up to more of a sitting position.

"Eddie saved me," I said rapidly while I adjusted the bed. "He stopped those guys. They grabbed me off—oh no, my bike! It's somewhere on Williams."

My mind was so scattered. Thoughts flooded my head— Eddie, the accident, why did it happen, what was happening with the tracker problem. I couldn't lock in on any one thing.

"We've recovered it," John said, and it took me a second to remember what he was talking about. "A lot of people are investigating what happened."

"Eddie?"

"He's fine," Mom said. "Banged up, stitches on his face and on his side, and a slight concussion. He was very lucky. It sounds like he'll go home tonight, though."

"Can I see him?"

"In a minute. He's just down the hall and has been asking for you." Mom took my hand. "Listen closely, okay?" I nodded. "We're calling this a botched kidnapping attempt that Eddie saved you from, which is pretty close to the truth. It's what'll be in the police report, and it's the story we give to anyone who asks."

"Got it," I said.

Why anyone would want to kidnap me was a mystery, so I wasn't sure how I was going to sell that to Eddie or my friends. I guessed we'd figure that out later.

A nurse came in. "You're awake. That's good. Let's take some vitals and see how you're doing."

"Can I see my boyfriend?"

"When I'm done here, I'll see if he's still awake. I know he'll want to see you." She smiled and set about her tasks.

While she checked me out, my phone vibrated on the bedside table. It was Lorenzo or someone else from TOS. Clearly the nurse wasn't TOS-cleared because John didn't give me the phone.

"Everything looks good for you," she said after what felt like an hour. "You're going to have some bruises, and you've got a couple of stitches above your right eye, but otherwise you're okay. As soon as this IV finishes, we're clear to release you if your vitals stay stable."

"Thank you," Mom said.

The nurse patted me on the shoulder. "I'll see if your boyfriend's awake."

"Thanks," I said.

As soon as she was gone, John handed me the phone. There was a text from Lorenzo to call him.

"Doctor Possible. Winger here." The weariness in my voice stunned me. All my usual energy was gone.

"Thank God you're okay." Lorenzo sounded relieved. "Do you want an update or do you need some time?"

"Let me have it. I can talk. Only Shotgun and Snowbird are here. I'm still in the hospital, so if someone comes in, I'll be careful."

"Got it," he said. "You should know your chip's gone off the grid. When Shotgun called in to get your exact location, we saw it was out of the system. Checking the logs, we know your chip went off-line about two hours before you called Shotgun. We're running analysis on the logs and comparing to the others that have gone off-line."

"Can you send me my logs?"

"Already done. They're in your email."

I thought about the info. That explained why the van was at the school. They were going after someone. Did they know who they were getting when they picked me up? Were they just told to pick up the person with the tracker they'd locked on to? Why the grab? Was that why the van circled around? Were they trying to figure out if I was the right target?

We knew there were chips that had gone off grid, but the agents were mostly accounted for. At least I had two trackers I could test—mine that was off the TOS grid because of whatever's happening, and the new one that was working normally, or at least it was this morning.

"Thanks. I'll work on it tonight."

"I don't think that's a good idea," Mom piped up. "You need to rest."

"You can hit the ground running tomorrow," Lorenzo said. "Get your strength back. We'll keep new details coming to you in email."

The nurse returned, peeking around the door, and I pulled the phone away from my ear.

"Oh, sorry," she said, entering the room. "Eddie's awake and you can see him. He's right next door. If you want I can bring a wheelchair, or you can walk with the IV pole. I did bring you another gown so you can put it on backwards and cover up."

She put the gown on the bedside table.

"Thanks," I said. "I'll do the walk."

"I'll let you get changed and I'll be back to walk you, just to be safe."

I was about to say something, but John spoke up. "I can make sure he's okay in the hall."

I was thankful for that. I didn't like needing the help, but if I had to have it, I was grateful John volunteered.

"Great. I'll leave you to it."

She retreated.

"Sorry about that, Doc." I returned to the phone.

"No worries. Go see him. I'll email you later."

He disconnected, and John lowered the bedrail that was nearest him while Mom maneuvered the IV pole so I wouldn't pull the tubing out.

"Be prepared for how rough he looks, okay?" Mom asked.

I nodded. I couldn't imagine he could look worse than how he had in the crushed Jeep.

I groaned when I stood up. Everything hurt. It was impossible to keep the grimace off my face. John helped me get into the second gown.

"You sure a wheelchair wouldn't be better?" John asked.

"I'd rather not."

Mom gave me a light hug. "I'm so sorry, Theo. I...."

She didn't usually hold her words back. This wasn't easy for her any more than it was for me. Usually my TOS work happened behind the safety of my desk. This was the first time I was directly involved. Yes, it was weird that occasionally I rescued my parents, but I didn't actually see any of it. I just knew the outcome.

This time Eddie and I got hurt.

What had I done? If I hadn't called Eddie, he wouldn't be broken. I should've called John when I thought something was wrong. I'd put Eddie at risk. I owed him a lot, but what had it cost him? What if he couldn't swim this winter because of his injuries?

An eerie thought crossed my mind. What if TOS weren't the good guys? I'd never thought that before. But this situation was different. We *had* to be the good guys. I'd have to figure it out later. I had more urgent things to deal with.

This tracker problem was personal now. I had to bring down who or whatever had hurt Eddie.

SIX

"So you were just snatched off the bike?" Mitch asked. "That's crazy, man. I don't know what I'd have done in your place, or Eddie's for that matter. Dude, it was ballsy to stop them like you did."

"I had to do something since they weren't stopping. No one messes with my boyfriend like that."

Eddie sat up in his bed, propped up with pillows. Mitch and Iris were over along with me. I was on the bed next to him while Mitch and Iris were in his beanbags we usually played video games from.

Since neither of us was fit for laser tag, they'd come here to hang out. There was, however, a rain check for the laser tag takedown.

Eddie had gone home last night, and we video chatted when he got settled. Mom didn't want me driving last night either since I was just out of the hospital too. Thankfully she let me out on my own today, even though there might still be a target on my back because my tracker was still not in the TOS system.

Whereas I only had three stitches, the left side of

Eddie's face was swollen and peppered with stitches and butterfly bandages from the bits of debris caused by the crash. He also had a rib fracture, along with three bruised ones. A line of dozens of stitches ran down his left side where metal from the door had stabbed him. On top of that, he had a mild concussion.

As much as it pained me to move, I knew it was a lot worse for him.

My heart ached seeing him bandaged and bruised. His injury was because of me and he didn't even know the truth about why. He rolled with the kidnapping story we were using. There was no reason for him to think it was anything else.

"Why would anyone want to kidnap you?" Iris asked.

"No idea. That's what the police are trying to figure out. I'm nothing special. Yesterday I was just a kid on a bike, who got stuffed into a van. It's bizarre."

"Are they close to finding the guys?" Mitch asked.

I shrugged. I actually didn't know. When they briefed me this morning, TOS had reviewed traffic-cam footage. Mud covered the van's license plate, so other than knowing it was from Massachusetts, there was no number to trace. The vehicle had come out of a residential neighborhood when it first appeared on traffic cams. They'd combed through that neighborhood, but found no leads. The van went out of sight less than ten minutes after it hit Eddie. There'd been no sign of it since and a manual sweep of the last known area turned up nothing. With the tinting on the windows, it also meant the cams couldn't see the driver.

They were analyzing my bike for prints or anything else that might help ID the guys in the van. So far that was pointless as well. As I recalled, the guys wore gloves, so it wasn't surprising there were no prints.

It had been hard to watch Eddie's Jeep get hit. He'd turned right so close to the van that they had no choice but to hit him. TOS forensics thought the van was reinforced, due to the amount of damage caused when it was going thirty miles an hour. The van escaped with only dents while the Jeep was a total loss.

"I haven't heard anything," I finally said. "I just know, if it wasn't for Eddie, I don't know where I'd be."

I squeezed his hand.

"Like I said," Eddie coughed between words. "I couldn't let anyone just take you. And don't worry about me, I'll be up and around in a couple of days."

"We definitely missed you at the game last night, man."

Mitch had already told me about the loss. It had been bad. This was the first game I'd missed in more than a season. Mitch said he'd been out of sync with the wing who replaced me, and the team as a whole had been off its game. Coach downplayed it, saying it was only because of the surprising news about why I was out.

Another reason to be pissed off about the whole thing.

"Mitch!" Iris admonished. "Don't talk about that. Theo's got enough on his mind."

"It's okay," I said. "Next week we'll get a W."

"Here's what I don't get," Eddie said, without the cough. "Why would they grab you like they did? If they're so eager to get you, there's got to be so many easier ways to do it."

I'd thought about that a lot too. They were actually pretty smart about it. It was on a stretch of road where there wasn't a ton of traffic that time of day. Seeing the footage, they had me off the bike and in the van in less than twenty seconds. The van itself blocked the view from oncoming traffic. As fast as they moved, it could've looked like they were helping someone who had an accident.

"I don't know," I said. "Nothing makes sense. Unless someone's just grabbing teenagers."

"I saw a documentary on PBS a few weeks ago about human trafficking," said Iris. "Do you think they were going to ship you to some other country?"

That was an unexpected turn.

"But wouldn't you go for someone who wouldn't fight back?" Eddie asked.

"Right?" Mitch said. "He's a hockey player. He knows how to fight and defend himself."

"Not when they've got a gun," I said quietly.

"What?" Eddie asked, flinching as he turned toward me.

Iris gasped.

Maybe I shouldn't have said that. It was part of the official TOS report of course, but I didn't know if they'd added it into the police report. Now that I'd told my friends, I guessed I'd have to make sure they did. Dammit.

"Dude? Serious?" Mitch asked, his tone somber.

I nodded. The shakes started to overtake me. I knew I was safe in this room with my friends, but the memory of having the gun on me was suddenly all I could see.

"Theo? You okay?" Eddie asked as he squeezed my hand.

I took a couple of deep breaths. This wasn't the place to melt down. Not in front of these guys. Eddie already had enough going on. Mitch and Iris certainly didn't need to watch me freak out. I thought I'd gotten past this last night. Around three I woke up in a cold sweat. I'd screamed, though possibly only in my dream. There was no going back to sleep, because every time I dozed off, the scene replayed.

Sometimes it ended like it had in reality.

Sometimes I got shot.

Sometimes I got to the Jeep and Eddie was dead.

"I need some water," I said, bolting from the bed, and went to the bathroom across the hall from Eddie's room.

I closed the door and looked at myself in the mirror. I was flushed, which was a weird look for my pale skin. I gripped the sink as I quaked even more. I was wide-awake, but I couldn't push the scene out of my head.

What kind of an agent was I? Did Mom and Dad get this way after something happened to them? Did Lorenzo freak out after he was in the field?

I jumped at a knock on the door.

"Theo?" It was Mitch.

"Just a minute."

"Theo, let me in."

I really wanted to be alone, especially since I was on the edge of a meltdown. I also knew Mitch, much like Eddie, wouldn't let this go. I opened the door.

Mitch looked concerned, more than I'd ever seen him before. This was one of the things that made Mitch a great team captain—he always knew what his players needed.

"First I know I'm not Eddie, but this is from him since we wouldn't let him get up."

Mitch wrapped me in a hug. He was right. He wasn't Eddie. Mitch was my height so that was off, plus he didn't put his hands in the same places Eddie did. It didn't matter, though. The hug was perfect. I hugged him back and struggled not to cry. I didn't want to cry on anyone. I knew he wouldn't judge. He'd seen me cry before, just not in a long time—and it usually involved being hurt.

I was hurt. But it wasn't like any injury I'd had before. It wasn't physical.

I could've died yesterday.

"What can we do?" Mitch finally said as my shakes reduced.

"I don't know." That was true. I had no clue. "I guess it's just a matter of time."

"You should talk to someone? Mrs. Robbins, maybe?"

Mrs. Robbins was the school counselor. I suspected this was far outside her expertise. If I were pregnant, getting bullied, or failing classes, she'd be fine. Being captured and almost shot as part of a spy organization wasn't in her wheelhouse.

"I don't know." I couldn't say anything else.

"Or Coach? Eddie? Or me? You know you can tell me anything."

I pulled out of his grip so I could grab a Kleenex. "I'm sorry. I didn't mean to lose it."

"Dude, I can't imagine what you're going through. It was bad enough and then that thing with the gun. Jesus. That's intense."

"I'll talk to my mom about it. She knows people."

He nodded. "Do it," he said. "I'm here. Eddie's here. But you probably need more than we can help with."

I stared at him and gave a slight smile. He was a good friend.

"Thanks, Mitch." I offered a fist and he bumped it, but he pulled me into a quick hug too.

"If you need to get your mind off stuff, you can call too. Anytime."

I took a deep breath.

"Let's get back," I said.

I checked myself in the mirror. Color had returned to my face so my freckles weren't standing out on my skin anymore. My eyes were red, but at least I wasn't crying. We crossed back into Eddie's bedroom, and I settled back next to him.

"We're gonna go," Mitch said. "Let you two have some time."

"Thanks, Mitch," I said, "for everything."

He nodded. Iris gave Eddie a kiss on the cheek and then came around the bed to do the same to me.

"You two take care of yourselves," she said.

"See you later," Eddie said.

After we heard the front door close, Eddie turned and kissed my forehead.

"Are you okay?"

"Better," I said. "Too much going on in my head."

"Why didn't you mention the gun?"

"Because it's so surreal. Frankly I think I was trying to forget about it. The whole thing's insane anyway."

He adjusted himself on the bed so he was up against me. Each move came with a grunt, and those felt like a punch in my gut. It was worse than anything that happened yesterday. Eddie resumed holding my hand as he leaned his head against mine. Since I was shorter, my head was sort of a pillow for him.

As much as I needed to get home to work on some more tracker analysis, this felt so good. Just us trying to heal each other from all that had gone down. Plus I hadn't heard anything from Lorenzo since this morning, so it was a safe bet he had nothing new.

Eddie's breathing shifted, and it seemed like he was asleep. No way was I disturbing him now. I'd work later. I let my eyes close and hoped I could rest without any more freak-outs.

SEVEN

Eddie and I ended up resting for a couple of hours until his mom woke us so he could take some medication. Luckily she politely sent me home so he could rest on his own. I was glad she did. As much as I wanted to stay, I needed to work.

I'd woken up with some ideas I was eager to check out. I had all afternoon and into the evening to do whatever I wanted.

As I pulled Dad's car into the garage, I saw my bike. They must've gotten all the information from it they could and sent it back. Trashed didn't begin to cover how damaged it was. I gave it a quick once-over since it was already on the rack—bent wheels, dented frame and even a severed brake cable.

"Talk about a mess," I said to no one.

I pulled out my phone and made some notes. I'd need parts to get this fixed so I wanted to get the order in. The sooner I had it fixed the better, because I already missed my bike.

As I was typing, my phone vibrated with a TOS call.

"Winger. Defender here."

It was Dad!

"Hi. I.... Thanks for calling. I don't know where you are but thanks."

"Snowbird was able to reach me and told me what happened. Are you okay?"

"Um, yeah."

The silence lingered. I knew I didn't sell my condition well enough.

"No," I finally admitted.

"Are you secure? Can we go video?"

"Sure," I said and activated my video connection.

Dad's face filled the screen. I couldn't tell where he was, but it was good to see him.

"Winger, tell me."

He sounded like he always did when he knew I was holding back. He'd used the voice on me when I was eight and terrified of going back on the ice after I broke my leg. He'd used it when I was thirteen and trying to tell him I was gay. And here it was again. Of all the people I could talk to about this, Dad was the best because he got me so completely. And he always set me on the right path.

"I keep reliving yesterday. Crashing my bike into the van. The gun aimed at me. Eddie in the crushed Jeep." I sat on the hood of the car. "Sometimes it ends differently—with one of us dead."

"I'm so sorry. That shouldn't have happened to you. When you started working for TOS, we didn't like the idea of you getting too involved, but I don't think we envisioned anything like this."

"I didn't either," I said quietly. "I tried to fight back, as best I could, Da—"

"I have no doubt." He cut me off before I could call him Dad, which I desperately wanted to do right then. "If you need to walk away from this, I think we'd all understand."

"No. I can't. Too many years helping on too many projects. Besides I want to make sure no one else gets picked off like I did. Even with your training, getting abducted still can't be easy."

"You're pretty amazing, Winger. I don't know if I'd have felt the same way at your age. Take care of yourself. I'll be home in a few days, but if you need anything, pick up the phone. Okay?"

"I will."

"Good. I gotta go."

Dad put his hand on the screen and a wave of nostalgia crashed over me. He'd done this when I was younger as a way to hug me via video chat. I placed my hand over his.

"I love you, Winger."

"Love you too, Defender. Thanks."

The call disconnected. Even though my phone's home screen was peeking out behind my hand, I left it against the glass as if it could soak up any remnants of Dad's presence.

After a couple more notes about the bike, I went inside. Mom was in the kitchen making coffee. I gave her a hug, which she returned gently.

"You okay?"

"Yeah. I just talked to Dad."

"Good. We're both worried about you, you know?"

"Yeah." I swallowed hard. "I'm a little worried about me too. I don't even really know how to describe it. I've had dozens of hockey injuries, but I don't have dreams about those."

"It's bad?"

I shrugged. I was doing that a lot lately. "It's weird more than anything. It's so vivid. Like I'm there all over again."

"Do you want to talk to one of TOS's counselors? They're really good. I had one a couple of years ago who helped me."

"You?"

She gestured to the island and we sat on the stools. "I'm not usually in a position to have to fire a weapon. Even when I am, I try to injure not kill. But I ended up killing someone, and that was difficult for me. It didn't matter that there was no choice. I couldn't figure out how to talk to your father about it, but TOS provided someone. You can make the call or I can."

"Is there a manual for this stuff?" I asked.

How was I supposed to know there were counselors? I only know how to contact computer folks like Lorenzo, plus Mom, Dad, and John.

She gave a small laugh, which was one of the best things I'd heard all day.

"How's Eddie?" she asked, diverting the conversation.

"Hangin' in. He hurts. But he's tough. I'm glad we hung out. I think it was good for both of us really. I'm gonna go up and work for a while."

"Okay. Just don't overdo."

I nodded and took off.

In my room I shut the door and fired up all the computers to get down to business. First things first I dialed the bike shop to order the parts. As I talked to Monty, my favorite mechanic, I got the new chip out of my locked desk drawer.

Once I finished the order, I hung up and got to work.

I accessed the tracking system and narrowed down to

our street. There were two blips in our house. TOS cleared me to view four chips while I was testing. The test one, as well as the devices in me, Mom, and John. Since Dad was on a mission, I couldn't access his, but that was okay.

They were all ID'd with numbers. Mom's and the new chip were here. As Lorenzo had said, mine was missing from the TOS system. I entered John's ID and found him across town. Why was mine missing? What had changed?

I was curious about the logs from the Wi-Fi in the house. I had my own hub, separate and more secure from the Wi-Fi in the rest of the house. Mom and Dad used two other hubs—one for TOS work and the other a regular one from the cable company.

But the logs for all of them could be interesting. The trackers would ping off of all three at different times. Given my computers could see a dozen Wi-Fi networks from surrounding houses, they were probably pinging off those occasionally as well.

I started with the least used network. Sure enough, there were dozens of log entries over the past day. Some of these had to be the chips, although it all simply looked like phones denied access to get on a network.

The trick was, not even TOS had a way to identify what a tracker ping looked like in a Wi-Fi log. Nothing trans-mitted would give away what it actually was.

How could I filter out real phones? Maybe I didn't need to.

My hands flew over my keyboard.

I loved it when an idea popped into my head. I had been going about this the wrong way. The system kept track of what the trackers pinged against to know the location.

In the tracker system, I looked up the test chip and saw

where it had been pinging from. Dozens of its connections today came from my router, the others in the house, and the neighbors' too. It was all spelled out right there—the name of the router, the IP address, date, time, and GPS coordinates.

I wrote a quick program to match up the tracking system data against the logs from the three routers in the house.

The router data was fascinating. Each time the test chip pinged, in addition to masking itself as a phone, a long string of what looked like encrypted data went with it. This information transmitted in the background, not needing to be an authorized device. Very clever. It was the same concept as being on a plane and able to look at the airline's website even if you didn't buy the Wi-Fi. The encrypted string must have something in it that would convince routers to let it through.

The string was always the same, though. The only thing that changed was the device the router thought was trying to connect.

Quickly expanding my data to look at the other chips in the house, I saw the same pattern.

Most disturbing was that my chip was still pinging. While the TOS system hadn't heard from my tracker in over twenty-four hours, it was still active. It had signaled the router downstairs just a few minutes ago.

Where was the data from my chip going?

There was nothing I could see in the tracker's user interface to reactivate chips that were removed from the system.

What if I tried to bring it back online myself? Add it as a new agent just like I'd done when I received the test chip.

I went through the simple steps, which only involved adding its ID number and my codename.

ID 2739. Winger. Added

Current location: 42 23.083, -71 7.095.

That was easy.

It didn't answer how my chip got removed from the system in the first place. I stared at the screen as if it would offer the answer on its own.

ID 2739. Deleted.

What?

How had that happened? I pulled up the access logs for the tracker system and saw all the chip activity coming in as well as when I'd just added it. There it was. Something took my chip off the grid.

The log line disappeared.

Damn. There was an active breach in the system.

I spun my chair to another keyboard and pulled up the same log. My system automatically made a mirror copy of everything I looked at or worked with. Logs captured all the changes I made too. It was a safety protocol in case anything unexpected happened while I worked.

I called Lorenzo on video chat and made my screens visible to him.

"Doctor Possible. Winger here," I said as soon as he connected.

"Winger. Good to hear from you, and kinda chipper. How're you feeling?" As he spoke his face popped on to one of my screens.

"Better," I said. Lorenzo didn't need to know about the issues I was having. "Listen, I think I'm onto something."

I stepped him through what I'd seen.

"Good work, Winger. No wonder we couldn't see anything."

"But they're onto us. There's no computer attached to the IP in the logs. It never resolves. But it seems the user got in through our system in the first place. Look at this."

I put the emphasis on one of the screens I shared.

"Here's how they got in. The logs write out to a directory that has no security on it. From there they can get into the user interface. For some reason there's an assumption that if you're looking at logs, you got authorized at some previous point."

My hands were running over the keyboard, almost on autopilot, as I talked. I already had an idea for a patch, and I was coding right now. The logs had to be locked down. There also needed to be a locked door for anyone who accessed the tracker system to ensure they went through log-in. No more auto-log-in functions.

"Who wrote this code?" I asked as I typed. "I've never seen anything so sloppy in terms of security."

"Stand by," Doc said. "I'm adding Red Hat."

He turned away from his cam for a second as he placed another video call.

"Red Hat," he said. "Doctor Possible and Winger here."

Joanna's face split the screen with Lorenzo's.

"We've got, well, Winger's got the problem isolated."

"At least I think so," I added.

I went over everything again.

"I've just added code to lock down the access logs so we cut them off from there," I said once I'd finished the overview. "We need people testing that. I'm finishing up another patch that should force the tracker system to disallow any automatic access tokens. Once that's done, it'll need testing too."

"Doc and I can take the first pass on testing, and if it passes us, we'll get some others on it to make sure it's secure," Joanna said. "Great catch, Winger, especially catching the logs disappearing."

"I could only develop the fix because of the local backup copies I made. I recommend, again, that the agency put backup procedures in place across the board. That process was the only reason I was able to have the patches in place already."

"Noted," Joanna said.

It was the second time in a year I'd mentioned that. Initially it was just a good process. Due to this hack, perhaps the project would get some traction in the agency and get prioritized accordingly.

"We should also look for trojans in the system," Lorenzo said. "Sweep through everything and make sure there's nothing planted to help someone get back in. They'd have to assume we'd find the breach and fix it."

"Agreed," I said.

"We can get the other agents added back in the system too," Joanna said.

"I recommend against that for now," I said. "It might tip our hand that we've fixed the problem. I want to analyze the log data further and see if I can get a backtrace going. My chip may also point the way, since I know it's still transmitting."

"Okay," Joanna said. "I'll let Raptor know the latest."

"I've got the second patch in. The tracker interface should no longer allow anything other than a true log-in for access. I also added a ten-minute timeout to log out users so connections aren't staying open."

"Got it," Lorenzo said. "I see the new code. We'll get to testing. If we see any issues, we'll be in touch."

"Cool. I'll be online for at least another couple of hours, and then I'll be doing homework."

"Winger," Joanna said. "It's good to see you. I'm very sorry about what happened yesterday."

"Thank you," I said with a slight smile. "Signing off."

I cut the chat and sat back in my chair. Analyzing and creating the patch was the kind of work I loved doing. There was more to do, but at least there was progress.

EIGHT

"Hᴇʏ," Eddie said as he walked up to my locker after school. "Wasn't sure you'd still be here."

"Where else would I be?" I stuffed books into my backpack.

He shrugged.

It was hard to look at Eddie. It'd been four days since "the accident," as I was calling it, and while there were signs he was healing, Eddie still had new bruises popping up. I knew he was in pain too. It was obvious in the careful way he walked. His easygoing strides were gone, replaced by smaller steps.

Hurt was written all over his face. I couldn't decide if it was physical or mental, caused by the accident or by me.

I wasn't doing much better. Someone had accidentally dropped a textbook during American Lit and I jumped up from my desk, ready to take cover.

People laughed.

I'd tried to laugh it off too, but my heart pounded loudly in my ears for the rest of class. Afterward the teacher asked me if I was okay. I'd been getting that a lot because the news of what happened had spread among my classmates over the weekend. I kept my social media network small for a lot of reasons, but it was still obvious from my news feed that I'd become a hot topic.

"Come on," I said. "Let's go to Zinneken's and get some waffles. That'll help."

"Don't you have practice?"

I didn't like the edge in Eddie's voice. It'd never been directed at me before. I'd heard it when he was annoyed with people or upset with his performance in swimming. Maybe it wasn't *at me* but was because he was recovering. Maybe it was left over from yesterday when I couldn't come over after my afternoon class because I needed to get onto a TOS call. As usual I blamed it on client work, but I should've done something more to be with him.

He was in this condition because of me after all.

I shook my head. "I'm still a scratch. Coach wants my stitches out, so there's no chance of them getting ripped or infected."

"Then let's get some waffles." His voice became softer. He leaned in and kissed my cheek.

Once I shouldered my pack, I took his hand. "Come on. I've still got Dad's car, so I'm good to go."

"He didn't come back when he heard what happened?"

"Nah. I was fine. He still has work to do. We've talked a couple of times, though."

Out of the corner of my eye, I saw his confused look. Most dads would've come right home. I knew mine couldn't. I didn't have details on what Dad was working on, but it would take a lot more than what happened to pull him out. However, based on the talks we'd had over the weekend, I suspected if I told him I needed him, he'd make it happen.

I didn't pull that card, though.

Dad had calmed my rough edges. I didn't have any bad dreams last night. He'd told me about some of his bad dreams from when he first started out. On his very first mission, he'd been held at gunpoint and it tormented him for weeks. He told me about some calming meditation he always did before bed that helped him. It helped me too—or at least it did last night.

"My parents can't decide if they're pissed I did something as crazy as stopping the bad guys," Eddie said, "or proud because I was some kind of a hero."

"You were a hero. I'm certain I owe you my life."

"Then you can buy the waffles."

I faced him just in time to see a wink. "I'll buy you waffles forever if that's what you want. It's the least I can do."

"Theo!" I recognized that voice as Cullen Watson. "Wait up."

I'm sure Eddie saw my look of frustration as I stopped us so I could turn. I did my best to wipe the irritation before Cullen saw it.

"Hey. What's up?"

"Wanted to see if you had a chance to look over the envelope I left you."

Wow. He jumped right in. No regard for the injuries Eddie and I both sported.

"No," I said. "I already told you I can't look into that."

I might as well have kicked him in the stomach by the way his face fell.

"Fine!" he said loud enough his voice echoed against the lockers. "You were the only one I knew who would maybe help. Give it back, and I'll try to find someone else." He suddenly dropped his voice. "I have to go to *his* house today."

He was not only angry but crying too. Dammit.

"I told you I couldn't, but you gave me the envelope anyway."

"I was hoping if you had the stuff, you'd fix it."

This was not what I needed. At least Eddie had the sense not to say anything. He squeezed my hand, a great show of silent support.

"The only way I could do anything is if the agency who manages the computer officially asked me to take a look. Otherwise, it's all illegal and might even make things worse for you."

"Whatever. Gimme the stuff."

"It's at home. I'll—"

"Whatever!" Cullen stormed down the hall and turned a corner before I could say anything else.

I rubbed my hand across my forehead trying to diminish the headache that had formed.

"Do I want to ask?"

"Probably not." I gave him the details anyway. At least this was something I could share.

"Damn. That's intense."

"Yeah." I got us moving again.

"You really know how to drive, right?" Eddie asked as we got to my car. He was driving his mom's car, and it was parked a few spaces over.

"Jerk." I shoved him in the shoulder, and laughed a little. "You can buy your own waffles if you're gonna be like that."

He made an *ooph* sound, and I regretted the shove. It was playful, but it was also against his left side—the impact side.

"Shit. Sorry."

"It's okay. I'm glad we can goof around with each other."

"What do you mean?"

He sighed. "Nothing." Before I could ask again, he continued. "I don't know. It could just be me. Since the accident, I feel like there's a wall between us. Something's awkward, out of place. Maybe just because we're both dealing with the injuries and everything."

We shouldn't have to have this conversation. What would he say if he knew the truth? His boyfriend worked in IT for a secret organization and that was why someone rammed his Jeep. Whether or not the bad guys were coming specifically for me didn't matter, the fact was that it related to work he knew nothing about. Even though Iris had put that human trafficking story out there, it was a stretch to make it work in this narrative since that kind of thing wasn't known to happen. I knew the police were eventually going to abandon the case due to lack of motive and suspects. TOS was behind that of course. While I had some closure since I knew what was really going on with the trackers, Eddie was never going to have a resolution.

I needed to talk to Dad about this. There was a time he worked for TOS and Mom didn't. How did he deal with keeping stuff from her?

"I guess I haven't helped much, because I just went right back into things," I said. "We only had the weekend, and even then I was busy. I was freaked out, and I kept myself busy with client- and schoolwork so I wouldn't think as much. I'm sorry I wasn't paying more attention to you."

"No. No. I've actually tried to use you as inspiration to get back to normal. I'm sure I'm making something out of nothing. You've got no reason to put up a wall. And I'm sure you're dealing with more than I am since you were the one snatched."

"It's not a contest." Unwanted frustration crept into my voice. "We both got worked over, just in different ways. And you're right. I'm trying my best to forget it, especially the gun. Maybe that's what you sense. I'm trying to put a wall in front of that so I don't think about it."

He nodded and leaned in for a kiss, which quickly got a little heated. His kisses were comforting. A safe place to lose myself. I hoped he felt the same.

"I hope it's that. I don't like feeling that you're hiding something."

"Why would I hide from you?" I did my best to sound surprised.

"Like I said, it's probably nothing. I know you've always got work stuff you can't talk about and I'm probably hyper-sensitive right now. Let's get some food, and then maybe we can hang out at the park for a while."

The afternoon sun danced in his brown eyes as he talked, making me want to skip the food altogether.

I nodded. Homework and TOS could wait awhile. Time with Eddie was exactly what I, and maybe we, needed.

NINE

After we got stuffed on waffles, Eddie and I parked out at Danehy Park to make out. Because it was chilly, not many people were around. This empty parking lot was a preferred spot for us if we couldn't be alone at Eddie's. It wasn't like we were getting naked, so even if someone saw us, the worst they'd do was ask us to move along.

It was easier to fool around in Dad's car rather than the closer confines of Eddie's Jeep. Regardless of the bigger back seat, each of us occasionally grunted when we moved, and it wasn't a grunt of pleasure. It seemed being comfortable wasn't a primary concern right now.

We were in the middle of a deep, long kiss when my phone made the worst screeching noise I'd ever heard. I didn't know it was capable of making that sound. We tried to ignore it, but on its third wail, I grabbed it from the console between the front seats.

LOOKOUT

That single word terrified me. It was the highest TOS

alert possible, and it had been blasted out to agents across the world.

"What is it?" Eddie angled himself to try to see the phone.

"Amber alert," I said. "I guess I never turned on the blocker for those."

"Oh man." Eddie leaned back in the seat. "That's the first thing I do when I get a new phone. All it took was that tone scaring the crap out of me once."

I needed to get home, but I didn't have a way to leave Eddie without it being weird or pissing him off.

I swiped the phone clear and didn't know what else to do. It rang in my hand—Mom's ringtone. This might be the cover story I needed.

"Hi, Mom. What's up?" I tried to keep my voice even so Eddie wouldn't get suspicious.

"I figured you might be with Eddie because you didn't have practice."

"Yeah, we're getting something to eat."

Apparently I can lie to Mom pretty easily too. At least we'd been eating earlier.

"Tell him I'm asking you to pick up some stuff for dinner. Then get home. I want you here, and I'd imagine there's some work waiting for you as well."

"Sure. I can do that." I made my side of the conversation seem normal. "I'll be home soon."

"Okay. Be safe."

I disconnected. What was happening? Mom sounded nervous and that never happened. Was I in danger? Was she in danger? I tried to shake it off.

I sighed. "I need to go. Mom forgot stuff at the store and she's trying to make dinner—a perk of being hurt is Mom's been cooking."

Eddie smiled, apparently buying the lie. He knew I usually made my own dinner because everyone at my house was so busy.

"I should probably get home anyway. The 'rents are overprotective these days."

We kissed again, probably longer than we should've, before hopping out of the car so I could get in the front seat and Eddie could go to his.

"Wanna come over later?" Eddie asked. "We could do homework?"

"Homework or *homework?*"

"I need to do the first one, but I'd love some of the second. This wasn't quite enough."

"I've got a lot to do too, plus I know I need to check in with my crazed client. Let me call you in a couple of hours and let you know how it's going."

"I'll take that." He gave me a sexy smile.

At least he seemed less suspicious now. We kissed some more before I let him go. We both needed each other today, and it made the kisses insanely good. Once he drove away, I jammed my headphones into the phone and called Lorenzo.

"Winger, all hell's breaking loose," Lorenzo said after I identified. He sounded harried, far more than he had when all of this started. "The patch to make sure people are authenticated has either failed or they've found another way in. In the past ninety minutes, we've had four agents go off the grid. We've also...."

Lorenzo trailed off, which was unlike him. Reciting facts was one of the things he excelled at.

"Doc?"

"Sorry. I'm not sure you should hear this part. It's not really relevant to...."

"Tell me." I was coarser than I meant to be.

"An agent was found in London in her apartment with her neck cut open and the tracker gone."

I pulled into the grocery store. I decided to make this look good in case someone was following me.

"I see," I squeaked out as the shock from that sank in. "I'm headed into a public place. I'm putting you on mute and I'm gonna play some music. Stand by."

"Understood."

I did my best to walk normally around the store. I wanted to be home *now*. Because my chip was still transmitting and being tracked by someone else's system, I felt very exposed. My heart sped up so fast it felt like I was going to have some kind of attack. I slowed my breathing and my stride to try to calm down.

I got milk and some ground beef, which I knew we didn't need. I said hi to Roy, a guy from my history class, who rung it up, and then I was on my way again.

As soon as I was in the car, I continued with Lorenzo.

"Your code is still in place, and we're making instant log copies and we don't see signs that lines have been removed," he continued without missing a beat. "Oh, and one other weird thing. An agent was arrested in Montreal for robbing a drugstore using a TOS issued sidearm. He has no memory of doing it. As far as he knows, he had lunch at a café and then he was in the back of a police car."

That made no sense at all.

"Do you think these are related?" I managed a calm voice even though my heart pounded hard in my chest.

"Maybe. There was a project that used the trackers to make agents susceptible to suggestion. It sounds crazy, but it's apparently possible if the trackers were attached to a part of the brain. A few people here remember that project. It was scrapped ages ago."

"Wait. What? Did you really just say something about mind control?"

"Yeah." Lorenzo sounded like he couldn't believe it himself.

"And it worked?"

"That's what I'm told."

"Incredible," I said with no shortage of wonder in my voice. "We need to get a handle on that. If someone's controlling agents, we could all be screwed."

"Yeah" was all Lorenzo had.

"I'm a couple minutes from home. I'll call you when I'm online."

"Thanks, Winger. Talk to you soon."

If my patches were still in place and solid, the person must be accessing under legit credentials. I called Lorenzo back.

"That was fast," he said.

"I had an idea. Do the authentication logs show any unusual activity? Who's logging in and from where?"

"We're going through those now. Red Hat's also talking to Raptor about suspending all access until we can secure the system."

"Good idea. Can the chips be remotely deactivated?"

The silence meant Lorenzo didn't like the answer.

"No." He spoke quietly. "Once active, the only way they can be deactivated is to remove them."

"I see. I'll call you back in a few."

I hung up. These chips were clearly not designed with the idea that something could go wrong. And mind control? As much as I believed in what technology could do, it was difficult to grasp TOS had used something like that.

I pulled into the garage, and momentarily I was thrilled to see parts had arrived and were stacked next to the bike.

The feeling was short-lived, though, because it was a reminder of what had happened.

I put the groceries away as I called out to Mom. She responded from the office, and when I got there, I found Dad!

Dad was home and sitting at his desk like he should be. Why didn't she tell me that on the phone? I would've said to hell with the ruse of going to the store.

As I crossed the room, he stood, and I restrained myself from running to him. Instead it felt like I was walking through quicksand, because it took forever to reach him for a massive hug. Most guys, and most dads for that matter, wouldn't hold a hug this long, but he'd always given hugs that comforted and calmed. For most kids, I think, those kinds of hugs came from their mom. For me it was Dad.

"We'll let you two talk," Mom said when I finally released him. "Victor, we'll be ready for the briefing when you are." Dad nodded and Mom and John took their laptops and left the office. Mom shut the door behind her.

"I didn't know you were coming home today." I sat on the corner of the desk as he settled back in his chair.

"I've been reassigned to work on the tracker issue and coming home was on the way to the next place. And I wanted to keep my promise to be home, even though it's not for as long as I'd hoped." He looked at me for a moment. "How are you?"

"Okayish." I half shrugged. "Slept better last night than I have since it happened. Your tricks really worked."

"Good." While he smiled, concern etched his face. "I'm sorry I couldn't get back sooner."

"It's fine. You've got saving-the-world stuff to do."

We both laughed a little. It'd been a long time since I'd used that phrase. Once I knew their secret and they could be more up front with me, we sometimes referred to the trips as *saving-the-world stuff.*

"Are there any leads?" I asked.

"Yes. Some solid intel came in earlier today. It looks like Blackbird is behind it, and we think we've located their base of operations. I'm going in to help the team further investigate to make sure."

"Blackbird?"

He nodded. "It's an organization we routinely come up against. A truly nasty bunch that goes to great lengths to get what they want. This time they're going directly after our agents en masse. Speaking of, someone's coming to the house to remove your chip. You'll be untrackable within the next couple of hours."

"That's awesome." It was a huge relief that this thing was going to get out of my neck. "Am I getting another one?"

"Not right away. Until this is over and the system is secure, you're not going to be trackable. Your mom and I were very clear with Raptor that we weren't going to have you exposed like that."

"Can you and Mom get yours taken out?"

He shook his head. "Not right now." The look on my face spoke for me because he continued before I said anything. "I know. We'll all be upgraded as soon as possible. There's a shortage of the newer chips, and they're replacing the ones for agents on the most sensitive missions first."

"This isn't a sensitive mission?" It felt weird questioning Dad like this, although I supposed in this case I was really questioning Defender. "You're going into the middle of it."

"You'll just have to trust me when I say there are things going on that are even more important."

It was tough to swallow, but I knew Dad was telling me

as much as he could. As a tech, even when I was working on a specific mission, I only knew what I needed to in order to manage my specific objectives. I nodded because it was all I *could* do.

"I know Red Hat is counting on you to help on the tech side." He diverted the topic slightly. "I've made it clear that if you need to stop for any reason, that you must be allowed to."

Lorenzo hadn't said Red Hat had instructions. Maybe they had just come down and he was waiting for me to get here before updating me.

"I'll be fine."

"I know you think that. Look after yourself, and I don't mean just physically. Give yourself the okay to freak out if you need to. You may not be able to talk to me, but Mom and John can listen and connect you with others if necessary."

"Yeah, Mom's already told me that, and she's been great." I paused and just looked at Dad. "Thanks."

I don't know how Dad did what he did, always able to calm me down. I hoped I'd have that skill when I had kids.

"I should get back. I've got a lot of stuff to brief your mom and John on since they're providing support."

I nodded. "And I need to see what Lorenzo has for me."

"I'll check in later." He stood and gave me a quick embrace.

Before I got to the door, I stopped and turned back. Dad looked up, waiting for me to speak. I wanted to ask if we, TOS, were the good guys. It was a question that had been floating in my head a lot during the past few days, because I wasn't sure I knew. I thought we did. Dad would give me a straight answer if I asked, but it wasn't really the right time.

"Theo?" Dad asked.

I shook my head. "It's nothing. We'll talk later."

"Okay. If you're sure."

"Yeah."

He went back to his screen, and this time I left. Mom and John both looked concerned when I poked my head into the kitchen to let them know they could go back into the office. I'd seen Mom's expression a lot over the years. She's a mom after all. John was usually calm and cool, though, so to see him rattled was unsettling.

"I'll be upstairs. And I'm good." I smiled at her, trying to head off the question I knew was coming.

She nodded and tried to smile.

It'd been a while since we were all working on the same thing. Usually I enjoyed the collaboration, but I didn't like seeing my parents stressed like this. I suspected it was because I was more involved than usual.

Upstairs I fired up my equipment. As soon as I was online, Lorenzo rang me on the video link.

"We're locking the system down. We've seen a few different accesses this afternoon from Denver by agents who shouldn't be there or even allowed into the system. Once we do this, only IT is going to have clearance."

"Makes sense." I got myself comfortable at the desk. "I'll see if I can trace where in Denver the log-ins came from."

"Actually we'd like for you to look at the mind-control aspect. I sent you the details we have. From a gadget standpoint, you're one of the best we've got."

"I'll get on that."

This was one of my favorite things, and it was going to be kinda cool to dig into something I'd never seen before. While security and staying ahead of hackers was cool, working on gadgets was awesome. Over the years, I'd upgraded TOS phones to do things no other phone could, not just in terms of security for regular calls but also turning it into a long-range listening device, a keypad hacker, portable motion sensor, and my proudest achievement, an app that could take over a car's computer, allowing it to be driven from the phone.

Some of it was via apps and some of it was modifying the device itself. TOS had an incredible ability to get the necessary components. I suspected they had an in with the manufacturers.

We left the video channel open so we could talk as needed. I imagined Lorenzo had many such conversations going at this point as he directed people all over the world on various aspects of this fix.

I pored over the notes about the mind-control function of the chips. It seemed older chips didn't just sit innocuously in the neck. They had a small fiber that connected to the nervous system. This hadn't been part of the chips for seven years. Once they abandoned the idea of using them to control agents, they stopped making the trackers with the fiber connection.

I took the test chip from the drawer and, sure enough, there was no indication of a fiber connection. The chip was essentially a smooth, plastic bean, made out of a substance the body shouldn't reject, much like the polymer for replacement knees.

Given when I was chipped, I wouldn't have this fiber. John, Mom, and Dad would. I wanted to see one of those, or at least test it. As I read through the notes, more of the tech revealed itself. A small pulse of electricity sent whatever commands someone typed into the control console. It was possible to intensify the pulse for maximum effectiveness because people sometimes reacted differently to the control. Some people needed a stronger pulse to accept the command. Some needed lesser strength to avoid side effects like seizures.

This was unbelievable. The notes didn't cover how to stop it if someone was under the influence. Apparently no one thought this would be abused because only the upper reaches of the organization were authorized to activate it. The idea was to remove the fear factor for agents by planting the command in their heads so they would do it as if they'd come up with it. With the commands, they wouldn't question what they were to do. What I couldn't figure out was why the agent in Montreal couldn't remember what he did. There was nothing about wiping memory. Unless there was an order to forget.

I wanted to test this. None of these notes discussed where the commands were input. Was there something separate? Something no longer in the control panel? It would make sense to remove it when the program was terminated.

I spun around to my computer that was hooked up to the tracker system, and logged out of the interface. I went into the root directory to look for more clues. There were hundreds of file folders and, of course, nothing was obviously what I was looking for. I jumped over to the main repository of tech documents. I wanted the flowchart for the interface, which had to be in here.

The most recent flowchart was dated four and a half years ago. It was exactly what I needed. It showed several modules grayed out, including agent control. Going back to the code currently in place for the tracker system, I didn't find any of the subfolders for anything that had been decommissioned.

The code wasn't in the system, and yet it appeared that it was still being used.

"Hey, Doc?" I waited for him to look at the screen before I continued. "When code is decommissioned, where does it go?"

"We never throw anything out. I'll chat you a path to the code junkyard. Whatever you're looking for has got to be in there."

"Thanks."

The path appeared on my chat screen.

I muted myself again and used the information. There were lots of folders in there, but thanks to the alphabetic listing, I found *agent control* right away. I reviewed the contents, and it seemed like a complete, ready-to-run module. According to the docs, I could reintegrate this with just a couple of keystrokes. I liked the elegant way the code could be added and removed, very plug-and-play, to make it easy.

I unmuted my mic and called out to Lorenzo again. "I want to reintegrate this to the system for a few minutes and test it out. Do you see any issues with that?"

He thought for a moment, scrunching his forehead as he did so. "Should be fine. We've got the tracker system restricted to just a handful of log-ins now. I'd recommend removing it as soon as possible."

"Agreed. I just want to try it out and see what kind of calls it makes. I'll let you know."

"I'll let Red Hat know you're doing it."

I nodded and muted him again.

It took just minutes to bring the code back into the main tracker system and start it up. *Agent Control* showed on the main-menu interface as if it'd never been removed.

According to the documentation, all I had to do was enter the agent ID I wanted to control and then type the commands.

Typing was so old school. Why not voice commands?

Anyway. I plugged in John's ID.

He wasn't going to appreciate this, but I needed to see what would happen.

What could I have him do? It had to be something so random that it couldn't be anything but this.

The perfect thing snapped into my head.

I typed in the command and then went into the hallway to listen. Before I got to the stairs, I could hear him shouting the first lines from *Ragtime*.

Remarkable. And crazy that he actually knew those lines.

Mom kept asking him what he was doing. Just as she was getting hysterical, he stopped and apologized. The confusion in his voice was unmistakable.

"Sorry," I called down. "I was testing something, and it was better to not give you any warning."

John and Mom appeared in the foyer. John scowled at me. He was either pissed, freaked, or both.

"What was that?" he asked.

I thought about what I could say. Was this classified tech even though it was decommissioned? "I'm not sure I can talk about it. It won't happen again."

I slipped back into my room and closed the door before they could say anything else.

"Doc, that agent control works. It's freaky." I went through the steps to remove it from the tracker interface.

"What did you do?"

"Made Shotgun recite some American lit."

"Wow," Lorenzo said. "Even while we were talking about it, mind control didn't really seem possible. You just proved it, though."

"Right? If I hadn't seen it work just now, I'm not sure I'd

have taken it seriously, even though I've read the documents." I paused as I finished typing some system commands. "I've removed the code so no one can use it. I'm going to review the logs and see how the commands are transmitted. We might be able to use that info to help find who's behind this. If we can't zero in on them taking over chips, maybe we can locate them when they're sending these control signals out."

"Yes!" Lorenzo shouted and then flinched. "That's a great idea."

"Kinda scary since it means they'll actually have to be controlling people, but it might be a way to track them. Or maybe even shut the other system down. I have to get some homework done. I'll be online later."

"Catch you later." Lorenzo disconnected our call.

"Will do."

I hated that there were times when I had to step away from TOS work. Keeping up my schoolwork was one of the requirements my parents had for allowing me to have this job and sometimes it got in the way.

TEN

I STAYED home to do the homework even though I really wanted to go to Eddie's. It was the right choice, though, since a doctor came over and removed my chip. I had a bandage that I was going to pass off as covering an area where my helmet chafed me.

Once I'd done as much school stuff as I needed to, I headed downstairs to check in.

"How's it going?"

"We've almost got everything done that the field team requested." Mom looked up at me and smiled. "How was homework?"

"Good. I got ahead on a couple of things to free up time for me to work on the tracker issue. I'm going to look into some ideas I had while I was working on the math assignment."

"Don't stay up too late. You still need your rest."

I smiled at her. "I'll be in bed by midnight. I promise."

"Night, honey," she said.

"Sleep well." John briefly looked at me. At least he

didn't seem to be holding a grudge for the impromptu performance I made him do earlier.

Once in my room, I flopped down in my chair, and studied the screens. Of particular interest was the information I'd pulled from the transmission logs when I sent the control commands to John. It had bounced around the Wi-Fi and cell networks for a couple of seconds before it locked on to him. Cross-referencing the last few pings his chip had made before I sent the command, it looked like the system used the last known location to send it. It was a pretty good way to do it since the chips reported back often.

Could I send a command outside the system? It would explain a lot if that were the case.

I went into the hallway and called downstairs, "John?"

"Yeah?" he yelled back.

"I need another quick test."

"Okay." He was in the foyer. "What do I need to do?"

"Just hang out right there."

I plucked the command code out of the log file and went to the command prompt on one of the PCs. I gave the instruction to send the string of information, which would blast it off my secure Wi-Fi into the world.

I went to look down to John.

It took a few seconds, but he spoke the passage over again.

Damn. That wasn't secure at all.

"Is that it?" he asked.

"Yeah. Thanks."

"I 'spose I should be thankful you're not making me do something embarrassing." He went back to the office.

In my room I reviewed the documentation. How were the messages encrypted? Digging through the less-than-organized information, I found that it was a pretty simple bit of cryptography, at least by today's standards. When the system was built, it was probably as good as it got. But with today's advances in technology, the algorithm was easy to hack. Of course the encryption had never been updated because the project had been terminated.

I wondered....

I pulled up the engine I'd developed last year as an MIT project and ran the command line through it. In less than a minute it was decrypted. I saw the exact words of my command for John, along with other details like his ID number.

If someone knew this existed, it wouldn't be that hard to write commands and blast them out without using the actual interface. If someone had a chip, and someone certainly did given the agent they'd found with the chip removed, could you reverse engineer the mind control program?

I pulled my phone and pinged Lorenzo because he wasn't on video.

"Winger, I thought you were done for the night. What's up?"

I could tell by the sigh that he'd been asleep.

"Sorry, man. Just haven't gone to bed yet."

"S'okay. What's up?"

I told him what I'd figured out. "Are there any of the chips around that interfaced with the controller? I'd love to get one for testing."

"I don't know. That's before my time. I can ask Red Hat. She'd know for sure. What're you thinking?"

"I think they figured all this out using the chip they extracted from that agent. It's why they're still able to get people, even though we plugged the hole we found."

"Hmm. And she would've had one of those chips.

Other than that, the chips work exactly like what we use now."

"Would that agent have known the IDs of any of the other agents who are missing or off grid?"

"I don't know, but I'll find out."

My mind raced full tilt now. "Even if they don't, though, they could make guesses on IDs and see what they get. Why the hell weren't those chips replaced when agent control was decommissioned?" I kinda didn't mean to say that the last part out loud. Luckily it was just Lorenzo.

"Good question," His tone gave away that he'd been thinking the same thing. "I'll see about getting you one of the original chips ASAP."

"If not, maybe we could get Shotgun's or Snowbird's removed and upgraded?"

"On it. I'll keep you posted." Lorenzo yelped as a number of alarms went off on his side of the phone. "Dammit. Winger, agents are going off grid, several at a time. We're losing four a minute."

I brought up the tracker interface, and as I watched, the count of active agents decreased by two.

"How?"

"Don't know." The clicks of his keyboard were almost deafening.

How could we stop this? The IDs were the key. If you had the IDs, you could take over the signal. You didn't necessarily know who the agent was, but you'd know where they were.

"What if we change the IDs?"

"That's a few thousand, Winger. We'd never do it fast enough."

"Algorithm to change them, make them more complex,

letters and numbers. Write off the original IDs to a secure location so we can translate later."

I imagined Lorenzo's scrunched-up thinking face as he considered. Meanwhile my hands danced over my keyboard to write a simple program to do this. I used a varied length sequence, which was also alphanumeric. It would take too long to make the program recognize special characters, but that could be a future upgrade. I planned to write the original IDs into my backup log for now so we'd have the list of the transformations. I could send that securely over to Lorenzo later.

"Winger. Red Hat here. Doctor Possible added me. Do you think you can get this done?"

"We're losing six a minute now, with about one hundred fifty off the grid from this event," Lorenzo said.

"Yes, ma'am, I believe so. I'm working on the code now."

Silence from her for a moment. "Get the code done and send to Doc and myself. We'll help test it."

"Got it. Stand by."

I always typed quickly anyway, but it felt like I'd gone into warp speed. It was simple code, but I needed the algorithm to be tight to make sure there were no obvious patterns in case information got into the wrong hands. We could sort out the usability of the long IDs later but for now, we had to stop the agents being removed from TOS view.

I added in a secondary algorithm that would create new IDs each day. By the time that started, we'd have a better place to write the secure information translating back to the original IDs.

I was pissed I didn't have any Dr Pepper in my fridge. Actually I had nothing in the fridge, because I tended to munch as I worked and I'd been working quite a bit the past couple of days. I should've restocked when I made that grocery trip for Mom. I couldn't even yell downstairs to get something because of the soundproofing in the walls. Oh well. I'd get by.

Twenty-six minutes later, I sent the code to Lorenzo and Joanna. It looked pretty solid in my own testing.

"Okay. You've got it. See if you can break it." I filled them in on all the features I put in.

"I can't believe you wrote this so fast," Lorenzo said after a few minutes. "It's tight. So far my tests look good."

"Mine too," added Red Hat. "How will you apply this?"

"I'm going to rewrite directly in the database, and I'll output the translations onto one of my secure servers. Then you tell me where to send it and I'll upload a copy there. I think it should be a location outside the network where the tracker system is housed."

"Agreed," she said.

It was quiet as we all continued testing. I was confident in the code and the plan, but I kept testing to make sure it was performing as I expected it to. This had to be it. The takeover had to stop. It was still six per minute, and it was still too many. Hundreds of agents were vulnerable and easy to pick off, kinda like I'd been.

Less than fifteen minutes later, Lorenzo and Joanna reported they were satisfied with the code. Of course that meant another ninety agents had gone off the grid during their testing. I quickly ran the code on the database, and it transformed the few thousand remaining IDs in just a couple of minutes.

"Done," I announced as soon as the completion notification came up.

"Now we wait and see," Joanna said.

While we waited for reports to come in to see if we'd lost more people, I further encrypted the conversion list for safety, because I was going to transfer it over to the TOS servers.

"So far, so good," Lorenzo reported. "Couple of minutes with no further loss."

"What happens to the ones that went off grid?" I asked.

"We're working to get in contact with those agents to find out where they are," Joanna said, "determine their status, and let them know they may be at risk. We'll get their trackers replaced as quickly as possible. Also we've got an older chip on the way to you, Winger, so you can do further analysis. You'll have it by morning."

"I'll make it a priority."

Checking the map, I saw Mom and John were still in the TOS system. I was glad I stopped the problem before they were lost. I wanted to ask about Dad, but I knew that was inappropriate.

Once Lorenzo and Joanna were satisfied we'd stopped the takeover, I told them I was signing off. "If anything comes up, though, call."

"Thanks, Winger," Lorenzo said and Joanna echoed him.

It was quarter to twelve so I had a few minutes before when I wanted to be in bed. I wandered down to Mom's office and found her and John there, just as they'd been nearly two hours ago.

Mom saw me before I could speak.

"Theo? Everything okay?"

"Yeah. Just been a busy couple hours. Wanted to come down and—well, just to say good night again."

Mom got up and came around the desk as I walked toward her. She wrapped me in a hug. Being a mom, she knew I needed it.

"I know there's things you can't talk about. But you're doing okay, right?"

I nodded, still enjoying her embrace. "I am. Just some really intense work and...." I didn't know what I wanted to say.

"It's okay," she whispered, "to need a hug from Mom sometimes. Doesn't matter how old you are."

She kissed the top of my head.

"Thanks, Mom."

She let me keep hold as long as I needed. When I finally let go, she gave me one more kiss. I went over to John, feeling a bit silly but going for it anyway.

"Old times' sake?" I asked as he looked up from his screen.

"Of course." He stood and gave me a bear hug.

I'd known he wasn't my real uncle for some time, but he still seemed like family to me. His sturdy embrace reminded me of Dad's and that was comforting.

"I'm here anytime you need me, Theo. For anything."

"Thanks."

We did a fist bump once we'd released each other.

"I'm going to call it a night. See you in the morning."

"Night, sweetheart," Mom said.

"Later, Theo," John added.

Going back to my room, my mood was improved. It was silly to want the hugs, but I suspected I was going to sleep better because of them.

ELEVEN

AFTER PRACTICE I had a secure message on my phone from Mom saying she and Joanna wanted to talk to me. Joanna *and* Mom? That was a weird combination. The message was from Mom, but I couldn't remember a time they'd talked to me together. Even if I was working on a mission with Mom and Dad, Lorenzo usually did the tech briefing.

I hurriedly stripped off the top half of my pads, grabbed my phone from the locker, and went into the hallway. Looking around, I called Mom on her regular line so she could get Joanna and call me back.

"Theo, hi," Mom said.

"I just got out of practice and saw the message."

"Can I call you back? I'm in the middle of something here."

"Sure can. I'll keep the phone close."

We hung up, and she immediately sent me a secure text telling me she'd get Joanna and call right back.

While I waited, I looked through my TOS email, and there was nothing out of the ordinary. They'd managed to talk to 223 agents of the nearly 400 who were off-grid. They continued the work to contact the others. Some were on leave, and that occasionally made them more difficult to reach. There were twenty-seven off-grid agents that were *of concern*.

The phone vibrated in my hand and I answered immediately.

"Winger. This is Red Hat."

"Winger. This is Snowbird."

"Hey." I sounded upbeat as if I might be talking to a friend. "I'm just off the ice and not able to talk much but wanted to check in."

"Understood," Red Hat said. "Snowbird, I'll let you take it from here."

"Winger, we thought it was important to let you know some news sooner rather than later." Her breath caught. Mom was upset. What happened? "Defender is missing."

I slumped against the wall. My hand holding the phone dropped to my side and bounced off the cinder blocks. My legs threatened to buckle, but I managed to remain standing. I composed myself, walked farther away from the locker room to lessen the chance of someone hearing, and raised the phone again.

"Sorry." My voice cracked in the middle of the word, making it sound like a whimper.

"It's okay." I'd never heard Joanna sound upset, which only made this worse. "He's one of the agents that went off-grid last night in the takeover."

"No," I said softly.

Even when Dad was in trouble before, TOS had always known where he was. Now he was missing, and it was my fault. I hadn't moved fast enough.

"Winger," Mom said. "Can you skip your afternoon engagements and return to base?"

Sometimes I hated protocol.

"I'd rather keep my schedule."

"Winger, I...."

"Please, let me finish. If there's surveillance on me, which is very possible since they know who I am, I think I should follow my regular schedule so it doesn't appear anything is amiss."

It made sense to me. My old tracker hadn't left my room since they'd taken it out. What I didn't know was if there were actual people watching me. As much as getting captured again worried me, I also didn't want to succumb to fear and just hide. Silence on the other end of the phone said they were struggling with it too.

"He might be right, Snowbird," Joanna said.

"Okay." Mom struggled with the suggestion. "I'll see you in a couple of hours, then."

I spoke quietly. "Red Hat, I'll get to work on what you sent as soon as I'm at my station."

"Some people here are working on what you mentioned in this morning's email as well. I'll make sure they send you any findings, so you have them when you get there."

"Thanks. I need to go."

"Understood," Joanna said.

I disconnected and sent Mom a text on our regular line with no security: *Don't worry. I'll be home regular time.*

Sorry I'm being such a mom came the reply.

It's okay. I understand.

Coach Daly walked by and must've seen the look on my face as I headed to the locker room.

"Reese?" I stopped and turned back. "You look like you might be sick. You okay?"

I nodded, but it didn't feel very convincing. He gazed at me as if he were trying to get a more accurate reading.

"Hit the showers, maybe that'll help."

"I'm sure it will."

So much ran through my head as I got out of the gear, put it away, and entered the showers. If I'd done more, Dad wouldn't be missing. And what about all those other agents? The ones that TOS couldn't find were my fault.

"Hey, man," Mitch said. "Good stuff today. I'm glad you're back at full speed."

"Me too." It was hard to keep it together. It felt like my chest might explode. "Looking forward to a kickass game this weekend to make up for last week."

Luckily Mitch was nearly finished, so I didn't have to make a lot of small talk. My mind continued to race. I hadn't figured out how to trace the trackers that had gone missing. I could see the traffic going back and forth, but I couldn't figure out how to find the originating computer based on the chips' return transmission. There had to be a way. It was older tech. I was just missing something.

Even stranger was that the TOS documentation didn't mention how the device made and received transmissions. It was as if that information had been deleted. Lorenzo looked in other repositories, but the only documents that he found were the ones I already had.

As I came out of the locker room, I found Eddie talking to Mitch. Wordlessly I went up to Eddie and wrapped him in a hug. After a grunt of pain, which I felt bad about, he hugged me back.

"Hey. What's up?" he asked.

"Nothing." I tried to quash the emotions that threatened to escape. "Can't I just get a hug?"

"Of course," he chuckled as I hung on. "It's just not like you to throw yourself on me like that."

"You sure something's not going on?" Mitch asked. "You seemed off after that call."

I let Eddie go and looked at my friends. "It was an update from the cops. They've got nothing new. It kinda brought everything back. I don't know. It's stupid."

Mitch clapped me on the back. "That's messed-up. How does a van disappear? How does no one see a guy taken off his bike? Is this going to make you switch to a car so you'll have steel wrapped around you for safety?"

I laughed. I appreciated how it just popped out because it broke my sadness. Mitch often ragged on me for riding my bike everywhere, given the effort it took and the extra time required. I liked how he was trying to turn this into a procar moment.

"No way. It's *the* best way to travel. I've got all the parts, and I'll fix it up over the next few days so things will be back to normal."

"Which is too bad. We've had some nice times in cars over the past few days." Eddie wore a big grin.

"I'm sure Mitch doesn't need to hear about that."

"What's to hear?" Mitch asked as we walked toward the lobby. "I've had *plenty* of good times in a car. Eddie makes a good point, Theo. Go with a car and you guys can do that anytime."

"Or if I got Eddie on a bike, we could ride to some pretty excellent, secluded places."

"We're not going to win this one," Eddie said as Mitch rolled his eyes.

"His loss." Mitch gestured to me.

"Mine too," Eddie sounded a little disappointed. "You have no idea."

"And I really don't need to," Mitch raised his eyebrows at Eddie. "Okay, I'm outta here. See you guys later."

He took off toward his car, and Eddie and I went to mine.

"Do we have any time before your class to hang out?"

A quick look at my watch provided the answer. "Sadly not."

"Maybe after?"

"Maybe." I left it vague and hopefully there'd be no discussion when I said no later. I should've just gone home so I could start working again, but I knew going to class was the right choice, even though it was going to be difficult to keep my mind on the lecture. Maybe I'd have an epiphany and the answer to all this would magically drop into my brain during class. It'd happened before and this would be a great day for it to again.

TWELVE

"I THINK I may need to launch an intervention." Eddie fell in step with me in the hallway between first and second period. "Don't take this the wrong way, but you look like hell."

I already knew that. I'd seen myself in the mirror before I came to school. There'd been very little sleep last night. Even though I tried, it didn't happen. Instead I'd made breakthroughs on how to trace the mind-controlling aspects of the trackers. It was clever how the program accomplished the masking. It took me hours to uncover it, watching how the signals bounced around the internet.

Around five this morning, I sent Lorenzo all the information so he could run tests on his end to make sure it worked like I thought it did. Even when I lay down, I thought about Dad or had flashbacks from my abduction.

I tried calling him, both secure and nonsecure. I knew it was stupid, because he wouldn't pick up for me if he wasn't picking up for TOS. I did it anyway.

I knew his phone was in a downtown Denver hotel, but it hadn't moved in hours. I traced it right after I got home from class yesterday. If TOS figured out I'd done a trace, there'd be trouble. I'd re-designed the phone security system after I'd cracked it originally. However, I'd left a backdoor to my parents' phones.

I hoped TOS knew he was in Denver.

I set it up so if his phone moved, I'd get a text. If that happened, I was at least going to tell Mom regardless of what the consequences might be for me.

"Ton of homework," I tried to stifle a yawn as I spoke, "plus a client deadline that's insane."

He pulled me out of the hallway traffic and leaned against a wall. He embraced me, and I rested my head against his chest. If I wasn't careful, I'd doze off on him.

"Don't run yourself ragged."

We stood silently for a while as the bustle in the hallway intensified as next period drew closer.

"Are you sure that's all that's going on?" he finally asked.

"What do you mean?" My voice was muffled since I didn't move.

"I've seen Hurt Theo a lot over the past year, with all the various hockey injuries. I've also seen Stressed and Tired Theo when you're overworking." He gently moved my head so I looked at him. "You say you're getting past what happened, but it feels like something else has piled on."

I craned my head up farther and planted a kiss on his lips. I wished I could tell him what was going on. Mom, John, and I talked a lot last night. Unfortunately there were so few other people I could say anything to. My kidnapping attempt had been public, but what was happening with Dad was top secret. Mom said it'd be okay, but the fact John didn't echo that proved exactly how bad it was. I suspected Mom was on mom autopilot.

"Nah. I'm just straight up tired. The client work is more than usual. It's a tough project, and it's not getting done as fast as they want."

I rested on his chest again because I liked it there. The warning bell rang. We had two minutes to get to class.

"I don't know how you manage to do all this, or why you do it." I shrugged in his arms. "Is there anything I can do?" he asked. The concern in his voice tugged on my heart.

"Let me stay like this for a few hours."

He gently hugged me tighter.

"I'm pretty sure that wouldn't go over well. You know how teachers can be. How about we go off campus for lunch and you can rest for a few minutes and I'll make sure we get back on time."

This guy was awesome. I'd planned to see during lunch how things were going with Lorenzo, but the truth was that I couldn't do much while I was at school other than listen to Lorenzo or respond to text messages. Hanging with Eddie would be perfect. He might be less suspicious of what I wasn't saying, plus I could close my eyes for a few minutes.

"I'd love that. Meet on the front steps at twelve fifteen?"

"It's a date. We'll get some food and maybe you can grab a quick nap or something."

"You think of everything."

"If I did that, I'd have a way for you to not look like the weight of the world is on your shoulders. I don't like it. But if I can't fix that, I'll at least get you some lunch and a few minutes of rest."

I pulled out of the hug and gave him another kiss.

"You're awesome."

"Yes, I am." He kissed me again. "We gotta get goin' or there's going to be a tardy mark."

"See you in a few hours."

"Yup." He gave me one last kiss before he sprinted off. As I walked into class, which was just a couple of doors away from where we were, I made a promise to myself to do something special for Eddie once this madness was over. He was being a saint. This was the first time since we'd been a couple that I'd had something major going on with TOS, and Eddie was being patient even when he knew I was holding back. Meanwhile, I was learning the art of deception, using him for practice.

THIRTEEN

I GOT HOME from practice and found an extra car parked behind John's in the driveway.

What if there was news about Dad?

I parked in the garage and couldn't get out of the car fast enough. The seat belt tangled me. My backpack caught on the center console. If something could get in my way, it did.

Entering the house I found Mom in the kitchen, leaning against the counter with a concerned look on her face. She'd looked like that for days now, but this look had an edge to it. She didn't like whatever was going on.

"Hey, Mom," I said hesitantly. "Do I get to know what's going on? Or should I just go to my room?"

A sad chuckle came out. "We've taught you so well." She sighed. "Maybe too well."

She gave me a quick, very motherly hug.

"You get to know. Come on, we're in the office."

She behaved so oddly, splitting between agent and Mom, and between proud and concerned. It was confusing.

In the office the first person I spotted was Lorenzo. We shared a handshake that morphed into a half hug.

"It's been too long."

"Yeah, man! When I had the chance to come here, I jumped on it."

Nearly six months had gone by since I'd done a month-long internship with Lorenzo in his lab at TOS HQ, which was in a plain-looking office park outside of Richmond, Virginia. It'd been a blast being around all the tech, not to mention working directly with him, the director of encryption, and others on the IT team. We learned a lot from each other. While my mind usually worked in very out-of-the-box ways, I learned some good logical thinking from him that I tried to mesh with my own process for working through a problem.

It was cool that he was here. He was so professional when we were on the secure channel, but he was a fun guy during off hours. He was only ten years older than me, and we had a fair bit in common, between video games and our techiness.

"Theo," Mom interrupted our reunion, "this is Yoshi, codename Yong Chi. He's running the operation to recover the missing agents, including your father."

I dropped my backpack into a chair and went over to Yoshi to shake his hand. He stood as I approached. "Good to meet you."

"The pleasure's mine."

He was a thin man and a couple of inches shorter than me with jet-black hair and a nose that looked like it'd been broken more than once. It instantly made me wonder if he was a hockey player, but more likely, he'd gotten the breaks working for TOS.

"I've heard a lot about your work on this matter so far, and I'm hoping we can have you join us to put a stop to this and recover our agents."

"I'm always down for helping, and for this one, I've got more than a little personal investment."

"Yes, I understand Defender is your father."

I nodded as Mom's hand came down on my shoulder.

"Theo, there's a lot to talk about, and before we continue, I want you to know that your involvement is totally optional. It's important you keep that in mind. I know your father would agree with me that you're too young for this." She swallowed hard. "But it's also important that the choice is yours."

What?

This scene was already strange, and now it was completely bizarre. I usually got my TOS assignments from Joanna, or Lorenzo passing down information from her. The details usually arrived in an email or Lorenzo and I talked. Sometimes I briefed other agents before they went on missions, if they were using my tech. No one had ever come to the house. Even Mom and Dad didn't get assignments like this.

The doorbell rang.

"Oh, good, that must be our last person," Yoshi said.

Mom left to get the door. I hadn't ever seen the office this full. John was there of course. And with Yoshi and Lorenzo, plus whoever just arrived, it was a crowd.

The voice I heard talking with Mom was familiar, but I didn't place it right away. The person who entered surprised me.

"Coach Daly?"

"Reese. Or should I say, *Winger*?" He smiled and gave a nod. "I'm D-Man."

"Nice! Cool to find another hockey-named agent."

Coach had played for Ohio as a defenseman in college, so it was great to hear he used that in his name in the same way I used *Winger*. Coach Daly had joined the Tigers as an assistant coach at the same time I started as a freshman. He must've been there to watch over me in the same way John did at home.

"I had no idea," I said.

"And you weren't supposed to." Coach gave the same pleased look that he did when we correctly executed a play he'd taught us.

"If we could all take a seat." Yoshi's commanding voice got everyone's attention. "I'd like to get this briefing underway."

Mom and John settled at their desks. I perched on the edge of Mom's side of the desk. Dad's empty chair was a big void in the room. Lorenzo and Coach took seats while Yoshi remained standing.

"Theo, as you're aware, we've been unable to locate a number of agents since the system breach. In the short time since then, several executed crimes against very secure targets. The ones we've managed to capture before police or other security got to them, tell us they couldn't stop what they were doing. We've already taken their trackers out to prevent further influence."

Yoshi took an oversize tablet from the desk and displayed a map to everyone.

"Based on the information we have because of the work you've been doing with Lorenzo, we know the commands are originating from Denver. Specifically in a facility that's near the Ice Centre. The servers are behind a firewall that we can't reliably penetrate from the outside, so we're going in to disable it. We believe we can do that from service tunnels we can access from the rink." Yoshi fixed his gaze on me as he continued. "We'd like you to be part of the team. There's an invitational high school hockey tournament happening this coming weekend. With your approval, we can set up to have you there, and you'll work with Lorenzo to infiltrate and deactivate the rogue tracker setup. We'll have other agents in place to take people into custody. Everyone in this room will be on the mission to support."

Everyone looked at me expectantly.

Mom and Dad would say yes without hesitating.

I was scared. Whoever had the tracker technology had already tried to take me, and they'd hurt Eddie. This was a chance for revenge. I couldn't think about that, though. My focus needed to be solely on the mission, and probably the hockey too since I'd be on a team looking to win.

Fieldwork was something I'd never considered. What did it even entail?

"Can I talk to Lorenzo privately?"

Mom raised an eyebrow and Yoshi looked annoyed.

"Whatever you need," Mom said. "Do you want this room?"

"No, we'll go to my office."

I'd said "office" because that seemed better than saying "my room." If I was going to be an official-agent type, I might as well upgrade myself to "office."

I gestured toward the door and Lorenzo got up and headed for the hallway. I grabbed my pack as I left. We didn't speak as we went upstairs. I closed the door once we were in my room... office.

"Nice. I always wondered what the rest of this room looked like." Lorenzo looked around the room. "Sweet setup."

"You know, I would've given you a three-sixty view if you'd asked."

"Yeah, but it seemed weird to ask. It's already strange seeing it under these circumstances."

I tossed my pack on the floor next to the desk and sat back in my chair. I gestured toward one of the gaming chairs across the desk from me.

Lorenzo sat and I studied him for a moment. His hair was more tousled than usual, like he'd boarded a plane before he'd really had time to get ready. At least he was in his trademark superhero T-shirt and black blazer.

"Have you been in the field before?"

"Not like this. I've worked around the world for TOS, but usually in front of a keyboard, at a distance from where things are going down. I've never faced a request like this."

"Are you…?"

I hated even asking the question. What would he think of me? Hell, why were we having this discussion? I had to do what they wanted. What if I didn't go and they didn't get Dad back? I'd never be able to live with that.

"Scared?" he finished for me. "Sure. There're a lot of variables in a mission. But whether it's backing you up or doing it myself, this mission must happen."

He was right about that. There weren't other options.

"Theo, I don't know what I would've said ten years ago. I wasn't even thinking about this life when I was sixteen. I knew I was good with a computer, but I had no clue what I was going to do with that. I figured I'd end up making video games."

I smiled because I knew his passion for games. He was always introducing me to something new to play.

"This is a lot more cool than that," he continued, "even though there can be lots of risk."

"I should do this."

"And I'll have your back. Just like everyone else down-stairs will." He moved so he sat on the edge of my desk. "Don't let me talk you into it. This is major, especially since you haven't had field training and you'll only be able to take in so much while we get set up."

"You've had field training?" That was a surprise.

"Yeah, back when I started. And I take a refresher every six months."

I nodded.

"I'm gonna do it anyway. I need to get my dad back. And I probably know the agent-control system better than anyone else at this point."

"That you do."

I stood and Lorenzo followed my lead. He gave me a very brotherly hug along with a slap on my back.

"Thanks for the chat," I said.

"Anytime. And when we're done, you gotta show me all this equipment. I think you might have better stuff than I do and I'm not sure I can allow that."

"Deal."

Once we were downstairs, I took a deep breath before we went in.

"Okay," I said, interrupting whatever Yoshi was saying. "I'm in. What's the plan?"

"The first thing is getting you into the tournament," Yoshi said.

"I'm already taking care of that," Coach said as he typed on his phone.

"We're working on getting good schematics of the rink," Yoshi continued, "so that we know the perfect place to get you tapped into the network. Ideally you're going to be able to connect, find the exact location of the main system, and at the same time, shut it down."

"You make it sound so easy," I said.

"There'll be more briefings on the way to Denver, and

you'll have someone with you when you try to make the takedown."

I turned to Coach. "I need to know about this tournament too. Am I skilled enough to play in it, or is it going to be weird that I'm there?"

"No, you'll be great," Coach said. "The only reason we didn't send any Tigers is because it's typically for students who are looking to continue into high-level college hockey or straight into the NHL, but haven't been seen. It's a chance to show off for a number of scouts all at once. If you were on that track, we'd have submitted your name for consideration. There are a couple of wild-card slots, though, where scouts can request invites for players they want to see. We're getting you one of those."

I wasn't going to ask how they were making that happen. It was probably better I didn't know.

"Okay. But, I don't want to mess up anything for other players who need this opportunity for college."

He nodded dismissively and went back to his phone. My concerns about the tournament were probably not among the top mission objectives.

This was crazy. I was headed to Denver to play hockey and thwart a bunch of hackers.

"Before we go, I'll make sure your teachers and the team know why you're gone," Coach said.

"I'll talk to my professor too, so he won't think I've just bailed on class for a couple of days. When do we leave anyway?"

"Tomorrow morning," Yoshi said.

"Tomorrow," I said quietly. It made sense and yet I didn't think it'd be quite this soon. "Okay."

Mom shot me a concerned look that I didn't respond to. Another week missing a game, which Coach would take care of, and another weekend that wasn't going to work right for me and Eddie. There was no choice, though.

"If you've got time, we can start figuring out how we're going to hack into this network," Lorenzo said. "I've got some ideas and I bet you will too. The more we work out in advance, the more time we'll have if we need to try any outside-the-box concepts that I know you'll come up with."

I couldn't decide if the butterflies in my stomach were more excitement about the adventure or terror at the possibility that it could all go very wrong. The nerves could also be because I was going to have to explain to Eddie that I was suddenly leaving for the weekend to play in a tournament that wasn't even on my radar an hour ago.

FOURTEEN

"Let me get this straight," Eddie said, voice filled with irritation. "You're going to a tournament—in Denver—that Coach Daly just told you about a few hours ago. How's that even possible?"

This was even worse than I'd imagined. Between all the "client" work and now this, Eddie was getting shortchanged unlike any previous time in our year together. I couldn't blame him for being upset, but I couldn't change the situation either.

"Were you just not telling me about this because you didn't think you'd go, or because I didn't matter enough to know you were suddenly thinking about playing in college?" As he talked his voice grew angrier and his brow furrowed. The part that upset me most was the hurt in his eyes. "We've talked about this, Theo. You didn't want to put the time into playing in college with all the travel. Does MIT even have a team? Or have you decided that's not where you're going now?"

We were in the beanbags in front of Eddie's television. After Lorenzo and I worked out our initial plans, I excused myself because I couldn't just leave in the morning without seeing Eddie. It'd pissed Yoshi off, but Mom at least understood and made it okay for me to go. I clearly wasn't making a good first impression on Yoshi, but Lorenzo and I would have plenty of time to get our strategy together since we weren't going to try our hack until Friday between tournament games.

"Well, yeah, MIT has a team, and that's still where I want to go. Coach said a scout from Ohio wanted to see more of me and...."

"More of you? When did they see you the first time?"

Shit. I was rapidly getting in over my head. Coach had said the cover was that an Ohio scout invited me. I didn't think through telling this to Eddie who knew a lot about my college plans to this point.

"They scouted one of the seniors early in the season and they wanted another look at me. Since they're going to be at this tourney, they reached out to Coach to invite me."

He sat up in the beanbag and scowled at me. "I don't get it, so now it's Ohio? I thought we were staying here. That's all we've talked about. And you've scoffed at playing competitively because that's not the direction you wanted to go."

"Coach and my parents think I should consider all my options." We were quiet for a moment before I turned away to stare at the blank TV. "I thought you'd be kinda excited for me that someone thinks I'm good enough to play at that level."

Out of the corner of my eye, I saw Eddie's expression soften as he let go a sigh that sounded like he'd been holding in way too much air. I hated that I played him with the gee-I'm-sorry move and tone. I kept stuff from Mom and Dad all the time, but at least they knew the bigger secrets that were in play.

"I am excited, Theo, because I know how much you love to play. But I don't get why I'm not in the conversation, for the trip or for maybe going to a different school. How is this thing just coming up now? You can't tell me that you didn't have an idea that Ohio wanted to see you, or that it was even a possibility. What kind of tournament gives a player less than a day's notice they have to travel, especially halfway across the country?"

"I don't know what to tell you," I said, and at least that was the truth. "Coach told me today and my parents were all for it."

"Stop lying to me, Theo," Eddie said tersely. The hard look was back, and my insides tensed up. I'd never heard him like this before. "Is this what you were hiding yesterday? Why you seemed so stressed out? You couldn't figure out how to tell me that you were making new plans? I don't expect you to ask permission or anything 'cause that'd be stupid. But I wanna know what you're thinking. Maybe help you work through things. You listen to me all the time. It should be a two-way street."

"Maybe I want to see if I'm good enough," I said, locking eyes with him. I was going to have to go on the defensive if I was somehow going to save this. "Is that okay? I haven't changed any plans. I'm just checking out this possibility."

"You're good enough, and I hate that you don't know that." My tactic did nothing to lighten his anger. "It's bad enough you've got all this work stuff that I know stresses you out, and now this. What else is knocking around your head that I know nothing about? What goes on in the secret life of Theo Reese?"

And there it was. What would he think if he knew exactly how many secrets I had?

"It just wasn't important enough to talk about. Nothing's set yet."

"Or maybe I'm not important enough to talk to. Who else knew? Mitch? I bet he knows."

"Actually he doesn't. I was gonna call him *after* I talked to you, because you're the one who should know first."

More silence. I was so out of my depth here. Eddie and I had enjoyed pretty smooth sailing, usually only disagreeing over the weird hours. This was a flat-out fight, and I didn't like it.

I sat forward and reached for his hand. He jerked back when I made contact, as if I'd burned him.

"I think you should go." He rolled out of the beanbag, struggled to stand up, and moved across the room—about as far away from me as he could get and still be inside the four walls. He didn't let his healing ribs keep him from getting distance from me. "I'll see you when you get back."

"Eddie...."

Before I could get up or even say more, he interrupted me. "Really. Just go."

With that, he retreated to the bathroom across the hall. It wasn't lost on me that it was just a few days ago that I ran in there when I couldn't deal with being in this room.

I really messed this up. I quietly left the room and slipped out of the house. Luckily his parents weren't in the living room, so I didn't have to make an awkward goodbye to them.

I didn't think we'd broken up, but we were teetering on the brink. I had every intention of going through with my plans for MIT. Why would I change that? Not only was I already earning credits there, but I loved everything about the place. Once I was back, I'd make it clear that I'm not pursuing college hockey—outside of pickup or intramurals anyway—and that MIT is my college. Denver will have just been a lark.

I needed to come up with something big when I returned. He wanted to go to that fall dance. Maybe I could turn that into something super cool for us, as a way to apologize for all the stuff going on.

I'd expected him to be happy for me getting put into the tourney. I hadn't thought about how it looked that I was going, though. Usually all the available scenarios clicked into my head so I could sort through to find the right one. Of course this was unlike anything I'd dealt with before, even though thinking through things was something I typically excelled at. This time I'd really botched it.

Maybe I was too engaged thinking about the mission. There were so many ways for that to go wrong, and it went far beyond hacking into the enemy's network. There were agents to find and bad guys to capture. It didn't seem possible to cover all the permutations.

I couldn't bail on this mission; getting Dad back was too important. His capture was my fault because I hadn't stopped the hack fast enough. Mom and Dad might be right. Once he was home, though, maybe I should actually set up a computer consultancy and live the lie I've been using as a cover for the last few years. Or I could just finish high school and be a regular guy.

It was a lot to think about. Hopefully my brain's processors wouldn't overload.

FIFTEEN

By the time I got to Denver, I thought I might be more nervous about meeting the team and being a good player for them, than about anything else that was happening. Of course the other thing on my mind was Eddie. He didn't text me back last night, and he hadn't today either. He also sent my calls straight to voicemail.

It'd been a while since I was on a team where I didn't know anyone. The roster announcement would take place at the welcome dinner. I'd never done a tournament like that. I was going to have to prove myself to a coach and teammates that I didn't know. I played good hockey. I knew that. Hopefully I'd be able to focus on the games when it was time, rather than getting distracted by the mission.

I had a lot to worry about. I didn't want to let my teammates, fellow agents, or parents down.

Our group was staying in the host hotel, which was near the rink. My gear went straight to the rink and was being placed in my locker, which made me a little uneasy since I liked things to be a certain way. I'd deal with that tomorrow by getting there early.

Surprisingly I had a room to myself. I figured Mom or John or Coach would stay with me, but the room was all mine. I liked it for the privacy, but I also felt vulnerable, even though they were in the rooms surrounding me. I refused to let on about that, so I did my best to bury my uneasiness.

I'd brought my secure laptop as well as a tablet. Lorenzo and I had spent hours enhancing the iPad for the mission. It had customized apps that should let me get into the covert network, provided the intel we had was right.

A knock on the door made me jump as I was setting up the normal laptop at the desk. Looking through the peep-hole, I saw Mom.

"Hey," I said, opening the door.

"How're you holding up?" she asked.

"What do you mean?"

I went to the desk to set up the laptop so it was ready to go if I needed to use it. I figured it was good to have it out for show too, so the room looked properly lived in.

"I'm not blind, Theo," she said, taking a seat on the edge of the room's king-size bed. "You're stressed, more so than I've ever seen you. You can still walk away from this, or change places with Lorenzo."

I swallowed a laugh I knew she wouldn't appreciate. Lorenzo couldn't take my place. Not now.

"How would he? He can't play hockey, so he wouldn't have easy access to the parts of the rink we need to be in." I finished with the laptop and closed the lid so it'd sleep. "Besides, even he thinks my skills are a requirement to work through the network security we're going to encounter."

We looked at each other silently. I didn't know what she expected me to say, and I couldn't read her expression. This was a new thing. Usually she was an open book to me, but during the past few days, I hadn't always been able to sort out what she was thinking. It's like she'd put up new security protocols I hadn't figured out yet.

"You're growing up so fast," she said with a sigh. "I haven't reconsidered involving you in TOS for so long, because you've thrived working on whatever they give you. It's been behind the scenes and mostly safe. You're out here in real danger now. As Snowbird I know it's one of the best possible things for the mission, but as Mom I'm terrified."

Damn.

"It's going to be fine," I said. "There're a lot of people here who won't let anything happen to me."

She opened her mouth and then didn't speak. It just hung open for a moment.

"Can I be completely honest with you?" she finally asked.

I couldn't say no, even though I was pretty sure I didn't want to hear what she was going to say.

"I hope you always are, at least as much as the job allows."

"You say that, about people watching over you, and yet you still got abducted."

"I know. I've thought about that. I'm hoping it just looks like I'm here to play hockey and that they don't know that I'm any kind of agent. Maybe they'll think I had a chip because I'm the kid of an agent. In other words, I'm trying not to freak out about any of that."

"How did I get a son who's so smart?" she asked.

"Smart would've been to stay home. I'm scared too, Mom." I stood up from the desk chair and went to the window to look out on the leaf-covered grounds. "I have no field training. The computer stuff isn't a problem, but what if something else happens? The only thing I know is what

I've seen in Bourne and Bond movies, and I'm not sure that's helpful."

I turned to face her but stayed by the window.

"I don't suppose you can stuff all your training into my head in the next few hours?"

She smiled, and it made me happy.

"I wish it were that easy. Theo, you're one of the smartest people I know. I think you've got a lot of common sense too. Just apply all of it."

Another knock at the door. This was probably Coach, because we had to go to the opening reception in the ballroom.

I once again looked out the peephole. Indeed Coach had dressed sharp in his game-day attire of dark suit, dark shirt, and colorful tie. I always thought he looked red-carpet ready in this outfit. I dressed a lot more casually in a light blue T-shirt with dark jeans and dark sneakers. I had a jacket to wear too, just to dress up the whole thing.

"Come on in." I held the door open for him.

"Katherine." He acknowledged Mom. "Before we go, I want to set you up for comms so you'll always be in contact."

He pulled a case from his pocket. Inside was a small black object, scarcely bigger than a sprinkle on top of a cupcake. I'd seen these before because Lorenzo and I did an upgrade on them six months ago, but I'd never used one. He also pulled tweezers out of his pocket.

"I'm gonna put this in your ear and we'll test it. You should know that once this is in, the six of us will hear everything you say, and you'll hear everything we say, unless you modify the settings with the app."

"Got it. So no late-night partying and such."

I struggled not to laugh since I was not exactly the party

type. Coach laughed first, though, and then Mom, so I couldn't contain myself.

She slapped my shoulder as she walked by, headed for the door. "I need to check in with John. You"—she pointed at me—"behave!"

I grinned at her as she left. We needed more light-hearted moments to break the tension.

"Now be still and I'll get this in place." Coach picked up the tiny device with the tweezers and went to work.

It was hard not to move because of the tickly sensation in my ear. All I could think of was that gross scene in *Star Trek II* where Khan put those little mind-control critters into Chekov and that captain guy.

That's what this whole mission was, trying to zap and get control of little critters. Where was Captain Kirk when you needed him?

"Okay," Coach said. "You should hear my voice in your ear."

I nodded. It was weird hearing him twice. The earpiece had a bit of delay, but it worked. It itched a little too, like a bug crawling around. I resisted scratching at my ear.

"You'll get used to it." He apparently noticed my discomfort. "I promise."

Again I heard him twice. That, more than the itch, was going to take some getting used to.

"So when you are addressing comments to someone on channel, you'll refer to them by their codename," he contin-ued. "That way there'll be no guessing who you're talking to. Lorenzo's already sent the app to your phone. It turns it off completely, or lets you mute yourself or the external conversation."

"Oh, so I can party and no one will know?"

"As long as you don't forget the mute part," came Mom's voice in my ear.

"Lastly anytime you activate yours, you should always come on with your codename. That way everyone knows you're on channel."

"Winger here."

"Better late than never." Coach clapped me on the shoulder. "Shall we get going?"

I grabbed my jacket and took a look in the mirror. I fussed with my hair just a bit, trying to get it to lie right. I wanted to make a good impression on my soon-to-be teammates and opponents.

I crossed in front of Coach, and he fell in behind me. Before I opened the door, he put his hand on my shoulder. "Don't worry, Theo. You're going to be fine. Nothing's going to happen tonight."

"Except I'm about to meet a hundred-something hockey players who are going to wonder why I'm here. I'd almost rather there was something techie for me to do."

Coach chuckled under his breath. "It'll still be fine."

We chattered about the game we were missing back home as we went downstairs. I hated missing two weeks on the Tigers, but at least this was better than sitting out for an injury. We should win this game pretty easily, unless something went wrong. By next week the tracker matter should be solved and life back to normal.

Players and coaches packed the hotel ballroom. No scouts were allowed. This was just a mixer for the players, most of whom were here with coaches as chaperons. As far as they would know, Coach was my only guardian here. John and Mom had tickets as spectators and would blend in with parents here to watch.

Just inside the door was the check-in where I got my

official name tag. I was branded: *Theo Reese. Left Wing. McKinley High Tigers, Boston, Mass.*

Thankfully my arrival didn't make the entire room turn and look, which was a fear I'd had. Given the small number of tags left on the table, I was among the last to arrive. We were stuck down here until they made opening remarks and team assignments. I also had visions this was going to be like grade school PE. I was usually picked midpack back then, and while I didn't know how this was going to work, I dreaded being the last pick.

"I'm going to mingle," Coach said. "Try to have a good time. Remember you're just as good as the rest of these guys. Don't sell yourself short."

I didn't know what I was doing. I played a good game, but being in this situation gave me the jitters. I wandered over to the buffet and picked up some little meatballs and some chicken strips along with a bottle of water I stuck in my jacket pocket. At least the food looked good.

I scanned the crowd, trying to size up the group. It pretty much looked like any gathering of high school athletes I'd ever seen. There were a couple of huge guys, who had to be defensemen, who I hoped I wouldn't come up against. The players gathered together while the coaches had a cluster of their own.

"Hey. Glad to see I'm not the only one standing on the edge of the crowd."

Luckily I didn't flinch, even though this guy had snuck up on me.

"Yeah. Just getting the feel of the room. Theo Reese." I turned to look at the guy.

He raised a fist, which I happily bumped in the universal hockey-player greeting. "Jamie McAllister. You're another one of the wild cards. Cool."

"Nice to meet you." I hoped I didn't sound too enthusiastic. "How'd you know I was a wild card, though?"

"Player bios went up on the website yesterday. The wild cards were all flagged with asterisks. How'd you get your ticket punched?"

"Ohio wanted to see more of me after they scouted a McKinley game looking at a couple of my teammates." It rolled right off my tongue like it was the truth. "I hadn't planned to play in college, but I guess we'll see what comes of this."

"Well done, Winger. No hesitation at all."

It was almost a total freak-out when Coach's voice came booming into my ear. Hopefully Jamie didn't see a reaction.

"Cool." If Jamie noticed any change in me, he didn't mention it. "I was too wishy-washy at the top of the season. I wasn't sure if college was even what I wanted, but if I can get a scholarship, it'd be worth it. My coach got a contact of his to invite me. We'll see. Maybe I'll get on someone's radar."

According to Jamie's tag, he was a goalie. He was my size and had his long brown hair pulled back in a ponytail.

The main program started, sparing us from any additional conversation. Over the next thirty minutes, they divided us up into teams. There were six, and it was a double-elimination tourney. Beyond the medals for winning the tournament, there were going to be most valuable player awards for forwards, defensemen, and goalies.

Right after the team assignments, the players and coaches gathered under the colored banner for their team. I was assigned to gold. There were sixteen of us—mostly juniors, although we had one senior. Jamie was our goalie, so I wasn't completely among strangers.

"Nice to meet you all," said our coach, Martin Bayliss.

"I'll be studying up on everyone tonight to make our initial lines. Our first game is tomorrow morning, and we have the potential to play twice each day, so recovery and rest between games is critical. We'll meet for breakfast at seven to go over lines and strategy. In the meantime, enjoy the next hour or so and get to know each other before you hit the sack."

A round of "yes, sir" and "yes, Coach" followed before he walked away.

"So how many points this season, Reese?" asked Donny, a winger from a school in Maine.

"I've played four games so far, and I've got seven." I was glad I'd actually checked my stats before I left. I didn't usually keep up, but Coach said I might need to know.

"Not bad." Donny sounded smug. "I've got nine in four."

Everyone started throwing out stats.

"Winger. Doctor Possible here. Need to talk when you can break free."

How would it look if I walked out while we were still supposed to be bonding? I was mostly listening and only answering what I had to. But I was ready to go. Posturing over stats was boring.

Finally Donny put an end to what he'd started. "We seem pretty well balanced in stats. That should help us get some wins."

"Stand by Winger. I'll extract you."

Even though it was jarring, there were clearly major benefits of the earpiece. Why didn't everyone have these? It'd be so awesome to have a network with your friends to bail you out of situations without having to rely on a sly text message. You could simply say a code word, or someone else could step in. It'd be awesome.

"Not sure I'm thrilled that we ended up with two of the wild cards." Donny's commentary just kept going. "They should've evenly split them across the teams rather than landing two on one. That means there's at least one team with none."

"Don't worry about me," Jamie said. "I'll have your backs."

"Not you I'm worried about," Donny continued. "I've researched everyone here as soon as the player list came out. It's going to be a close tourney. All the players have a ton of great stats and press coverage showing their achievements. But even with his stats, it's hard to find anything more on Reese." I stared him down like I would if we were in a face-off. "I can read more about your work at MIT than I can about you on the ice. You sure you wouldn't be more comfortable in a computer lab for the weekend?"

Great. I'd been Googled and most of what he found were my papers. It's not my fault MIT had better search-engine rankings than my team's website or the school newspaper. At least TOS had done a good job keeping the kidnapping thing out of the media so he didn't find that too.

"You know my stats, so you know what I can do and that I hold my own in a strong division. If you researched as thoroughly as you say, you'd have seen a couple of vids of my scoring on YouTube. If that's not enough, you'll have to wait until tomorrow."

"Coach better not put you on my line," he said.

"Sorry to interrupt, guys." It was Coach Daly. "I need to borrow Theo to go over some stuff."

As we walked away, I heard Donny continue to disparage me. Apparently he didn't think a geek could play hockey.

"Good timing," I said to Coach. "Otherwise we might've been trying to have a shootout in here."

"You'll show him tomorrow. I'm sure of that."

"Doctor Possible. It's Winger. Headed to my room if you want to start talking." Whispering to myself was weird.

"Come to mine, Winger. It'll be easier to show you here."

"Got it."

We headed to the elevators.

"Get your sleep tonight, okay?" Coach said and I nodded. "You'll need it tomorrow, between the two games and the mission."

"I will."

"Good." Coach got off at the floor our rooms were on. I stayed on and went up four more to where Lorenzo was and hoped he had some good things to show me.

SIXTEEN

I DIDN'T GET to bed as early as I wanted, but I compensated by sleeping late and giving myself only twenty minutes to eat. It wasn't like I had to look great since we were having breakfast and then going straight to the rink to get ready for the tourney's first game.

I was up late with Lorenzo going over some new intel we had on what was under the rink. We were going to tap into the fiber-optic network that ran in the service corridor right behind the locker rooms. It would keep us from having to go into the sublevels. I also practiced making the tap into the network to ensure the connection would go unnoticed.

Luckily my lack of sleep didn't impair me on the ice. The gold team was great to play with, although when Donny found out we were on the first line together, he groaned. He quickly changed his tune when I scored the first goal of the game. He found me even more useful in the second period when I set him up for a goal of his own. With less than ten minutes to go, the game was going brilliantly.

How long did it take agents to get used to the chatter in their head from the earpieces? The TOS agents were here watching the game because we had work to do right after. They were talking up a storm in the stands. Nothing related to the mission, of course, but their voices filled my head. It was fascinating because I could still hear everything around me on the ice, but what Mom, John, Coach, Yoshi, and Lorenzo said went straight into my brain. I had to work to keep my focus on the game.

Out for one of my last shifts, I got a breakaway when the opposing team's defense mishandled the puck. I wasted no time barreling down the ice. As I crossed into the offensive zone, a defenseman caught up to me. I saw him in my peripheral vision and noted I had no one to pass to. I got a shot off just before the D tripped me.

I spun out and ended up crashing the boards. There was a whistle, but as I turned over the ref didn't have his hand up. The goalie, however, had the puck in his hand. Apparently none of the refs saw the trip, because there was no penalty call.

"Winger, you okay?" It was Mom.

Oh my God. I would have to mute the earpiece for the next game. The chatter was bad enough, but Mom asking questions was not cool. I was hoping they'd let me take it out for the games. After all, I didn't want it flying out if things got physical. But apparently they're designed to stay put even under the most extreme conditions.

"Yes," I said quietly as I stood up.

I wasn't really okay. That hit rattled everything that had been hurt during the kidnap attempt last week. No way I was going to admit that, though.

I shook it off and set up for the face-off, which was just to the right of the goalie.

"Okay?" our center asked.

"Yeah. Let's do this."

He nodded.

We won the face-off and got a shot on the goalie, which bounced off him and landed right on my stick. I made a low shot, sending it just between the goalie's pad and the post. It was perfect.

The team piled on me. The score was five to three, and with that safety goal, the chances of us winning just went up considerably because there were less than five minutes on the clock.

As we headed back to the bench, from our net Jamie raised his stick in salute. The wild cards were proving pretty valuable so far.

My last shift was a bust—lots of chances but no scoring. Their goalie kept us at bay even while his defense crumbled.

We'd won our first and now had a few hours off before we'd go again.

"Winger, let us know when you're in position," came Yoshi's voice before I even left the ice. *"D-Man will meet you just inside the service entrance."*

"Yup."

I tried Eddie again as soon as I got my locker open. He'd never been this angry. Was I going to have a boyfriend when I got home?

When I got to the showers, my teammates were dissecting everything about the game.

"Great job out there," Jamie said as I took the stall to his left.

"Thanks. You too. Hell, we all did great, especially for that being our first time together."

"At least we should have the *wild card* branding off us now."

"Hope so. Be good to get through the rest of the weekend just being able to play."

"Although you might have a different target on your back now after the points you racked up out there."

"I'm okay with that." I grinned. That was one target I could deal with.

The hot water was great, relaxing the muscles tense from the impact of that hit. I closed my eyes and let the water soothe me while the chatter of my teammates kept me engaged. The talk shifted to strategies we should use this afternoon.

"Winger, we're all in position," Yoshi said. *"Snowbird is in the Starbucks two doors down, and Doctor Possible and I are in a van in the parking lot. No response required."*

I couldn't delay any longer. I'd have to take care of the aches later.

"You wanna grab some lunch before the next game?" Jamie asked as I turned off the water. "We're going to see what we can find nearby."

"I'll catch up with you later. Some of my family came in and are waiting for me."

"Got it. See ya, Theo."

I grabbed my towel from the hook just outside the shower room and dried off as I headed to my locker. I quickly stored my gear, hoping for the best drying possible before the next game, and got dressed.

After the last of the gold team headed out, I made for the service corridor that ran behind the locker rooms. Coach Daly met me just inside the door as planned. He had a gun drawn, which I hadn't expected even though he was there to make sure I stayed safe while carrying out the mission.

I moved as if I knew exactly where I was going, which I did since I'd studied the maps. I also acted like I belonged here, looking authoritative and feeling the part. Coach and I went through the Employees Only door and closed it behind me. No one was in the corridor.

"Winger here. I'm in. Moving with D-Man to the designated point."

"*Copy that,*" said Yoshi.

Okay, this was cool! Yeah, I'd had the earpiece in for a while now, but this was using it for real. And I was using my codename for more than phone calls. It was pretty badass.

"*Doctor Possible here. We're tracking you, Winger.*"

We'd modified my phone and earpiece so the team would be able to monitor my movements.

There were a lot of conduits in here, far more than it seemed like the rink should need. Last year I had a behind-the-scenes tour of my rink at home. There were lots of refrigeration pipes to move coolant. But here there were far more electrical conduits for this three-rink facility than in our six-rink one. We walked for what amounted to a couple of blocks before we made a right turn where there was a steep set of stairs. Coach stayed at the top of the stairs to keep watch as I descended.

On the lower level, the conduits were larger and often marked as high voltage. There was a huge junction box about 150 feet ahead, which contained the fiber optics I was looking for.

As soon as I was in front of it, I took off my pack and pulled out my tool kit.

First thing I used was a device that affixed to the keypad on the front of the locked box. Given the display, the sequence was six numbers. I made sure the sensors went over the keys and then activated it. It figured out which keys were used most—using fingerprints and wear patterns—and then it rapidly pushed the buttons until the box popped open.

Next I used the wire stripper to remove the casing from the fiber optics. I carefully did the work like I'd practiced with Lorenzo—making sure not to damage any of the fibers, but giving me easy access to them. My hands started shaking as I handled the thick casing that wrapped the fibers. I tried pretending this was just another practice.

"I've got the casing open, and I'm ready to apply the fiber tap."

I swapped tools for the TOS-designed fiber tap I got last night. It automatically sliced into the fibers, provided the tap I'd plug into, and maintained the fiber connection so it'd appear uninterrupted even as it made the connections.

As soon as the tap device was near the wires, it began whirring. It practically jumped from my hand as it grabbed the wires and began its specialized task. It was a simple-looking device with only three lights on top. Currently the yellow light showed, meaning it was doing its job. I waited for the green one to illuminate, because if it went red, things were going to get messy.

I took the tablet from the pack, along with the cord that would allow me to plug into the tap. Lorenzo and I had made modifications to the tablet last night to make sure it could handle the speed of the data flow. Luckily Lorenzo traveled with a lot of extra tools and parts.

The tap was taking longer than expected.

"The tap isn't done. Doc, are you able to track its progress?"

"*No. Damn. We should've added that function to the tablet.*"

"It's still yellow, so I guess it's okay."

Suddenly it snapped into place and the green light

popped on. The snap reverberated in the corridor, making me cringe. I shouldn't worry. The likelihood the sound alerted anyone was minimal. Plus D-Man was standing ready to take care of anyone who showed up.

"Got it. Tap complete. Stand by. Hooking tablet into the data stream."

We'd modified the tablet to feed Lorenzo everything via the same frequency the earpieces traveled on, so we weren't reliant on Wi-Fi or cell networks.

I plugged the tablet in and went to the app to get onto the fiber network. I had access, which meant the tap had done its job perfectly.

"Starting the search to see what's on the network."

I brought up another app, this one of my design, so I could analyze the traffic on the network. This was serious stuff, because everything was hard-core encrypted. But I knew exactly what I was looking for, based on my knowledge about the tracker chips. It only took a few seconds to see we were in the right place.

I found the firewall—the one we couldn't see from the outside because of its masking. Inside its home network, though, it wasn't hidden.

"Starting the firewall breach."

Using another program of my creation—which I'd used to show TOS the vulnerabilities in its own network, I started pushing on the firewall, looking for vulnerabilities I could exploit. All I needed was one way in, and then I should be able to force a door to stay open for me.

"*Time check, Winger,*" Yoshi said. "*You've been down there twenty minutes now.*"

"Copy that. It shouldn't be too much longer."

Different versions of my algorithms continued to bombard the security measures, and I added new variations as I saw the results. This was fun. I hadn't hacked a firewall like this in a long while, and it was more exciting than I remembered—changing things up to look for the security holes as authorized data moved through the firewall, but I was being turned away.

"Winger, I'm seeing some odd data streams coming through the tap. Are you seeing them? Started about thirty seconds ago."

I moved from the firewall program to a program where I could see the data flow. It appeared data was being sent straight to the tablet as an attack. Something was wrong. The tablet shouldn't be visible to anyone monitoring the datastream. Lorenzo and I had customized our attack to stay in the background. This incoming data to the tablet was acting almost like antibodies coming after a parasite.

"What the hell? I've never seen anything like this. Are you capturing, Doc?"

"Yeah and working to analyze."

The tablet flashed a notification that the program found a way through the firewall and was establishing a connection on the other side.

"I'm in. Doc, watch those odd flows. It seems like the tablet is being flooded, from what I can see. I'm going to try—"

Suddenly the display pixelated. I worked the small keyboard, as I accessed the tablet's root functions. I needed to insulate it from the incoming attack.

"Ahhhhh!" I couldn't stop the scream, even though I needed to be quiet.

My body spasmed.

I couldn't let go of the tablet.

"Winger!"

"D-man? What's happening?"

I couldn't respond. My body wasn't listening to my brain.

Even though I heard Coach say something in the earpiece, I couldn't understand.

The tablet shattered in my hands just before I slumped to the cold floor.

SEVENTEEN

I opened my eyes and tried to focus.

"Theo? It's Mom. Can you see me?"

"Blurry" was all I could say.

My body shifted as the surface moved beneath me. I must've been on a bed and someone had sat down. A hand ruffled my hair. That was definitely Mom.

I blinked, and she came into focus, along with the room behind her.

I was back in the hotel.

How'd I get here?

Behind Mom stood John, Coach, Lorenzo, and Yoshi. Everyone crammed into my room.

I was getting past the firewall and then....

I jerked and sat up.

"They were ready for us. They zapped my—"

"Easy, Theo." Mom used her mom voice as she pushed me back.

"They did," Lorenzo said. "We hadn't expected that. I—"

"I think I know how we can prevent it." I sat up again

despite my body's demands to do otherwise. "We can cloak the tablet and make the push on the firewall look like it's coming from somewhere else."

"Theoretically possible. We'd have to make some modifications. Might be hard to test that, but maybe."

"Theo, stop," Mom said. "You've been seriously injured. That shock you took was similar to what a high-power stun gun generates, plus you've got some cuts and minor burns from the tablet exploding in your hands. You're lucky this isn't a lot worse."

That explained a lot. Not only was I sore from that check this morning, but I was reeling from some hundred thousand volts of electricity.

"If I were any other agent, we wouldn't be having this discussion."

"We would," Yoshi said. "Just long enough to make sure you were okay before continuing."

"Why would you say that to him?" Mom shot Yoshi a death glare, which would be a hell of a superpower to have.

"Because it's true."

She gave a frustrated sigh as she stood up and walked to the window.

Did I need to be the agent or the son?

We still had to find Dad.

"Do we have the equipment?" I opted to be the agent even as a wave of nausea came over me.

Lorenzo thought a moment, consulting his tablet. "Yeah. Most of it. Testing, though...."

"My MIT adviser has contacts at the university here. Let me figure out how to ask for that without raising suspicion."

I looked to my watch, and it was gone. Weird.

"All the electronics on you fried," Lorenzo offered. "Watch, phone, earpiece."

"Fuck."

"Theo!" Mom snapped, turning from the window. "Regardless of the situation, I won't have that language." She was furious, and it was more than my word choice.

I paused for a moment, considering the options.

"Okay, here's the deal as I see it." I looked to the clock on the nightstand. "I've got a game in ninety minutes."

"Theo, no. I can't—"

I held up my hand, stopping Mom. If I was going to be an agent, I had to be all in.

"Being in the tournament is our easy access to where I need to work. If I don't play, we lose that. We don't know if Blackbird knows I'm the one who made the attack this morning, but if they do, I also want to show that they didn't win. It'll be rough to play, but I'll get through it. Lorenzo, if you can get the parts together and start work, I'll join you as soon as I'm done with tourney events. We need to make another go of this tomorrow. Do we know they won't try to move out?"

"We're watching all the traffic going and coming from the area," Yoshi said. "We're not completely satisfied that we've got the place buttoned up, but we're monitoring everything we can. We suspect the facility is too large to move on short notice, even if they know we're here."

"Okay. We get the equipment ready and make another run tomorrow. Coach, when do I need to be at the rink?"

"I'd say you've got forty-five minutes."

I nodded.

"I need some time with Mom and John. Coach, I'll see you in the lobby to go to the rink."

"Theo," Yoshi said, "we should further debrief."

"We can do some in the car on the way to the rink, or we can do it after the game. Not right now."

Yoshi looked at me. It was obvious he was trying to decide if he was going to challenge me. I was certainly on the verge of insubordination, because he was the team leader.

He ultimately nodded. "Let's leave them."

Coach and Yoshi headed for the door. Lorenzo held back a moment and handed me a phone from his messenger bag.

"It's exactly like yours. I uploaded everything from the cloud, so you should see no difference. I'll pick up a watch while I'm out and I'll have a tablet later as well."

I smiled. He had my back.

"Thanks, man."

He nodded and headed out with the others. The door was hardly closed before Mom let me have it.

"Theodore Reese, what are you thinking? You're in no condition to continue with this mission, much less play. I can't—"

"Mom." I spoke quietly. I couldn't be mad at her. "Dad's somewhere and we've got to find him. This is our best chance—"

"There're other people—"

"No. There aren't." I stayed calm. "If Lorenzo and I trade places, the response time will be down. He doesn't think as fast as I do about these types of things."

"Lorenzo is a highly trained, and I emphasize the word *trained*, operative and computer tech, what makes you think—"

"He's right, Katherine," John said. "Lorenzo's trained for the field, but Theo's the better tech for this scenario."

Mom leveled the death glare on John.

"Exactly," I continued. "There are situations where he'd outthink me, and we'd be better if I backed him up. This isn't one of those."

I went to the closet and looked at myself in the large mirror. I looked like crap. Dozens of small cuts marked my hands, and there were a few on my face too. My palms were a vivid red, clearly first-degree burns.

I thought I looked older too. Maybe it was how I carried myself because of the pain vibrating through me. Maybe it was because life had changed so much in just a few days.

I needed to come up with a story about how this happened, because I wasn't going to be able to cover up the damage. It was also possible in a group of strangers that no one would ask.

Meanwhile, the story I really wanted was how they'd managed to get me back to the room while I was unconscious. For some reason I imagined a slapstick comedy. I'd have to hear about that one later.

Strangely I wasn't scared. Not like I'd been after I was bikejacked. Was that normal? All I felt right now was the need to complete the mission.

"It's going to be okay, Mom."

I wrapped her in a hug. Since the kidnapping attempt, she'd been taking care of me and trying to work the case. Now her husband was missing and I was more in danger than ever. She needed that hug, I think, based on how tight she squeezed. It hurt pretty badly, but I didn't let her know that.

When she finally let go, she seemed calmer.

There was a knock and Mom let Lorenzo in.

"I wanted to get you a new earpiece before the game, just in case you needed it."

He handed me the device and I just stared at it. I'd never gotten the info on putting it in and taking it out.

"Oh. Okay." He caught on that I had no clue, so he took tweezers from his bag.

"Does everyone carry those? Are they agency issue?" I asked. "Shouldn't these just come with the earpiece as part of the package?"

"I got mine at Walgreens," Lorenzo said.

"Me too." John nodded.

I looked at Mom to finish this odd bit of sharing. "I actually use my mom's. I remembered playing with them at her makeup table when I was little, and when she passed, I decided to take them. I've used them specifically for the earpiece ever since."

I simply nodded. It was the best response to the surreal conversation.

Lorenzo showed me how to put it in and take it out, and I practiced a few times. I dropped it more than once. Frankly I worried about putting it in wrong and having it end up in my brain or something, which they promptly told me wasn't possible.

"And with that I gotta get going." I returned the tweezers to Lorenzo.

I stripped out of the sweatshirt I'd been wearing and fished another out of my bag. I caught myself in the mirror again and noticed several small lacerations on my chest and stomach. I could see the slits in the shirt when I further examined it.

Mom turned her head away. How did she deal with Dad on missions when things got rough? Or was this because I was her son? How did Dad do it when it was her in trouble? As I pulled the shirt on, my hands were tight and stinging. Putting them in hockey gloves wasn't going to be pleasant.

"Okay," I said. "Time to meet Coach."

"What are you going to say if anyone asks about the injuries?" John asked.

I shrugged. "I'll make it up on the fly. I'm thinking no one's gonna ask. It's not like I know these guys." I turned to Lorenzo. "While you're getting parts, can you get me some tweezers?"

"Of course." He chuckled.

"Thanks."

We all left the room with our various assignments. I knew Mom and John would be at the game and Coach would be there of course. Lorenzo and Yoshi would be gathering what we needed to make another go at the mission.

EIGHTEEN

The game was even tougher than I thought it would be. The pain was insane. Every stride hurt, not to mention the stinging sensations in my hands. It took everything I had to bury it. I was sucking at the game too, with my response time just enough out of sync that I made a lot of errors. While I didn't care what the scouts saw, I did want to support the team, and that wasn't happening.

As I suspected, however, if anyone noticed I was more battered than before, no one said anything. It probably helped I deliberately arrived late to the locker room, so everyone was already focused on getting ready.

Sitting on the bench and drinking water, I gazed through the crowd on the opposite side of the ice. The attendance was higher than I thought a high school tourney would be.

Crap.

Sitting right at center ice, about halfway up the stands, I discovered Eddie. What was he doing here? Were my eyes playing tricks on me? Huge coincidence if that was the case, because the guy sat exactly where Eddie liked to sit for Tigers games.

A stop in play brought a line change and my turn to go out on the ice.

"Winger here." I spoke softly as I went to my face-off spot. "Snowbird and Shotgun, why do you suppose—" I stopped short. I shouldn't say a real name on the comm. "Look one section to your right and three rows down."

"Did you know about that?" Snowbird asked.

That was all the confirmation I needed.

"Nope. He hasn't been talking to me."

Talk about complicated. Was this an apology for the other night? It was cool he was here, but I had things to do too. Eddie was going to want to hang, especially since I had a room to myself.

Damn. I had a room to myself and my boyfriend showed up. This should be the best thing ever. How was I going to put him off when I couldn't give a good reason for it?

As the puck dropped, my mind raced on what to do. Somehow, even with the distractions, my game-playing sense finally kicked in. I received the center's pass and one-timed it at the goalie. While the goalie deflected my shot, Donny was right there for the rebound and scored. He came at me and gave me a bear hug.

I struggled not to cry out when he tackled me with the embrace. I was going to need a vat of ibuprofen tonight.

"Man, I thought your head was in a computer somewhere with the way you were playing," Donny said. Was that condescension or concern? "Can we see more of that, please?"

We headed back to center ice. Since we were only out for a few seconds, we planned to stay at least another thirty.

The opposition won the face-off, so we were immediately on defense. I managed to block a pass from their center to the winger, but I ended up grappling for the puck because the winger wasn't giving up easily.

The winger kicked my skate out from under me, which sent me crashing on my butt and back. I don't think my body had ever taken as much punishment as it had in the past few hours. This time the ref saw the trip and called the penalty. I took that as my cue to end the shift and head back to the bench.

"You holding up?"

It was Coach Daly.

"Barely." I could hardly hear myself while I talked. "Hopefully I can stay on my feet for the next six minutes."

I looked across the rink to Eddie. He appeared to be solo. How'd he get here? It's not like it's easy for someone our age just to show up in Denver from Boston.

The opposing team managed to tie up the game with four to go.

My next shift was intense as I sprinted the length of the rink three times in less than forty-five seconds. It was the worst suicide drill ever because I was already exhausted. We didn't break the tie, and the second line didn't either.

Next shift out was more of the same as both sides kept turning over the puck and rushing back to the other side. I called on energy reserves I didn't know existed. No scoring again, so when the final buzzer sounded, we shifted to four-on-four overtime.

Ultimately the game went to a shootout. Coach decided I was going to go first. I stepped out and waited for the ref to place the puck at center ice and blow the whistle. I'd already gotten a goal on this guy, and I'd watched during the assists I'd picked up too. I had a fairly good idea on how he moved.

I started slowly as I picked up the puck from the dot and moved directly toward the goalie. As I crossed the blue line, I sped up a bit but didn't divert my path. We locked eyes but I watched the puck in the very edge of my vision. As I got aligned to the face-off dots, I diverted to my right and he stayed center, but our eyes focused on each other. I drifted farther right and maneuvered the puck with me, winding up to shoot.

He committed to the left, blocking up the net, but I shifted back to my left at the last moment and ultimately backhanded the puck right into the post. The *clank* echoed in my ears.

Fuck me. I had a wide-open net, and I managed to hit the post. I slammed my stick into the ice as I returned to the bench. As I sat down, several teammates commented that it was just an unlucky break. Thankfully Jamie stopped the opposition.

The second-round shooters also failed, though not as spectacularly as I did. Donny finally got a puck in the net, and the bench cheered for his return. We'd win if the opponent didn't score.

I stood on the bench, watching Jamie. He was the picture of cool, just like during both games. The skater came in, zigging all around. Jamie didn't commit. I wasn't sure what he looked at—the puck, the player, the stick. All he moved was his glove hand. The shooter got close, into the deep slot, before he let the puck go. Jamie confidently caught it in his glove, which he held up defiantly as he skated out of the crease.

We erupted into cheers and spilled off the bench. After we swarmed Jamie to thank him for keeping us in the game, we shook hands with the other team. We'd snagged our second win, no thanks to me.

I was among the first into the locker room and into the shower. I stood under the spray, enjoying the water running over my weary body. The water felt like pinpricks where I had cuts and burns, but I ignored it because the rest of me needed it.

"Hey, Reese," called our coach. I turned to find him in the doorway to the showers. "Someone's here to see you."

Dammit. Really? It had to be Eddie. Everyone else would've just called over the earpiece.

"Thanks. I'll be right out."

I quickly soaped up to get the hockey stench off me.

"You okay, Theo?" Jamie took the shower to my left. "I know I've only played one game with you, but you seemed off."

"I'm more banged up from this morning than I thought. And that trip in the third just made it worse." I rinsed and regretfully shut off the water. "I gotta get going. I'll see you at the dinner tonight."

"All right. Take care." Jamie sounded concerned, which I ignored.

In the locker room, I moved quickly to stow my stuff and dress. Despite the fact I had things to do with Lorenzo, I put on my best great-to-see-you face. Eddie was leaning against the wall across from the doorway.

"I thought I saw you in the stands." I came up and wrapped him in my arms—a move which came with a fair bit of screaming from my muscles. "What a great surprise."

He kissed me and squeezed me tight. My body didn't know what to do with the mix of sensations, between the awesome kiss and the painful squeeze. Hopefully the moan that escaped sounded like enjoyment. Truthfully I wasn't sure which one it was.

"You too." He continued to hold me. "I'm sorry I was such a dick before you left."

"Don't be sorry. It's on me for not telling you about this when Coach first brought it up. You should've known this was a possibility."

"It's behind us." He waved his hand, as if I needed the extra emphasis. "Are you doing okay, though? You looked rough out there."

"I got slammed pretty hard in the morning game and it's painful. Come on, let's get out of here. There are better places to hang out." I took his hand and headed for the rink lobby. "So how'd you get out here?" I asked. "It's an epic surprise."

"My dad's here for a conference, so I asked if I could tag along so I could apologize. He shocked me by saying yes."

Eddie's dad is an insurance and financial consultant, and while he's nice, he never seemed like someone who would bring his son along on a business trip.

"Guess what?" I shouldn't say what I was about to, but I was going to go for it and deal with the ramifications later.

"It must be good. You've got such a wicked look on your face."

"I've got a room to myself."

"No way." The excitement in his voice nearly matched mine.

"Winger, mute yourself before you say stuff like that."

Dammit. Mom. I forgot about the stupid earpiece. I'd already gotten used to it in my ear and for this game, they said they'd keep their side muted unless it was important.

I nodded, smiled, and raised my eyebrows at Eddie, going for silent communication.

"Winger"—this time it was Lorenzo—*"sorry to break up this minireunion, but I need you. I've got some stuff to test if you've gotten access to that lab."*

I hadn't looked at my phone since the game ended, so I didn't know yet if we had the lab. The lab would have to take priority.

"Winger"—now it was Coach—*"I'll call you to help extract you from this conversation. Stand by."*

Could nothing go right? Just a few minutes with my guy would be great to improve this crap day. But I'd asked for this since I was playing secret-agent man. My phone vibrated.

"It's Coach." I showed my phone to Eddie. "One second." We both stepped to the side of the hallway so we weren't blocking traffic. "Hey, Coach."

"Your mom's going to kill you, you know?"

I sighed. "Yeah. Not my smartest move."

"So tell Eddie that you need to meet me to go over some game-play stuff and that I've got some physical therapy lined up to help with the previous game's injury. That'll give you a few hours."

As I talked, Eddie touched my hand that held the phone and then took the other one in his. Concern crossed his face, and I shrugged trying to make it seem like nothing.

"Sounds good, Coach. I could use the PT for sure. I'll see you in a few minutes."

I clicked the call off, and Eddie took the phone and turned my hand over, studying the redness.

"What happened?" he asked as I tried to grab the phone because I don't like it being in anyone else's possession. "These look awful."

He kissed the palm of my right hand, which was redder than the left.

"Scalded myself this morning. The water went superhot all of a sudden."

"Damn, Theo, you gotta be more careful." He handed the phone back, and I immediately pocketed it. "How did you manage to play like this?"

"Just did. Didn't have a choice, you know? Look, I hate to do this, but I've got to get back to the hotel to meet with Coach Daly to talk about today's games, especially the mess that last one was." I didn't have to fake disappointment. I really wanted to spend time with Eddie after all that had gone down since we arrived in Denver. "He's also got me an appointment to get worked on because of the hits I've taken."

"It'd be more fun if I worked on that." He laid a red-hot kiss on me, which yielded a whistle from someone that passed us in the hall.

"There's a dinner and mixer thing I've got to go to tonight. After that we should be able to chill."

The slightest frown played across his lips. "Can I come with you? Hang out? Meet your teammates?"

"I don't know if I can bring a guest. I'll find out, though." Since holding his hand would be uncomfortable, I hooked my elbow around his and started walking. "I'd love to just go do stuff with you, but between the games and some of the other tournament stuff, it's kinda busy."

"Don't worry about it." His usual smile returned. "I didn't even know what your game schedule was until I got here, so I'll take whatever I can get."

"I love that you're here." I truly meant it. "It's a perfect surprise. We'll get some time for sure."

As we walked the dozen or so blocks back to the hotel, the hum of pain increased. The adrenaline from the game was wearing off, leaving me sore. I wondered if Coach could really set me up with some PT.

"Are you really okay? I swear you seem like you're in more pain than after the whole kidnapping thing."

"The therapy will help—both the professional *and* yours."

"Anything you want." Eddie took my hand.

"I love you."

He kissed my hand and smiled.

It was awesome to see Eddie. But we were going to have to figure out how to manage him. At least he and I could grab nights together, I'd just have to be stealthy to avoid Mom.

NINETEEN

The hours postgame were exhausting but beneficial. Lorenzo made some great advances on our tech before we went to see Dr. Abbey, director of the Computer Science and Engineering Department at CU Denver. I managed to play everything off as an experiment about fiber-optic data flow, and she left us to our work. Apparently my prof gave me such a rave recommendation she was good leaving Lorenzo and me on our own.

We had good results making it look like we weren't on the network at all. It wasn't foolproof, but hopefully they wouldn't be able to detect our masking. Since Lorenzo created it, I spent some time trying to break it and could do it easily only because I knew it was there in the first place. We didn't know what kind of tech the bad guys had available, so we still needed to be careful.

By the time the evening dinner and mixer rolled around, I wanted a nap. I was almost late, having lost track of time with Lorenzo. It was only because Coach called me that I managed to get to the hotel and change in time.

Tonight was a more formal banquet, so I actually threw on a real shirt as well as the tie I'd ignored last night.

Eddie met me in the hallway that led to the ballroom. He was so handsome decked out in a dark purple shirt, black coat, and black jeans. He was almost monochromatic, but the shirt had just enough pop to make a nice contrast. Neither of us liked to dress up. In fact I absolutely shunned it as much as I could. He looked amazing.

"Oh my God, I forgot to check to see if you could be here." I felt bad that he was all dressed up and might not be able to get in.

"Not to worry." He pulled out a lanyard and badge from his pocket. He put it around his neck, so he matched me. "I took care of it. You can bring guests, just had to pay fifty bucks. Totally worth it to hang out with you looking all sharp."

I gave him a quick kiss. Truth was, I needed this. An evening with my boyfriend was a great end to a less-than-stellar day. I'm glad he took the initiative to find out if he could come along.

"Next to you, I'm far from sharp. You look stunning."

"Dad made me bring something dressy since he's taking me to some speech tomorrow. I thought it'd be perfect for tonight too."

"Go Mr. Cochrane."

Instead of a tournament banquet, I felt like I was going to prom.

Prom? He'd already mentioned that once. Would he ask me? Or should I ask him since he'd asked me to the fall dance? How does that even work when you're both guys?

"Where'd you go just now? I recognize the look of you solving a problem."

My face heated. He'd caught me plotting the future.

"Oh man, it's something good too," he added. "I haven't seen you blush in a long time."

I looked away and willed the blush to fade as I checked out the crowd assembling in the ballroom. It looked like there was an array of guests, from parents to girlfriends.

"Come on." He reached under my jacket so he could tickle me. With only the dress shirt between my skin and his fingers, I giggled and squirmed. "Tell me."

"All right." I relented since I didn't want him to go too far with the tickles. "My mind flashed forward to prom and thinking about how great we'll look."

A soft, wonderful smile replaced his mischievous look. "Is that your way of asking me to prom?"

"I guess it sorta is, yeah."

"Cool."

"Very cool." And just like that, I had a prom date. "Let's get some dinner, I'm starving."

We walked into the ballroom and I looked around, trying to decide where we should sit.

"Theo! Over here."

It was Jamie sitting a couple of tables away. He waved us over. Other teammates sat at the table, but there were three chairs still open. Most tables had some spaces left, but this was a good choice since Jamie was cool. The other two guys were both defensemen, one was Chuck, but I couldn't remember the other's name.

"Hey, Jamie. These free?"

"Yeah, man. Hoping to get a table full of teammates." He looked at Eddie, and it was obvious he was trying to resolve if Eddie was on our team or not. Given that I didn't know everyone on sight yet either, I understood his confusion.

"This is my boyfriend, Eddie. He came to town to catch some of the games. Eddie, this is our goalie, Jamie."

"S'up?" Eddie said with a quick nod of the head. "You were great in that shootout."

"Thanks, man."

"And this is Chuck and...." I pushed my brain one more time to see if I could get the name of the other guy, but it wasn't happening.

"Billy," he said.

I nodded and we sat down. I attacked the salad in front of me. I'd had a couple of protein bars after the game, but they weren't enough.

"That's cool you could come see the games," Jamie said to Eddie. "The only person that came with me is my coach."

Donny joined us. If Eddie was uncomfortable being at a table full of players who were strangers, he didn't show it. It was different from any gathering we'd had with the team back home, which was usually a party at someone's house where we could drift around. Here, we couldn't leave the table.

Dinner was good, but it went on way too long. Eddie was a champ listening to all of the strategy we talked. Donny's coach had looked at some of the other teams' play, so we had some intel that we dissected to be ready for tomorrow.

"You better be on your game tomorrow, Reese," Donny said. "We can't have the mistakes you were making this afternoon. You got that one assist, but the rest of the game was like peewees on ice."

"Everyone has bad games." I appreciated Jamie came to my defense. "Why are you being a douche?"

"Because we don't get to have bad games here. These are too important—for all of us."

"I can tell you from firsthand experience that this afternoon was a fluke," Eddie chimed in.

Stealthy, I placed a hand on Eddie's knee, hoping he wouldn't add fuel to the fire.

"He's right." There was no bravado in my voice like I had last night when we were going over stats. "I played like shit."

"Glad to see we're agreed."

Donny and I stared at each other for a bit before I looked away. I was too tired to play his games, especially since he was right.

Finally people started to exit, and that was the signal we'd stayed as long as we needed to. We'd already had a couple of desserts, and while Eddie was doing okay, I could tell he was as ready to go as I was.

"Guys, I'll see you in the morning," I said, standing.

"Good to meet you all." Eddie raised a hand to say good-bye. "I'll be cheering tomorrow."

Coach was still talking with some of his colleagues, and I gave him a nod as I left. Mom hadn't come down for this, and I wasn't sure what she was doing.

"Would you be up for that?" I pointed to a sign at the elevator bank that indicated a fitness center with a sauna.

"I've never been in one, but sure why not. Plus you'll be—"

I put a finger against his lips so he'd be quiet. I didn't want him to say anything else while Mom was potentially still in my ear.

I simply nodded.

While we were in the elevator, I pulled out my phone and went to the app that controlled the earpiece. I muted myself so I'd still hear if someone needed me, but I had privacy.

On the third floor, we got out and walked quietly to the fitness center, where we found one woman working out on an elliptical. I looked around to see where to go, and when I found it, I jerked my head toward a hallway leading farther into the facility.

The sauna was inside the men's locker room. I hadn't thought this through very well, because we needed to do something with our clothes. Luckily we found free lockers. There was a stack of towels too. I could get into real trouble for this on a couple of levels. I wasn't sure it was cool to mute my side of the earpiece without telling anyone. Plus Mom probably wouldn't be too happy that I planned to make out with Eddie here.

A grounded agent. Could that happen?

I opened a locker and stripped while Eddie stared at me.

"What? You've seen me naked before."

"Yeah, but never somewhere that wasn't my room or a car. This is sorta public."

True. That made my heart flutter, adding to the overall excitement of the moment.

He continued to watch even once I was just down to boxers.

"Are you planning on steaming yourself in that?" I pulled on the lapel of his coat and got a grin out of him.

"Um, no."

Eddie hustled to catch up to me, getting out of his clothes, and stuffing them into the same locker as mine. Once I'd gotten rid of my underwear and locked the locker, I went to the stack of towels and covered myself. It was a challenge to be modest given I was tenting the towel. Wasn't much I could do about that. It was a side effect of getting naked with Eddie.

I tossed him a towel and saw he was going to have the same issue. I swear his face reddened a bit as he tried to cover himself. He got embarrassed even less often than I did, but it was always so cute watching the red push through to the surface of his dark skin.

The sight of the scar on his left side made me pause. I hadn't seen it with the stitches out. It was still an angry red line against his smooth skin.

"It's okay. It doesn't hurt anymore."

I didn't know what to say. I brought two fingers to my lips, kissed them, and touched the scar. Hopefully in a few weeks you'd never know it happened. At least his face was mostly healed, and you could barely see any remnant of the accident there.

"What about you?" He touched my chest. "You've got new injuries all over. How'd you get all these little cuts?"

"I had a klutzy moment yesterday." I lead us into the empty sauna and it was heavenly. The dry heat seeped into my tired, sore muscles.

"Jesus, this must be what the desert feels like." The high temperature distracted Eddie. Hopefully he'd stay that way since I had no explanation for how I looked.

I climbed to the upper bench to sit down. I pressed my back into the warm boards and a moan escaped. "Isn't it awesome?"

There was one of these in our home rink, and I some-times used it to relax knotted muscles.

Eddie stood in the middle of the ten-by-ten box, and we looked at each other. He'd already lost the battle with hiding his arousal as his erection stood straight out behind the towel. I wasn't surprised it wouldn't behave. Mine was difficult enough to contain, and his was longer. Watching beads of sweat break out across his forehead and chest was ridiculously sexy.

"Come up here," I said. "Sit down and just let the heat soak in."

"Are you sure we're not going to melt?" He sat next to me, his leg touching the edge of my hand, which was on the bench next to me.

"Oh, I'm sure," I said, sounding like something between a moan and a sigh.

He put his hand on top of mine as we sat quietly. I closed my eyes as I let the heat work magic on my soreness.

"You look so relaxed, like you might disappear into the boards," Eddie said after we'd been quiet for a while.

"Are you staring?" I didn't open my eyes to find out.

"Yes. The beads of sweat rolling down your chest look very lickable. Plus it's hard for me to ignore this." He grabbed my boner through the towel.

"Hmm." That got my attention, and I opened my eyes to find him smiling as sweat poured off him. "Two can play that game."

I gently grabbed his head and brought us together for a kiss. My back came away from the boards, and I instantly missed the direct contact with the heat. However, I enjoyed the deep kiss and the light stroking through the towel.

The room, with a glass panel in the door, wasn't the most private place for doing too much. The last thing we needed was for someone to find us making out in here.

"Let's go to my room," I said when I could finally allow myself to break the kiss.

The locker room was still empty, which was perfect. We toweled off, dressed enough not to look too out of place, and headed to the elevator. In the mirrors around the elevator, we looked disheveled, clothes slightly wrinkled and untucked, as we held our jackets in front of us so nobody could see the tents in our pants. Eddie's hair, usually a fairly poufy afro, was slightly deflated from the heat and sweat. Meanwhile, my hair was plastered to my head.

"Shower with me?" I asked when we got to the room. "Cool ourselves down."

"I'll do anything that gets us out of these clothes."

He stripped off his shirt, and there were new beads of sweat rising from his skin. I quickly followed his lead and let clothes drop all over the floor. A small part of me wanted to tidy up the clothes, but I was mostly fixated on Eddie.

We got a cool shower going and made out under the spray. It was the beginning of several hours together alone. I was willing to catch hell for it tomorrow because it was exactly what I needed.

TWENTY

As ROUGH AS yesterday's second game was, today's morning game was a million times worse. Hours in bed with Eddie was great, except I probably didn't sleep as much as I should've to help my body recover. He'd left around six to get back to his hotel before his dad woke up. That gave me a couple of hours of sleep on my own, but it wasn't enough.

Thankfully Eddie had to go to the speech his dad wanted him to see, so he missed the worst game ever. I'd be long done with the mission by the time he'd be back, so we'd be able to relax together. Tonight's team stuff was optional, which was good, because I doubted they'd want to see me.

Nothing I did on the ice was right. I couldn't tell if it was from being too tired, or all the physical and emotional stuff that had gone down, but it was like I'd forgotten how to play. The rate at which I made errors was appalling, and it was a relief, midway through the first period, when the coach dropped me back to the third line. I hated letting the team down. Luckily we still won and would advance to the championship game tomorrow.

As soon as I could get away from the team after the

game, I met up with Coach in the same service corridor as yesterday. My backpack was extra heavy because I had more stuff this time out. Lorenzo had picked up some insulators to help keep me grounded to avoid any shocks. I also carried an extra tablet because I wanted to set up a two-pronged attack this time, with Lorenzo coming in through the second tablet.

"You holding up?" Coach asked, breaking the silence as we walked along the corridor.

"You saw that game, right?" I said with thick sarcasm. "Worst game I've played in five or six years. Those guys deserved better than that."

"The team still won. Don't beat yourself up—"

"Please don't." I stopped, spun around, and looked at him. "Let's focus on this, and we'll deal with the hockey mess later."

He gave one curt nod before I turned back and kept going to our target. Luckily no one listening on the earpiece chimed in about the game. As he'd done yesterday, he stayed at the top of the stairs.

Someone had fixed the junction box I'd breached to the degree you wouldn't notice anything different unless you knew how it'd been before. They'd upgraded the keypad to a fingerprint system, which I was ready for thanks to the tech I'd recently tested with Dad. Hopefully whoever installed the new system had tested it and left me a print to grab.

"Winger here. They swapped the keypad for a single fingerprint ID. Trying out the new app now."

"*Perfect,*" Lorenzo responded. "*Another field test.*"

I grinned as the phone read the panel. There was a print, which the app grabbed and was able to project back. The panel popped open just as it had yesterday.

"That's another positive test completed," I said. Was it bad that tech working correctly improved my mood?

Everything inside the box looked the same as when we started yesterday. They'd even made a clean patch of the wire I'd cut into. I went through the same motions as yesterday, and it seemed to take less time today.

"Winger here. I'm in. Setting up the remote tablet now. Stand by."

I quickly unspooled the connector wires from my pack and attached it to the tap. My hands shook as I pulled the tablet from the pack and tried to hook up the small connector to the port on the tablet. It was far more difficult than it should've been. Where'd the calm go all of a sudden?

"Come on," I said to no one in particular.

"Winger, what's wrong?" asked John.

"What do you need?" I heard Coach in the earpiece as well as a whisper from his position.

"Nothing!" I snarled. "Just need to calm down. I'm shaking like I'm on a first date or something."

"Or like a scared teenager. Take a deep breath. It'll be okay." It was Mom with possibly the most soothing voice she'd ever laid on me. Even more than when I'd had chicken pox and nearly clawed myself out of my skin.

Mom's voice did the trick and the shaking subsided.

"You should be online, Doc."

"Checking."

I got the other cable and connected it to the fiber tap. I was moving fluidly now, like I'd expect to.

"Connection stable," Lorenzo said as I got my tablet hooked in. *"We look good, and we should be stealth. I can't read our connection on my monitors."*

"I'm online as well. Starting to go for the firewall."

The steps were the same, and I quickly got myself up to

the firewall and started my attack. This firewall wasn't very good. For all the work they'd done getting into TOS's systems, they didn't have much protection up once inside their LAN. I guess they figured it was only the LAN that needed protection. Too bad they didn't have me as their security consultant. I couldn't help but grin.

"I'm at the firewall."

"*Me too.*"

I liked having Lorenzo, "virtually," right behind me. In this case, he'd follow my path into the network so that if I got taken out, he'd still be in there. He'd be harder to detect since he wasn't the one making the intrusion.

"Defender?" Coach sounded very confused. "What are you doing here?"

Dad?

I turned slightly, keeping one eye on the tablet screen as the program did its work. I saw Coach in position, but I couldn't see beyond him. I wanted to sprint up the stairs, but I had work here. Mom wouldn't leave her task, so I looked between the tablet and what little I could see above.

"*What's happening?*" Yoshi asked. "*Defender's there?*"

"Defender, put the gun down."

Coach extended his gun, but I couldn't see anyone near him. I hadn't heard Dad either.

The tablet beeped. The parameters around the firewall changed. I quickly typed commands to compensate so the program could continue.

"Defender, you're here!" I shouted so he'd hear. Dad couldn't be on our channel as it was private to those on the mission. If he'd been added, someone would be talking to him. "You're just in time. I'm about to get inside this network so we can find the missing agents."

"*Winger, he's not part of this mission,*" Yoshi said. "*D-*

Man, give Defender the code phrase. If he doesn't give the response, treat him as hostile."

"You need to stop, Winger." Dad's voice echoed through the corridor, with a tone that made me cringe. That *did not* sound like Dad.

"What? Why?"

"Defender, stand down." Coach used the voice I recognized from when he wasn't happy with the team. "Green grass, red sky."

"Defender, we're here to rescue you and stop this," I said as the tablet beeped again.

"*Winger. Stop engaging Defender. That's an order.*" Yoshi sounded furious. What did he expect me to do with Dad up there?

Damn it. The firewall was morphing faster than the program could keep up. This was better tech than it initially looked.

"I can't let you continue. Drop your weapon D-Man." Dad hadn't responded to the phrase.

Coach was backing down the stairs carefully, aiming his weapon on a target I still couldn't see.

"*Winger, you need to get out of there,*" Mom said.

"Nowhere to go," I said quietly. "Doc, we need to take this firewall down together."

"*On it,*" Lorenzo said.

If we both attacked while the program ran, the firewall shouldn't be able to keep up.

"Winger, disconnect those tablets." Dad appeared at the top of the stairs. "Now!"

His voice boomed through the hallway. It was the voice he used when I was in trouble and it scared the little boy inside me.

"I don't want to shoot you." Coach was at the bottom of

the stairs. Dad and Coach aimed at each other as Dad started his descent.

"*Take Defender out,*" Yoshi said. "*Now, D-man.*"

"Don't do it!" I was in a panic. He couldn't shoot Dad.

My fingers flew over the tablet's touch keyboard. I couldn't stop now. I was too close. Dad was in trouble and I had to help him. He had to be under the mind control. No way he'd act like this otherwise.

"*Shotgun's on the way for backup,*" Yoshi said.

"Theo!" Dad roared. "I said disconnect the tablets."

"*Winger, do as he says,*" Mom said. "*It's not worth it.*"

"No, Dad," I said, dropping the codenames. Maybe he'd listen to his son. "Just a few...."

Dad fired and the tablet on the floor next to my backpack went dark. I pressed myself against the wall, hoping to be less of a target. My eyes burned with tears.

"*I'm out,*" Lorenzo said, his voice quivering. "*I can see what Winger's doing, but my direct connection's gone.*"

Dad shot at me. He hit the tablet, but what if he'd missed and got me instead?

I wiped at my eyes and turned my attention to the tablet in my hand and the firewall. I had to get in and make Dad stop.

"*Winger? D-Man?*" Yoshi called out.

More shots were fired. Out of the corner of my eye, I saw D-Man drop to the floor, clutching his shoulder. His gun clattered on the concrete as he dropped it.

"*Someone answer!*" Yoshi called.

"D-Man's shot." My voice shook worse than Lorenzo's had.

"*He's in,*" Lorenzo said.

I tried to focus on what I was doing. I found the agent control directory, not even renamed.

Dad kicked Coach's gun out of reach.

"Defender, you don't—" Coach went silent as Dad kicked him in the head.

I was so close.

"Shut it down, Theo." Dad leveled the gun at my chest as he walked toward me.

"Just a couple more seconds, Dad."

"I said shut it down!" He ripped the data connection from the junction box.

"*Winger?*" Mom sounded desperate.

"Take the earpiece out and give me your phone."

"Dad, no." Tears fell as my body shook. "You know this is wrong."

He slapped the tablet out of my hands and stomped on it with the heel of his shoe, shattering the glass.

The gun shook in his hand. It was as if some part of him was trying to fight against the commands he received.

"Dad, come on. We can walk out of here, get you help, and then I can finish this."

"*Winger, it's Shotgun. Almost there. Doors got locked, and it slowed us down.*"

He pressed the gun against my chest.

I shook my head and tried to find a voice that wasn't scared.

"You can't do this," I said.

"I'm sorry, Theo, but I have to."

We looked at each other. A tear escaped his left eye.

"Help's coming," I said. "Stay with me, and we can—"

"Give me your phone!"

I'd lost him. The moment was gone. I didn't move.

He pressed the gun harder against my chest. He jammed his hand into my jeans pocket where he knew I kept my phone. Once he had it, he smashed it into the wall, cutting off one more connection I had to the people who could help.

"You've got fifteen seconds to get that earpiece out."

The gun wasn't shaking anymore.

I nodded, relenting.

He produced tweezers from his pants pocket with his free hand and gave them to me.

I took them and acted like I was going to do as he asked. At the last second, I changed tactics and tried to jab the tweezers into his eye. It was the only thing I could think of that would cause enough pain to get him to drop the gun and buy time for John to get here.

It didn't work. I must have telegraphed what I planned because he deflected the attack and sent the tweezers tumbling to the floor. I quaked, unable to calm myself.

"Fine. We'll do this the hard way."

"*Winger? Just do as he says!*" Mom's voice shrieked in my ear.

"*Winger, I've got eyes on you.*"

"Defender, stop!" It was John. I heard him loud and clear with and without the earpiece. He was coming down the stairs.

In a quick and fluid move, Dad pulled the gun away from my chest and knocked me in the side of the head. Once again I dropped to the floor before the mission was complete.

TWENTY-ONE

THIS WAS WRONG. I hadn't even opened my eyes and I could tell things weren't right. The percussion in my head wouldn't stop. The left side throbbed unlike anything I'd experienced before. My right ear was ringing as if I'd been at a concert that was too loud.

I convulsed as my brain kicked in, providing the missing details.

Trying to hack into the enemy's network again.

Coach shot.

Dad had put his gun to my chest.

Did I really try to stab him with tweezers? What had I been doing? Trying to blind my father?

The shakes overtook me.

What had I gotten myself into? I should've done what Mom said and let the guys with the training handle it. Being safe behind the scenes was where I should be. I hadn't signed up for this.

Hot tears burned my eyes as I gasped for air, the emotions running free.

I had no choice but to do this. Dad was in trouble and it

was my fault. I had to do whatever I could to get him back. And now Coach had been hurt too. Where was he? And John? I hadn't seen him before Dad knocked me out, but he'd said he saw me.

And now I was... somewhere.

I slowly opened my eyes. The single fluorescent light in the ceiling gave off so much light that my head unbelievably throbbed more. I held my hand to the throbbing place and hissed at the pain of simply touching my scalp.

Dad didn't do this. Not really. Someone was behind it all, and it was still up to me to stop it.

How I was going to do that was a mystery. I was lying on the floor of a room barely bigger than a closet with off-white cinderblock walls, a single air vent near the ceiling, and a video camera mounted in one corner, or at least a black dome I assumed was a camera or something else to monitor me.

The crying needed to stop.

I took some deep breaths and sat up. The pain in my head intensified, and the rest of my body cried out from the other impacts it'd endured over the past couple of days. Stars danced before my eyes as I tried to get control of the hurt. I needed to play through this, just like I would if I was on the ice.

Dad had really clocked me good. I've had head injuries from hockey, but this hurt the most.

I maneuvered so I could sit with my back against the wall. Glaring up at the dome. Who was watching on the other side?

Dad? The bastards responsible for all this? All of the above?

"Winger here. Anyone?"

I said it, even though I didn't expect a response. Dad

must've removed the earpiece. Was that why there was a ringing in my ear? Hopefully he didn't cause permanent damage.

I dropped my head against the concrete wall.

I was screwed. I had no equipment. Was I even still near the rink? Had John been able to follow to know where I was?

I stared at the camera. There were no wires running to it. I looked around the room, analyzing my options. The one electrical outlet had a steel conduit running up to the ceiling. The camera had nothing visible. Was it a fake? Or was it battery powered and running on Wi-Fi? Could I modify it to put out a beacon? Modify it with what, though? It was at least half a foot higher....

Wait.

I still had my watch. I pushed up my sleeve and checked it out; it seemed undamaged.

Was it really after five? Dammit. Eddie was gonna hate me.

Knocking the back of my head into the wall was a mistake, as it set off a new round of throbbing. I had to close my eyes because it hurt to look at anything. I stayed still, took some controlled deep breaths, and waited for it to pass.

I couldn't even think while the pounding scrambled my thoughts.

I pulled my knees up to my chest, folded my arms across them, and laid my head down. It was slightly more comfortable than the wall. My chest tightened, despite the breathing exercises. I couldn't stop the tears.

I wanted my mom. I wanted Dad. I wanted to be playing on the ice. I wanted not to know all the stuff I knew.

What would it be like to be just a normal kid? Doing homework. Hanging out with my boyfriend. Getting in trouble for staying out too late and simply being grounded from video games or whatever. So many scenarios of normalcy swirled around my head.

"Stop being ridiculous," I said out loud.

That wasn't who I was. I became Winger for a reason.

Theo was a good guy, but Winger was more. Winger helped people, like my parents did.

The throbbing seemed to agree because it backed off just a little.

If someone was watching me, they could think I was still curled up freaking out. The way I positioned my arms, I could see the watch face and move my fingers to operate the controls.

There was Wi-Fi in here. What I couldn't tell was if it was for the camera only or if it went to the outside world. Either way it wasn't locked. I tapped to make the connection and the watch attached immediately.

Really?

I went to Twitter and the Tweets flowed in.

What could I send that was meaningful?

Lorenzo could lock on to the watch like he did a phone. He just had to know to do it. Would he even monitor Twitter of all things? I needed to make these watches do more for agents. Most people still didn't think a watch could do a lot, even though wearable tech was evolving fast. TOS should be outfitting the watches as well as they tricked out the phones.

I activated the voice system. "Send Tweet," I said quietly.

"What is the message?"

I flinched at the volume as the electronic female voice echoed in the room. If the camera had a mic, this plan would fail.

Involuntarily I shrugged. It was still worth trying.

"Watch me."

"Shall I send it?"

I looked at the message on the screen.

"Capitalize the first word."

"Shall I send it?"

The message was about as good as it was going to get.

"Yes. Send it."

The watch vibrated.

"Sent."

As long as I stayed on Wi-Fi, there was a chance Lorenzo could find me.

I swiped back to the Wi-Fi settings and adjusted them so the watch would attach to any open signal. If the IT guys were stupid enough to have one unsecured network, maybe they had it throughout the facility.

I laid my head back on my arms for only a moment before I jerked myself upright.

I was stupid. I got to my feet despite the dizziness that swept over me. Why was I just sitting around?

I went to the door and found it locked. I ran my fingers over the door. It was steel, and I pounded on it. Why not act like the kid I was?

"Hey! Let me out of here!" I screamed ignoring the rolling thunder it set off in my head.

I suspected this is what a hangover felt like.

"Come on! Hello?"

It didn't take long before the locking mechanism clicked. I stepped back. No way was I going to try to take on whoever came in. It was doubtful I'd win a physical battle. Not only was I untrained, I was sure my body couldn't handle it.

Dad came in, gun drawn. Plus there was that. These

guys had guns and I had no defense against that. Given what had happened earlier, I was sure Dad wouldn't hesitate to use it on me.

"Dad," I said, rushing him, taking a chance. I wrapped my arms around him. "We need to get outta here. This isn't right."

"It's about time you got up," he said, forcing me away from him. "There's work to do. Let's go."

His voice was monotone, even more than it'd been before. So much for that idea.

Dad stepped back and waved his gun, gesturing for me to leave the room ahead of him. I'd seen this movie too many times, and deep down I felt like laughing because it was absurd I was in this position.

"Where're we going?"

"The control center of course. You've got a job to do."

"What kind of job?"

"Finish what Blackbird started. Control the TOS agents we can and identifying and taking out the others. It's time to bring TOS down."

A chill washed over me, as if all the heat in my body rushed out. I knew exactly how to do what they wanted, given the research I'd been doing. They already had most of the technology, and since I'd set up the system that encrypted the TOS database, I'd be able to give them both.

Was I willing to die to protect that?

Mom and John had old chips. I couldn't let Blackbird get them like they'd gotten Dad.

We walked down what seemed like endless corridors, going past many closed doors. Every now and then, others would pass us but no one spoke.

I had to shut this down from inside. There had to be a way to do that. If I worked inside their network, I'd be able to do anything. I just had to make sure they weren't watching too closely.

As we passed yet another door, Dad suddenly grabbed my shoulder, jerked me back, and shoved me against a door. The moves were so fast, I nearly tripped over my feet.

"We're here." He jammed the gun into my back to make his point. "Open it!"

"Dad?"

"Do it." His tone was low, evil, and scary.

I sighed and fought to keep myself in check. I had to learn how to stay calm and focused. Does TOS teach that? It seemed like it'd be an important quality for an agent. Hopefully I'd get out of here to ask.

The room he shoved me into was enormous. "Control center" indeed. It looked like they could run the International Space Station from here. Huge monitors on the wall filled the front of the room. Without context and time, I couldn't decipher what all the data was.

There were individual computer consoles all around the brightly lit room. My eyes initially rebelled at all the light and movement. There were dozens of people manning desks, while six guards stood at the perimeter of the room.

"Theodore Reese, also known as Winger," said a man who didn't seem much older than my dad. He wore jeans and a dark shirt. If it wasn't for the gun at my back, I could have been at a tech startup, talking to the boss. "Glad you're up and around," the man continued from his desk at the center of the room. "We've been waiting for you. We should've met last week, but you eluded my men. They didn't think you were an agent. Foolish of them since we employ teenagers when it's required. Your father let us know that you could help us achieve our objective. You saved us a return trip to Boston by coming to us."

Dad shoved me toward an empty desk. Catching myself on the desktop, I stayed upright and did my best to look defiant.

"You might as well have a seat. No one's going anywhere until you give us control over the remaining agents. You've certainly given our team a handful, trying to keep up with you. Now you'll just do what we say. No chip required."

The calm tone was unnerving. He was right out of a movie, too, just laying out his expectations. I really wanted to offer a smartass action-hero response, but I didn't want to make this worse. I had to buy time so Lorenzo could find me.

"You're looking for a way out," the man said. "There isn't one. You've got no weapon, and your father has you covered. He's ordered to shoot you if you go near the door. Your only option is to sit down and do what you're told."

Dad pushed the gun into my lower back.

I hoped I was good enough to pull off a double cross that would end this. And free Dad.

TWENTY-TWO

Two of Blackbird's techs, identified as Angel and Westside, flanked me. Both watched what I was doing on my screen and monitored their network.

I burned a little time making them show me around their setup even though I'd already caught a glimpse of it during my investigation. After all, I needed to see as much of their configuration as I could if I was forcibly going to give them the rest of the TOS system so they'd control it.

Angel and Westside showed me a lot and it was very helpful.

As they gave me the tour, I contemplated if I was going to be sloppy and make it painfully obvious to Lorenzo what was happening, or if I was going to try for a solo inside takedown. I didn't like either option. There were too many variables that made them both risky.

"Enough chatter," the leader finally said after I'd been getting a rundown for nearly an hour.

"It's better for me to know everything now, so I don't damage your systems or trip any alarms within TOS," I said with an authority that surprised me.

"He's right, Raven, it will make this more efficient," said Angel, who was to my right. Her response led me to believe her skill set was likely lower than mine. She should know at least half of what I was asking didn't really matter.

Raven was a great codename. It fit a bad guy within an organization called Blackbird.

"I don't care! Get me those controls. Now!"

Okay. Raven'd had enough.

To emphasize the point, Dad jammed his gun between my shoulder blades.

"Okay, fine," I said, deliberately sounding like a petulant teenager. I didn't do that often, because it didn't usually get me anywhere. However, reminding these guys I wasn't an adult might be useful later.

I had open network access. Not only could I see theirs, but I was out on the internet too. As far as I could tell, I could get to anything I needed.

Time to get to work. The first thing was to transfer all the Blackbird information on this network to TOS's cloud. That alone should tell Lorenzo I was in front of a computer because not just anyone would be loading to the cloud, and if he figured out what was loading, it'd be all the better.

"What're you doing?" Angel asked.

"Yeah, that's a lot of data flowing out," said Westside from his desk on my left.

"Just making a backup. If anything goes wrong, we need a clean, recent backup to restore quickly."

Westside typed furiously across one of the keyboards in front of him. "We've got backups. We don't need another one."

I fixed a hard gaze on him, further asserting my expertise. "When was the last backup done?"

"We backup every day overnight."

"Exactly. So your last backup is more than twelve hours old. We're doing major work here. There's no reason to not have one that's more current."

"It's fine," Angel said. "We'll make sure it's wiped when we're done. But he's right. A fresh backup is a good idea before we do something this significant."

So far, so good. It seemed like Angel was going to play right into my plan. She wasn't objecting to anything I did and she kept Westside under control. Maybe she was in charge.

Next thing to do was get into TOS. Revoking my credentials should've been the first thing Lorenzo did after my capture. I wanted that to be true so I'd have to spend the time to hack into TOS.

Unfortunately I got on the TOS private network with no problem, which pissed me off. I helped create these protocols, and they weren't followed. Next I went to the tech group log-in and it worked too. That sucked.

What was Lorenzo thinking? The bad guys had me and, even though I was trying to control the scenario, I could get into TOS and do anything I wanted. If I got out of here, there'd be some serious discussions.

"That was too easy," Angel said.

"Yeah. They should've had that locked down so I couldn't walk right in."

"So much the better for us," Raven said. "Now get me what I want. I want every agent in our system."

"Well, the agent list is tough," I said. "I put an encryption layer on it that'll have to be cracked to make it work for your version of the system."

"You built it, so you can make it work for us."

"It's not that easy," I lied, sort of. "If you've made any configuration changes on your version of the tracking system, it may not be possible."

"You'll make it work," Raven said, barely keeping his temper under control. The guy seriously liked to yell.

"I might not be able to, at least not quickly."

"If a gun on you isn't inspiration enough, maybe this will be."

He typed into his console. Dad moved in front of the terminal where I was sitting and put his gun to his temple.

How much worse could this get?

"Theo, please." The look on Dad's face was pleading and his voice was normal.

"No!" I screamed as I slammed my hand down on the desk. Two could play that game. I pushed back from the desk and stood up. "You do whatever you want to me, but I won't do anything while you're putting him in danger."

Did I mean that? I was pretty sure I did.

I was the only guy who could get them what they wanted, and I wasn't going to have Dad standing in front of me ready to shoot himself.

Raven and I stared each other down with Dad standing between us.

Dad's finger twitched on the trigger as Raven typed.

"If you do that. I won't do anything for you." I surprised myself with how confident I sounded.

Our stare down continued. After a few moments, a grin broke out on Raven's face.

"You're good, Winger. You sure you're not a real agent? Maybe you'll consider joining our team once you finish this job."

Dad silently brought his gun back to his side and his

expression went blank. It was like he was dormant—neither himself nor the guy who had manhandled me earlier. Raven typed, and Dad silently moved to where he had been before.

At least that was over. I said nothing, simply took my chair. I was still in the TOS system. Maybe they were using it to trace back to me. That was a possibility.

"I'm scrambling our data stream," Westside said. "We can't let them trace you."

So much for that idea. At least these guys had some brains. As a geek, that made me happy. As an agent in trouble, I hated that I hadn't deceived them more effectively.

I had some ideas on how to destroy the entire operation, but it was going to take some noodling around in their systems to figure out the best way to do that. Meanwhile, I took my time going through the TOS system to get where I needed to be, and it frustrated my audience.

"I need to make sure they haven't laid traps," I explained. "You don't want me bringing a virus or worse back here."

"He's right," Angel said. "Caution is advised since TOS isn't following their normal security measures."

Thanks, Angel.

Perfect. Lorenzo was onto me.

He left me some clues in the TOS system. There were new directories, but he'd gone to the trouble to change up the time stamps so they wouldn't look new. The biggest clue was the Watch Me directory, which contained a replicated tracker system. I brought it online, and it looked perfect. I was confident he was monitoring my activity despite West-side scrambling the data.

My heart pounded like it was going to jump out of my

chest. I didn't know what the plan was. Hopefully Lorenzo and I had worked together long enough that we wouldn't surprise each other. I wanted to know who was around, so I brought up the map and had it triangulate on Mom's location. I saw her, Yoshi, and Lorenzo on the map in different locations, but John and Coach were missing.

"He's in," Westside said.

Raven left his post for the first time. He stood behind me, leaning in to look at the screen with the map. I had nothing suspicious on my screens, but Raven's presence made me nervous.

"Is that the entire team that came with you?" he asked.

"There're a couple missing," I said, keeping my voice even. It was true. There was no need to hide that.

"Indeed," Raven said. "We snagged two men when we got you. Why aren't they on the map?"

"We transferred them to our system," Westside said. "Once they were here, we could easily identify their chips. The injured one is in detention. The other is under our control."

Interesting. The patches I'd designed were still susceptible to hacking at close range. Curious.

Westside brought up the Blackbird version of the system. There were at least a dozen other TOS agents in this facility including the four in this room. Westside pointed out two dots. "That's them."

"What's next?" Angel asked.

"So we need to bring over the program and the database. Then there's the matter of the decryption system that's got to be installed. I need to run some tests to make sure I pack up everything that needs to go with this. If it's moved incomplete, you'll end up with something that won't work and could potentially be destructive to your system."

"Get to it." Raven returned to his central desk. "You've got twenty minutes to get it moved. I want you out of that system. The longer you're there, the more likely someone traces you even with our scramblers running."

I hoped Lorenzo knew what he was doing when he set up this fake system. I didn't have time to dig into it to see what he might have changed, because he had to have done more than just replicate it.

"I need some tools off my system. I'm going to tap into my private network."

"Watch him," Raven said. "Don't do anything you'll regret. I have no problem killing you and your father, because I suspect there's someone nearby who could finish the work for us." The menace in his voice sent shivers down my spine.

I didn't respond. I simply went about getting into my home system, where I had tools to package up and move code. If I didn't focus on what I was doing, the situation would overwhelm me for sure. Keeping to the mission and shutting all this down was the best way to stay calm.

"I'm in the TOS system as well," Westside said. "I'm going to do some damage as long as we're in there."

The grin on his face was horrifying. I had a feeling he'd be just as happy being a bully in real life as being one behind a keyboard.

I knocked the keyboard away from his hands. "You'll do *nothing* until I have what we need. If you just go deleting stuff, you could easily take out a subsystem that's required."

"Seriously. What's wrong with you?" Angel sounded annoyed as she looked to Westside.

"Hey, we're all on the same side." Westside raised his hands to show he wasn't doing anything. "Just trying to move this along."

"And to be clear," I fixed an icy glare on him, "we are not on the same side."

I returned my attention to the work and the plan I was hatching.

TWENTY-THREE

The twenty minutes went by way too fast. I did have time to think, though. I wanted to create permanent damage in the Blackbird network, just like Westside wanted to in TOS's. The biggest unknown was what would happen if I shut down the controller chips abruptly. Was there a proper shutdown sequence to bring someone out of the mind control?

I couldn't solve for that variable.

One of my screens flashed that the fake tracker system was ready.

"Now I can—" Westside flinched and stopped talking when I glared at him.

I suppressed a smile. There wasn't much good going on here, but at least I had one of the bad guys somewhat scared of me.

"No. You can't. I still have to get the decoder system, otherwise you won't be able to identify anyone." I turned to Angel, who I definitely liked better. "If you want to take the tracker package and deploy it in the same place as your version of the tracker, we can work together to get them merged once I have the decoder."

If I gave her something to do, she wouldn't pay attention to me. I was pretty sure Westside would be easier to deceive, so I didn't really care if he was watching.

Angel nodded. "Will do."

Turning my attention back to the TOS network, I saw the decoder algorithm I'd set up, but I didn't see a duplicate for me to take. I was pretty sure Lorenzo would've made a backup like he had of everything else, but even if he didn't, I had no choice but to pack this one up.

It occurred to me that an excellent project to work on would be safeguarding programs so moving them off a server would be more difficult. A system like that would've prevented this from the start, because any shred of code would've failed to work here. I'd have to think about how to do it, because there was a lot to account for, like server maintenance, but there had to be a way.

The decoder was quick to package because I'd written it to be very compact, even with the database that stored the information.

Without checking to see who might be watching, in a couple of keystrokes, I deleted my log-in to the TOS network and VPN. I couldn't get back in there now, at least not easily. I could probably hack in if I needed to, because I knew the network so well, but it wouldn't be fast. I quickly closed all the connections to TOS. I wasn't going to give Westside the chance to wreck things.

"Okay." I turned to Angel again. "Is it in place? I've got the decoder information."

"Very good, Winger." Raven sounded eerily happy. "Let's get it online and see how many people we can bring into the fold. How long, Angel?"

"The TOS package doesn't have the controller system" —Angel looked at her screen—"so we'll have to reintegrate that as we bring the data into our version."

Suddenly Westside spun my chair toward him.

"What did you do? I'm not in the network anymore."

"Oh, sorry," I said with deliberate snark. "I logged out."

"Well, log back in."

"No can do." Even as I talked, I wasn't sure where all this confidence was coming from, especially since my heart was thumping so hard. I could easily get myself hurt worse or cause someone else to get hurt. "I wiped out my log-in."

Westside flew out of his chair and pulled me up by my shoulders. It hurt, and I tried not to show that. I hadn't realized how big he was. The dude definitely worked out.

"Westside!" Raven called from his perch. "It doesn't matter. I'm sure there'll be someone in IT we can control to do the damage for us."

"But I wanted to."

He stepped back.

"Maybe you can take out your frustration on Winger once he's finished." As Raven spoke, Westside calmed down. "Now have a seat and pay attention to his activity so he doesn't get the chance to do something like that again."

"Yes, sir."

He slammed himself into his chair. He was seething, but at least for now, he wasn't going to be a problem.

"Winger?" I spun my chair to face Angel. "Faster to overwrite the existing data in our system or to merge the databases?"

I had to think about it.

"Show me what's in place in your system." I moved closer to Angel so I could easily read her screens.

"Our system's on the right and what you just down-loaded is on the left."

She passed me her mouse so I could scroll. There were a lot of similarities in the code, but some differences I didn't understand.

"I'm not sure a merge would work. There are differences I can't account for. What about just writing the data into your system? I'm thinking it would work much the same way as when you were hacking the individual chips out of TOS control. Doing that would keep your existing data in place and operational."

I wish Angel and I were working toward the same goal. Despite my first impression, she was thoughtful and smart. Was she the one who had set up what Blackbird was using? It wouldn't surprise me to find out she was.

"In theory it should. When we add chip IDs and send out the signal, it overrides TOS's and makes ours the primary. There's a security hole that—"

"Angel!" Raven called out and she flinched.

Damn, she'd almost slipped. But at least I had some clue about how all this was working. We would need Angel for a debriefing.

"Anyway," Angel shook off the admonishment. "The same theory should work as we put the data in. We'd just be doing it on a lot larger level. How many agents are we talking about importing?"

"I don't know. When I built the encryption, I tested on a finite number and turned it over. I don't know how many are in there."

That was sort of true. I knew it was in the thousands, but I hadn't needed to know, so I hadn't looked.

That was it!

I could design a decryption and import program that

could bring the whole Blackbird system to a halt.

"Can you write a decrypt and import script?"

Yes!

Angel played directly into my plan.

"One sec."

I moved through various screens on my monitor to put on a show about making sure I had everything to do what was necessary. *I* knew I had enough information. If I failed to bring their entire network down, which would be preferable, I could at least crash their tracker-control system.

"I should be able to," I finally said.

"It's gonna have to be all you since you designed the encryption." Angel gave a shy smile as if she was sorry she couldn't help. "Where's the decrypt usually occur?"

"The key is inside the tracker system so that it decrypts on the fly. It slows the job down a bit, but it keeps the data from being too easy to capture and do what you guys did."

"Nice." Angel looked lost in thought for a moment. "Really elegant since the control system is behind so many firewalls and security protocols."

"Exactly." I was sort of excited that she understood what I'd done.

"Okay you two." Raven spoke with a hint of sarcasm. "You can go make out later." It sounded like a parent giving us grief.

Angel actually blushed a little. I shrugged and cocked an eyebrow at her before turning to my screen.

"Where's your database?" I asked.

"Here."

Angel leaned over and typed rapidly on my keyboard. She brought up the database. I wasn't surprised to see that it looked exactly like the TOS one, the key exception being the information in the "control" column. That data was in more than a hundred of the database's rows. Wipe that data out, agents should be free—unless there was a safety I didn't know about.

I would need to be a magician to pull this off. I wanted to flood the database to crash the system, while looking like I was doing what they wanted.

Thinking under pressure was usually one of my strong suits, but this was a lot to process. If I messed this up, the consequences could be disastrous.

"Okay. Let me work on the decrypt, and then we'll merge."

Angel nodded. "Let me know if I can help."

The first thing I needed to do was set up a data loop so Westside, who I suspected was monitoring me more than Angel was, couldn't see what I was actually doing.

Essentially I needed to do three things at the same time, keep Westside in the dark, decrypt the database since Angel was likely watching that, and write the code to reduce this network to nothingness.

I tried to tell myself this was all in a day's work, so I wouldn't focus on this being make-or-break time. My fingers manipulated the keys in front of me as I worked quickly to set up the loop. I'd built one of these in computer science class years ago to keep the teacher fooled while I worked on more interesting things than the assignment. It was a little harder to set up here, because I didn't have a library of commands to pull from to use as part of the illusion.

Within a few minutes, I had Westside in the dark and Angel seeing what I needed her to.

"You're fast," Angel said.

I shrugged. "Years of practice."

"Is this kid for real?" Westside continued to look at his screens. "You're sixteen, so give it a rest."

"West, don't," Angel cautioned. There was an edge in her voice she hadn't used before.

"How about ten years?" I spun in the chair to face him. "You wanna test me, or do you want me to do this work that apparently you guys don't know how to do?"

Raven watched.

Westside stood, looking like he might punch me. This time I didn't care about his threat.

"You couldn't get past our security. We zapped you pretty good yesterday."

I stood and put on my hockey game face, a sneer along with a partially crouched stance that said *bring it*. He flinched just enough for me to know I had him.

Score one for the hockey player.

"Yeah, and when I came back, the only way you kept me out was sending someone to physically stop me."

"Boys!" Raven bellowed, apparently having enough. "Enough stalling."

Westside flinched even more as Raven yelled at us. I remained in place, glaring at him.

"Do you want to finish this on your own? Sounds like Westside can handle it."

I pushed my luck, but it was worth it. If I were in his head, he'd be even less likely to see how I was duping him. Westside tried to puff himself up. He squared his shoulders and expanded his chest. Even though it made him more imposing, I didn't move. I didn't need to.

"West, why don't you go? I got this." Angel was up now and stood between us.

"Westside! You heard her. Go!" Raven would make an excellent drill sergeant. That tone, plus the volume, would make anyone's blood run cold. It kind of reminded me of Darth Vader using the Force.

Westside tried to stare me down for a couple more seconds before he slammed his chair into the desk and turned to beat a hasty retreat from the room.

"Sorry about that," Angel whispered. "He gets too worked up sometimes."

I held my stance for a few moments, as if making sure he wasn't coming back. It couldn't hurt to show a little more alpha dominance. It might come in handy later. I didn't want to underestimate Angel. She was petite, but if she had fight training, she could be a problem since I had no skills outside of the occasional hockey brawls. Eventually I nodded at Angel and took my seat.

Dad seemed to ignore the entire exchange. As far as I could see in my peripheral vision, he hadn't moved. His gun remained leveled on me, but he took no action to get me to sit down or force me back to work. It probably would've been different if I'd made for the door, but Dad's instructions didn't seem to include stopping a disturbance.

It was time to get this done.

Angel watched my screen. I needed to be careful because if she clued in to what I was doing as I wrote code, I'd be screwed. I wrote more lines of code than I needed to, to bury the true intention.

"Any chance you could tell me what you're doing as you go?" Angel watched as lines of code scrolled up the screen.

"It'll slow me down." I stopped typing and looked over to her. "I can go over the code once I'm done."

"Makes sense, I guess. I don't really talk and type at the same time either. I'll try to keep up."

I nodded and went back to it.

It took longer than I expected. More than once I thought of something else to add to the code so I could really stick it to these guys. My concern was that I wasn't going to be able to test anything. It had to be right the first time because I was unlikely to get a second chance.

At least Raven didn't push. He must've known this part would take a while. Angel stayed quiet too. I had no idea how much she understood or if she was even keeping up with what I typed.

"Okay," I said after a couple of hours. "Just to be clear, once I do this you're letting my dad go."

I stood as Raven swiveled his chair my direction.

"Let's not jump to conclusions." His look was harsh and got the butterflies in my stomach going. It occurred to me too late that if I failed, I likely wasn't just going to lose Dad, but Mom too. "Let's make sure it's working first. After all I'd hate to let tech support go too soon."

I wasted no time. It was going to work. It had to. "Running the execute now."

I typed a few characters, hit Enter, and it was off. Angel went from watching my screen to hers. Part of the bonus code I wrote made it appear as if the database was being updated as Angel and I had discussed. In reality, though, the database was being corrupted.

I watched the real code lines scroll up my screen as they executed while I also had a display showing the fake information to Angel. Unfortunately I couldn't see what was really going down in the system. I could only assume the code was doing its work as it scrolled by.

The only good news I had was Angel wasn't saying anything and my program didn't get stuck.

"Raven, sir, we're seeing a database strain," called out someone across the room.

Damn. What were they looking at? I should've had that buttoned up.

"Looks fine from here," Angel said.

As far as I could tell, she was only looking at what I'd set up.

The database would be straining since I was replicating more data than it could handle. What had I missed that alerted that other person? Little tremors shook me as my nervousness became more apparent.

"Let me take a look." I willed myself to keep it together.

My heart pounded as I raced to track down what this random guy could possibly be looking at so I could jam it. I looked at the actual database output and saw the issue—monitoring software. Rookie mistake not creating the necessary script to fool the monitors.

"Found it. Stabilizing."

I swiftly wrote another program to handle making that alert look normal while I swept the system looking for anything else obvious that I should've accounted for already.

"It's returning to normal," the blabbermouth reported.

Suddenly Dad jabbed his gun twice in between my shoulder blades. He hadn't touched me since we'd come in here, so the jabs startled me and I hoped no one noticed my slight flinch.

Was it a sign he was free? Or was Raven silently reminding me he had control?

The program was far enough along so the controlled agents should be free. Because Dad hadn't moved for some time, the nudge might be the only signal he could give without revealing himself.

"I lowered the rate of adding new records and also made the decryption asynchronous, which should help the strain," I said, offering a reason why the situation appeared to resolve so quickly.

"Everything looks normal," Angel said. "Records are

flowing into the DB, and they look to be in the standard format."

Did the other TOS agents in this room free up? I knew from the earlier look at the Blackbird tracker map that there were four others in this room.

There were a number of guys along the walls with guns, who were like sentries, unmoving. I didn't think Angel had a gun. I suspected most of the others didn't either, since they appeared to be techs. I was sure, however, that Raven had a weapon. He had the look of a badass who carried at least one weapon.

In quick succession, red lights flickered on across the consoles in the room. Angel's screen, where she'd been watching the fake database load, went dark.

"What's happening?" Raven asked, remarkably calm, still facing the large forward screens as they all went black.

"Checking," said the guy who'd found the issue before.

The other techs and Angel sprang into action as well. My screen went blank as my program finished executing. The system was rebooting and encrypting itself.

"System reboot," Angel called, a frantic edge to her voice. "Did you expect that?" She turned to me expectantly.

I gave her my best confused face and called up the same system prompt.

"No." I feigned surprise. "That shouldn't have happened."

I typed. Except I wasn't typing anything useful. It was for show. I'd gotten this far, but I didn't know what to do next. The endgame was for Dad and any other agents to snap into action.

A klaxon went off at a station to my right. That couldn't be good, at least not for the system. But it really didn't matter. I figured it'd been at least a minute since the reboot, maybe more. If I'd done my job right, their system wasn't going to come back on in functional condition. At this point even I couldn't reverse it.

"Nothing's coming back up." Angel sounded more panicked. "Not even log-in screens."

She typed frantically, but her screen would only display the system prompt as she hit Enter again and again.

"I've got nothing." I worked hard not to sound smug.

"What did you do?" Raven swung to face me. Each word escalated in volume. "What?"

He stood, reached behind his back, and pulled a gun. I was going to be shot. Nearly point-blank. In the chest.

Gunfire sounded behind me and by reflex, I ducked. Raven jerked back, dropped his gun, and fell back into his chair.

"Do not threaten my son!" Dad commanded in a voice that rivaled Raven's.

Three others along the walls raised their guns to cover everyone else in the room. They had to be the TOS agents. Two Blackbird agents were shot in the arm when they tried to engage. It looked like I was right about the techs having no weapons. All of them raised their hands, including Angel.

I leaned back in my chair as my energy dissipated fast. It was over.

"Mountaineer, restrain Raven." Dad was very much in command of the situation now. One of the TOS agents moved quickly to Raven.

I shook uncontrollably. Everything that'd kept me going drained away. I really could've died here.

But I saved Dad. And the other agents.

Tears fell and I leaned forward so I could bury my face

in my hands. Relief flooded through me, but there was embarrassment too. This wasn't agent behavior.

"Make sure, for now, that no one can get in here." I wasn't sure who Dad was addressing. I certainly wasn't going to cover the door.

A strong hand settled on my shoulder. I moved my hands slightly and saw Dad sitting in Westside's chair.

"I'm so proud of you." Dad squeezed my shoulder with a reassuring grip. "I promise we'll get out of here as soon as possible."

I looked up, even more embarrassed that I was crying in front of him.

Three other agents moved around the room, securing everyone.

"You okay to do something?" he asked, voice soothing. Not at all like the command voice he'd used with the others.

"Of course. Anything." My stupid voice cracked. I swallowed hard, willing myself to stabilize.

Dad needed me. Defender needed me.

"Can you get a message out that we're okay and in control of the situation?"

"Yeah. I'm on it."

He smiled and that gave me the strength to get it done. He moved off to work with the other agents while I got busy.

I reconfigured one of the computers so it would boot up with its own operating system rather than attempt Blackbird's. Once that completed, I got on the internet and connected to my home network so I could call Lorenzo.

"Doctor Possible. Winger here." It was shocking how tired my voice sounded. At least it didn't betray my emotions.

"Winger!" Lorenzo shouted and then cleared his throat. "Situation?" he asked more professionally.

He was following protocol, although it was obvious he didn't want to.

"Under control and we're on speaker."

"Yong Chi and Snowbird are with me."

"Report?" Snowbird asked, trying to sound like an agent and not a worried mom and wife.

"Defender is here and in command," I said, struggling to decide what was important to say. I heard a sound of relief that had to have come from Mom. "I haven't seen Shotgun or D-Man since I was captured."

"This is Defender," Dad called out, loud enough so the mic picked up his voice from across the room. "We've locked down the control room we're in. I've got four TOS agents with me and there are at least eight others here, but it's unknown if they were able to lock down their sections. We're in an underground complex that's adjacent to the ice rink, but I'm not sure how best to get you our position."

"We've got it," Yoshi said. "We were able to lock on to Winger's watch after his rather unconventional message." Dad shot me a smile and it warmed me. "We've got a team on the way."

"We'll stand by," Dad said, moving toward the desk I was at. "We'll leave this channel open as well, since it's our only mode of communication."

"Very good. We'll see you soon," Yoshi said.

I leaned back in the chair, and Dad nodded at me. He said nothing and yet said everything. I knew we'd have plenty of time to talk later, but I took from that nod that not only was he proud of me as he'd already said, but was thanking me too.

TWENTY-FOUR

"You really did a number on these systems," Lorenzo said as he sifted through data at what used to be Angel's station.

TOS had been in control for about an hour now, and Mom, Yoshi, and Lorenzo were all here. They'd found Coach, unconscious but alive, in a room that sounded similar to the one I'd been in. At least the Blackbird agents had dressed his wound before they left him. He went to the hospital along with the other injured people.

John had helped with the takeover. Once I lifted the mind control, another TOS agent freed him.

The Blackbird agents taken from the control center had their hands zip-tied. I didn't know what was going to happen to them. What were the rules for one secret organization sabotaging another?

"I tried," I said, looking over Lorenzo's shoulder. "I figured maximum damage would at least keep them from grabbing more people, if I failed to release the agents who were here."

"It was super smart that you backed everything into the

cloud so we can analyze all of it," Yoshi said. "It appears that Raven was just working this cell. Blackbird's large and the data might give us a hint into taking out the entire organization."

I nodded and then grabbed for Lorenzo's chair as the world spun before me.

"Whoa," Yoshi said, stabilizing me before I fell into him.

"Here, sit." Lorenzo stood and then spun his chair my direction. "You okay?"

I took a couple deep breaths and tried to sort out what was happening. I still hurt and the pain only got worse as I calmed down. I needed food. When had I last eaten? I was a little dizzy, but I couldn't figure out the exact cause—hunger, tiredness, the day catching up, or all of the above.

"Winger?" Mom asked.

I hated that I was weaker than these guys. I used to think I could tackle anything.

"Sorry," I said, reaching for a bottle of water I'd been sipping from. "Doc, let's get back to it."

"No," Yoshi said, raising his hand. "Winger, Defender, Snowbird, we can handle this. Why don't you three go and we'll debrief later?"

"It's okay. I can finish with Doc. It'll be faster that way."

I refused to be the weak link.

"I'm just going to pack it all up and wipe the equipment. We can analyze everything when we're at home base," Lorenzo said.

Mom and Dad traded a look that I couldn't interpret.

"I'll stay behind," Mom said. "Yong Chi and I can lock it all down."

Yoshi nodded.

Damn. Whatever went between Mom and Dad got to Yoshi too.

"Come on, Winger," Dad said, putting his arm around me. "We'll get some food and clean up. I know I need that and I bet you do too."

I nodded, a little defeated I wasn't doing my job. I didn't have the strength to argue, though. Food would be good, and a shower would be kinda awesome.

"Shotgun's standing by to drive you to your temporary quarters and go over the cover story. Rosepetal will take you to him."

A woman who'd arrived with Yoshi and Mom stood nearby, clearly ready to take us to John.

"I'll see you soon—" Mom paused, clearly swallowing a word. "—Winger." She managed a smile but still looked troubled.

Dad still had his arm around me and it stayed there as we followed Rosepetal out. We were silent as we meandered through corridors.

"You did this" came a shout as we passed through an intersection. "I should've decked you when I had the chance."

It was Westside. He struggled against the two people who held his arms. His hands were behind his back so I guessed he was zip-tied like the others. He looked angrier than even Raven had when he was taken away. The agents stopped him and didn't allow him to come any closer.

"Come on," Dad said, trying to nudge me forward.

I debated giving him a smartass remark, but I didn't have it in me. We locked eyes for a moment before I walked away.

"This is far from over. I'll make sure people know exactly who did this."

"We'll see about that," said one of the agents restraining him.

"Owww." Westside cried out.

I didn't look back.

Finally we got to a loading dock where a single black van, with no windows in the back, waited, engine running. For a moment I flashed back on the kidnapping and had to stop myself from running away. It was ridiculous; Dad was at my side and John was visible in the side mirror. Dad and I got into the back, and Rosepetal closed the doors as we settled in.

Unlike the kidnapper's van, there were benches along both sides. I dropped onto one and Dad sat across from me and buckled his seat belt. I did the same. I was beat up enough. I didn't need a bumpy van ride adding to it.

"Here we go," John said. "We'll be to the temporary hotel in about fifteen minutes."

I wondered why it was a different hotel but not enough to ask about it.

"I'm so sorry, Theo," Dad said.

"Why?" I gave him a confused look. He'd done everything he could.

"I had a gun on you. I hit you upside the head. I shot Coach in front of you. If Raven had commanded me to shoot you, I don't think I could've stopped myself."

So many thoughts swirled in my head. I didn't know what to say. Between the kidnapping and the past couple of days here, life was unbelievable. I was in a movie I wasn't sure I wanted to be in.

But if *I* wasn't in the movie, what would've happened? Could Lorenzo have gone in and done what I'd done? There's a reason TOS had me working with them. Would this have played out the same? Would TOS have won the day? Or would Dad be gone? And maybe Mom too.

"Well, that didn't happen," I finally said. "We beat the bad guys."

"*You* beat the bad guys," he said. "There was no *we* there."

"Sure there was. After I brought the system down, I had no other moves. If you hadn't been there, I'd probably be... who knows. Locked up, beaten—"

"Stop," he interrupted. "Don't think about that."

I nodded. I'd rather not. I had a feeling I'd be thinking about it for a long time, though. I knew I was okay. I was confident Dad wasn't going to pull a gun on me again anytime soon. It didn't change that I could easily replay any number of scenes I'd rather not have permanently etched in my mind. If only I could wipe those out as easily as I'd wiped that network.

"It's more important than ever we get you into counseling," Dad continued.

"I'll be fine."

"No. This has been a lot, Theo. TOS will insist you debrief with someone and counseling will be mandatory. What you've just been through is a lot for any agent. For what it's worth, I'll be seeing a counselor too. What I've done is horrible, and I already know I need help with it."

At least he didn't call me a kid. I don't think I'd think of myself that way ever again.

I nodded. The nods turned into quakes. And before I realized what was happening, I was crying. Actually sobbing was more accurate.

Dammit.

I tried to wipe the tears away, but they wouldn't stop. Dad unbuckled, moved in next to me, and held me tight. It felt good. Sometimes you just needed a hug from family.

"I'm sorry," I said as it became more obvious I couldn't stop myself.

I hated falling apart this way, especially as some of the louder sobs came out. What would John think?

"Theo, you've got nothing to be sorry for. I couldn't be prouder of what you've done today, and I'm sure there's more to the story than I know."

He held me quietly for a few moments.

"And I'll tell you," he continued, "there've been missions where I had to walk away and cry. Your mother's held me many times, and I've done the same for her. Even when the mission ends up a win, you have to release the accumulated stress."

I nodded as he pulled me tighter into his chest. I buried my head there just like I'd done when I was much smaller.

"We're here," John said after he parked the van. He paused until I finally pulled back from Dad. "Here's a key." Dad grabbed it. "Go directly to room four twenty-three. Theo, there's a change of clothes from your luggage. Victor, we picked up some stuff for you."

I continued to shake, although I was calming down a bit. I feared this would be a recurring thing over the coming days.

"A doctor's on the way to check you both out," John continued. "I also took the liberty to have sandwiches delivered. They should already be there. One agent is in the next room, just in case. He'll bring electronics shortly. Lorenzo got some new things ready for Theo."

Lorenzo was awesome. And when did he have time for that? I dried my eyes with my sleeve.

"You ready?" Dad asked.

I nodded, afraid if I spoke, I'd end up crying all over again. We were at another loading dock, and Dad took us to the freight elevator. In no time we were in our room. The room was standard issue: two beds, a desk, and a dresser. It was a simple box, much like the room at the tournament hotel.

A duffel bag was on each bed and there was a platter of sandwiches on the desk. There was enough for a dozen people, but I guessed John was going for variety and not that he thought we'd eat that much.

I was hungrier than I realized. My mouth watered and my stomach rumbled.

"You should eat," Dad said. "You were down there for six or seven hours."

It was dark outside. I hadn't paid attention in the van. I grabbed a sandwich and went to the window, looking out through the gauze drapes.

The sandwich was chicken salad. Good choice for a blind grab.

A sharp two knocks sounded at the door. Dad's hand dropped to his gun, holstered at his side. He looked out the peephole.

"Yes?"

"Ranger here." I barely heard the response.

Dad opened the door and stepped aside. The two shook hands as Ranger came fully into the room and dropped another duffel on the bed.

"This has phones, earpieces, plus a tablet for Winger."

Lorenzo took such good care of me. I didn't really need a tablet here, but he knew I'd want one sooner rather than later.

"Thank you," Dad said.

"I'll leave you two," Ranger said. "I'm right next door, and once you're on comms, you can call if needed."

They shook again before Ranger left.

I took another sandwich and wolfed it down. It wasn't as good, tuna, but at least it was food.

"You want to hit the shower first?" Dad asked as he opened the duffel and pulled out a small box. From where I was, I could see the label that identified it as his earpiece.

"Yeah," I said, finally finding my voice again. "I'll probably feel better after."

"Probably," he said, nodding. "Theo, remember, anything you feel, you can just put it out there. I can tell you're disappointed with yourself right now, but there's no reason to be."

"Thanks," I said quietly. "It's hard."

"I know."

He hugged me again. I craved that contact. The hug in the van wasn't enough. I held this hug for a long time before finally turning my attention to the duffel bags to figure out which was mine.

I retreated to the bathroom and studied myself in the mirror. I was a mess. My shirt and jeans looked like I'd rolled around in the dirt. There was a massive bruise on the side of my head. I ran my fingers over the damage and flinched. It reminded me of Eddie's injury from when his Jeep was smashed. And what was I going to tell him about this? I hadn't heard the cover story yet, but I hoped it was a good one. He was going to be so angry that I just disappeared on him.

How did Mom say nothing about this bruise when she saw me? It must have taken all her resolve not to freak out.

I pulled the shirt over my head, carefully because my joints all hurt. The games plus the pummeling I took from Blackbird over the past two days compounded to make me feel awful.

There were new bruises on my chest alongside ones I recognized from this morning.

At least toeing off my sneakers didn't hurt, but moving to get my socks off and stepping out of my jeans and underwear pained me far more than I expected. I had a huge bruise on my right hip. Where'd that come from?

I looked awful, and I couldn't stop staring at myself. How was I going to explain not just to Eddie but the team for the tourney, not to mention back home? These injuries were much harder to ignore than yesterday's.

I shook my head at the reflection before finally turning away to focus on the shower. The water was just a touch under scalding. While the room itself was plain, at least the showerhead had a massage setting and good water pressure.

I stepped in. The heat coaxed my body into relaxing. The water stung as it hit tender areas of skin, but overall it felt great.

My thoughts were all over the place. I'd done good. I knew that. I'd sabotaged Blackbird's system and ended their control of TOS agents. But I could've been severely injured —or killed—more than once in the past couple of weeks. I'd been safe behind my keyboard, but now they knew about me because of a chip I hadn't even known I'd had.

It was a lot different saving Mom and Dad, or other agents, from the safety of my room. I knew what the stakes were then. I didn't like the feeling of being the target.

I didn't know if I could do this anymore.

I didn't know if I could stop doing it either.

TWENTY-FIVE

When I finally looked at my phone, I had a ton of messages from Eddie. Apparently Mom had only sent a single message to him about me being in the hospital after a car accident. No one else contacted him after that, and he was freaking out.

As we got back to the tournament hotel around two in the morning, I texted him back.

Sorry. Just got my phone back. I'm back at the hotel and okay. I'll see you in the morning.

My phone buzzed in no time.

Thank God! I was scared. No one told me anything, and it took me a lot of texts and calls to get your mom to tell me anything. Is Coach okay?

That was part of the cover story, since we both needed one. We'd been out, going to another physical therapy appointment, when we got hit. TOS set it up so if anyone went looking, it'd appear like it actually happened. I certainly felt like I'd been in a major accident.

Coach is still in hospital, probably for another couple days.

He'd gotten out of surgery earlier and was recovering, but he wasn't going to be coming back to Boston with the rest of us.

You want me to come over? I can sneak out of here.

Probably not a good idea. I'm wiped and my parents are watching me like a hawk.

Parents? Your Dad's here?

Yeah! He came in to watch the championship game.

Nice. Okay. I'll let you rest. If you change your mind though I can be there in like 15 minutes. Get some rest and I'll see you in the morning.

Will do. Love you!

Love you too.

At least he wasn't mad at me right now. He'd probably be furious once he saw what I looked like.

"Eddie doing okay?" Dad asked once I'd set the phone down. "I'm sorry we couldn't manage him better."

"S'okay. There was a lot going on."

I stretched out on my bed while Dad sat at the desk.

"The game's gonna be a bear to play in a few hours," I said as I flexed my limbs.

Dad sighed. Always a bad sign. "There's no way you can play. You may already have a slight concussion. You can't risk getting hurt even worse."

"What?" I flew out of the bed and over to the desk, ignoring the pain signals that came in from every part of me. "What are you talking about?"

"I'm sorry, but there's no way we can allow you to play. The doctor already advised against it and you're certainly not up for it. I saw how much pain you were in just getting off the bed. You need to rest and recover. And we have to make sure there's no chance of concussion."

I kicked the garbage can under the desk, sending it

crashing into the wall with a loud thump. Moving to the window, I looked out across the darkness lit up by the occasional street lamp. It was quiet out—no traffic or people were visible, but that wasn't surprising given it was past midnight.

"I needed to make it right by the team after the crap game I played yesterday," I said quietly.

"Do you really think you'd play well in the condition you're in?" Dad said, coming up behind me, his concerned expression reflected in the glass.

"I at least have to try," I said, without facing him.

He simply shook his head. He was right. There was no arguing it. I needed to play, but realistically the team's chances were better without me.

"Your coach already knows you're out for tomorrow."

Dad put his hand on my shoulder, but this time it wasn't comforting. I'd failed my team and there was no getting around that. I ducked out from his grip and crossed the room to slip into my sneakers.

"I'm gonna go out for a bit, just walk the lobby or something. I gotta process this."

"Don't," Dad said, stepping away from me. "I should let you rest. I can get out of here."

"Mom would probably like to get some time with you," I said. "But I need to walk a bit, clear my head."

"Stay in the hotel?"

"Yeah. The lobby's big, plenty of space to walk around."

"Okay." Dad and I both went for the door, but Dad stopped short. "I'm going to have Ranger keep an eye on you."

What? "I swear I'm not going to do anything stupid."

"I know." His earnest expression came close to starting up my waterworks. "Defender knows that. Your dad, on the other hand—" He stopped himself, and he pulled me into a loose hug. "I almost lost you today. I know you need the walk and that you'll actually be okay. But—" He paused again and I simply nodded. I couldn't argue his choice. "I promise you won't know he's there."

"It's okay." We smiled. His smile was tired, and I suspected mine was too.

In the hallway, we briefly hugged before going our separate ways. It was a bitter pill that I wasn't playing tomorrow. Two weeks in a row, I was on the bench due to injury. Not to mention how badly I'd played for the gold team in the last two games. It was only in the first one that I showed what I could really do.

Even though today was a win, it was hard not to feel like a loser.

Dad's been great with my emotional outbursts, but I seriously needed to be better than that. Maybe the counselor they were forcing me to see when we got home would help.

What would really get me in a better mood would be to play tomorrow. The tourney wasn't the point of the trip, but I *needed* to play. Skating helped get my aggression out and calmed me down. And I really owed the team more than I'd given them. At least they made it to the championship.

The lobby of course was quiet and that was what I needed. Hanging out in the small room would've made me stir-crazy. Being in a tired-but-not-sleepy state sucked. Maybe I should've asked Eddie over, although in the mood I was in, it probably wouldn't have ended well.

I wandered around the cavernous lobby, window-shopping at some of the upscale stores. Who really buys a thousand-dollar bracelet at a hotel?

"Reese?"

I turned to find Donny sitting in one of the high-backed chairs, phone in his hand and buds in his ears. The chair obscured him as I walked by. Had I seen him, I'd have gone another direction, because I didn't need his attitude.

"Damn, man." He pulled one of the earbuds out. "Coach told us what happened at dinner. Are you okay?"

He sounded sympathetic and maybe a bit shocked. I must've looked even worse than I thought.

"It's rough. I'm pissed I can't play tomorrow."

"Probably for the best, though. You don't wanna mess around with concussions. It took my brother months to recover from one."

"He okay now?"

"Yeah. And he's not as aggressive in games anymore. He was a really hard-hitting defenseman, now he goes more for snatching pucks from the opposition than slamming them. Do you have one, or are they just playing it safe?"

"If I do, it's minor, but they don't want to take any chances."

"Wanna sit?" he asked.

What was happening? Maybe I really had a concussion and this was a hallucination. I had expected to find dick Donny in the chair because I'd messed up for the team more than once.

"Might not get up if I do. Trying to stretch out and get myself sleepy before lying down."

He nodded, hit some keys on his phone, and stood up.

"Want some company?"

"Sure." We started walking. He let me set the pace, and I just meandered past the storefronts and the glass that looked out over the closed outdoor pool. "What's got you down here so late?"

"I get nervous before big games, and since I'm rooming

with my coach, I didn't want to disturb him. I came down here and decided to watch some *Mighty Ducks*. Kinda my movie version of comfort food."

"Nice. I use *Miracle* for that."

"USA," he said in a forceful whisper so as not to disturb anyone. He grinned and I did too. This was strangely what I needed—a moment with someone who wasn't going to ask too many questions or ask too often how I was. "I'm sorry you're not playing."

I stopped, and it took Donny a moment before he did the same. "I figured you'd be happy after that crap third game."

"Well, that was pretty bad shit. But I loved our flow in the first game and even the second. I was hoping it'd be that guy who showed up for the championship. Plus I looked at some of the vids. You've got good moves. I can see why you'd get invited here. How do you write those crazy technical papers?"

I chuckled. That was a question I got a lot when people found out about my dual identities between high school hockey player and MIT student. "Just the way my brain's built, I guess."

As we came up on the only open shop, we saw Jamie going inside.

"And even more of the team is up and around," Donny said.

Jamie was looking at the ice cream freezer when we came up behind him.

"Shouldn't our goalie at least be asleep?" Donny put his arm across Jamie's shoulders.

"Hey, guys." He had a guilty expression. "I woke up, couldn't go back to sleep because I wanted some ice cream." He turned toward me. "Theo, man, it's good to see you.

Dude, that's a major bruise." He raised his hand to my face but didn't touch me.

I nodded. "Ice cream. That's an excellent idea."

"Yeah, it is," Donny said.

We each got a different bar, and once we'd paid, we plopped down in chairs in the lobby.

"You're really not playing?" Jamie asked.

"Yeah. The doc and my parents aren't letting me. So I'll be the loud one in the stands, cheering."

"Gold. Gold. Gold." Jamie started the quiet chant and Donny and I joined in. We got one odd look from someone headed to the elevators, and that was okay. We hung out for about a half an hour before we headed to our rooms. Talking hockey with these guys thankfully got my mind to disengage so I could actually sleep.

TWENTY-SIX

"I'm working as fast as I can," I said, staring down the barrel of Raven's gun while Dad held his against my back.

"It's not fast enough!" he bellowed. "I've got a schedule to keep."

I tried to type faster than I already was.

"What are you writing?" Westside said. "This isn't decryption code."

He studied his screen. Had my deception failed? That couldn't be. I brought it up on another monitor in front of me. It looked like it was still running. Did I mess it up? I rapidly read through the lines of code.

"You're trying to wipe our system!" Westside shouted as he pushed me away from the keyboard. The chair couldn't roll far because Dad was right behind me.

"This is what happens when people play games." Raven was no longer yelling but spoke with an eerie calmness.

He fired.

I heard the bullet whiz past me.

Dad cried out. I turned as he hit the floor.

"*No!*"

"No! Dad!" I sat up, looking around. In the soft glow of my monitors' screen savers, I could see I was in my room.

We got back from Denver late. Mom and Dad had sat with Eddie and me at the championship game, which the gold team won. Jamie even got the tournament MVP for his work in the net. He also got positive feedback from two scouts who were there. Donny got some interest as well. I was very happy for them.

I'd slept through most of the plane ride. Eddie got home a couple of hours after we did, and I'd hung out with him and we caught up on homework. We were quite a sight since I had pretty fresh injuries and his were still fading.

My parents said I didn't have to go to school tomorrow, but I was always the kid who hated skipping. Plus I got cleared for noncontact hockey practice, and I definitely wanted to skate. MIT class was in the afternoon too. Since that class was my favorite, I didn't want to miss it.

If I didn't go to sleep, it was going to be a rough Monday. But because I wasn't sleeping at the moment, I decided to sift through some of the data we'd recovered from the Blackbird cloud drive backup.

It'd been about thirty-six hours since I'd crashed the system, and we still didn't know who Raven really was. He wasn't talking. As soon as he was out of the hospital, he'd go to a holding facility for more interrogation. I didn't want to think about what that meant.

Angel was more cooperative and said that she'd heard the intel Blackbird used came from someone who was formerly with TOS, but she didn't have a name. We were looking for clues about who it was in the mountain of data we had, as well as for how they'd broken through TOS's defenses. Westside, meanwhile, was being defiantly quiet.

My desk was a mess. As much as I use computers, I had a habit of scribbling notes on paper, and it was everywhere. I shuffled the sheets around looking for stuff I'd written while I initially tried to fix the intrusion.

What I found was the envelope Cullen had given me.

I sighed.

It'd be so easy just to fix his problem. But it seemed pointless if someone could just do it again?

A light knock on my slightly open door startled me far more than it should've.

"Come in," I said softly.

"I saw the light." Dad whispered too. "You okay?"

I shrugged. "Nightmare, and I haven't been able to go back to sleep yet, so I thought I'd do some work."

I didn't hide my issues from Mom and Dad. There was no need. I had an appointment with a TOS counselor after my afternoon class.

Dad sat on the corner of my bed. "I never planned this for you. Neither of us did. Over the years, I've rethought a lot about whether you should be doing all this TOS work. It's always turned out for the best. This time I'm pretty sure it didn't."

I leaned back in my swivel chair. Dad and I were strangely alike right now, both in a T-shirt and boxer shorts. His red hair as askew as mine probably was—actually his looked like my idea of styled, so I'm sure I looked worse. He had the same dark circles I'd seen under my eyes before I went to bed.

"I don't know what the right answer is. Getting in there and stopping that, I did what I had to. As scary as it was, I keep asking myself what would've happened if I hadn't been able to do it." I lowered my voice so it was even quieter. "I don't usually like the answer."

Mom appeared in the doorway.

"Is this a guys-only meeting?"

I smiled. Mom was amazing. So many choices I'd made upset her, but the only talking-to I got was about Eddie, safe sex, and being aware of what his parents would not approve of, and so on. It was a very mom thing.

We didn't talk about my decisions or the way I acted as a TOS agent. I was due to debrief with Joanna on Tuesday. She was giving me some time to decompress while she gathered other reports. I'd filed my written report while we were sitting in the Denver airport.

"Just a meeting of people who aren't sleeping," I said. "Come on in."

"Nightmare?"

I nodded.

"Me too," Dad said.

I looked at him with a raised eyebrow. "Really?"

This time he nodded. "Yeah. They don't necessarily go away when you get older. I remember everything. Shooting Coach." A pained look crossed Dad's face, unlike any I'd seen before. I thought he might cry. "Hurting you. Putting a gun to your back."

Mom sat next to him and wrapped an arm around his shoulders.

"We're certainly a different kind of family." I cracked myself up a bit.

When Dad chuckled, the tension broke and we all laughed. It wasn't a belly laugh or anything, but we were able to find a joke in a bad situation.

"What got you up?" Dad asked Mom.

"I just needed a drink of water. When you were gone, I went looking."

"Are we...?" I paused. I wasn't sure I wanted to ask.

"What?" Dad asked. "I think you've earned the right to ask questions. You've grown up at least five or ten years over the weekend."

"Are we helping the right people?"

I kinda couldn't believe I said that. I'd often wondered where TOS fit into the world, and I knew it was mostly on a need-to-know basis. Given what I'd just gone through, I wanted to make sure I was on the right side. At the same time, I didn't know what I'd do if I didn't like the answer.

Mom and Dad looked at each other. It was one of those moments where they said a lot, but I wasn't in on the silent communication.

"TOS is an unofficial organization that's funded by several governments around the world." Dad didn't seem upset by my question. "We do things the government can't officially do, although sometimes we work with agencies like the CIA, NSA, and MI-6. No government would ever admit that we worked for them."

"More like *Mission: Impossible* than James Bond?" I asked.

"I guess that works." Mom shrugged. "I can't think of another fictional organization to compare it to. So we do what's necessary to keep the US and its allies safe in ways a more official organization couldn't do."

I nodded. It seemed like we were the good guys.

"Blackbird often works to undermine commerce and destabilize parts of the world in ways that would benefit its own interests," Dad continued. "It would've been devastating if they'd put a lot of our agents under their control or killed them. As it is, TOS is going to have to change a lot of protocols because of possible breaches that our agents may have given Blackbird."

I knew about that. Between analyzing the data we had,

Lorenzo and I along with a lot of TOS techs were planning a massive overhaul. It was a big job that would take weeks. I was also working with another team on a new network-encryption system that would be less susceptible to any individuals leaving the fold. It was a wicked cool project that I wished I could turn in for an MIT class.

"Okay." I thought over this information for a bit, and Mom and Dad waited patiently. "Do we ever help individuals?"

"Sometimes," Dad said. "Though we usually work on a larger scale. Why?"

I told them about Cullen and handed them the information he'd given me.

"I know I could just fix this," I said after I finished the story. "But then I'm just as illegal as what happened in the first place. He needs a permanent, legit fix."

"This kid a friend?" Mom asked.

"No. He heard I'm good with computers and came hoping I could help. I really didn't want to know, but he snuck the envelope into my pack, and I haven't figured out what to do with it."

"Let me talk to some people." Mom took the envelope. "I think we can check this out and make sure he's where he's supposed to be."

I smiled. That was good.

"Thanks, Mom."

"You should get back to sleep," she said. "Your alarm will go off before you know it."

"Yeah." I gave the clock an evil look.

"You could stay home and get some rest," Dad said. "That's still okay with us."

"I'll power through."

"I wish you'd reconsider," Mom said. "I'm keeping an

eye on you, and if I think you're struggling, I'll pull a mom on you."

"Understood."

She came over, leaned down, and kissed me on the forehead.

Before she could walk away, I reached for her hand and stood up. I wrapped her in a hug, which she gently returned.

"I love you, Mom."

"Love you too, Theo."

I released her and went to Dad. He stood, no doubt sensing what was coming.

"Love you, Dad."

His embrace wasn't as gentle, but it felt safe, like the hug he'd given me in the van. Even though it was a tighter embrace, it helped more than it hurt.

"You too, Theo."

We stepped apart, and he put a hand on my shoulder.

"I was going to talk about this after you debriefed with Joanna, but I'll put it out there now. If you want to quit TOS, you have to know that your mom and I will support you in that decision. We'd actually prefer that you did, but it's one hundred percent your choice. We won't think less of you if you want to just be a smart teenager."

"Thanks." I hugged Dad one more time. "It's been on my mind. I know I'm in at least until we get the security protocols updated, but yeah, I'm thinking about where to go from here."

"Good."

"Night, Theo," Mom said as they left the room.

I dropped into my chair and spun around a few times, suddenly feeling like I was eight and twirled in Dad's chair.

There was a lot to think about. Meanwhile, I went back

to looking for the papers I'd been searching for, so I could get back to my analysis, which would hopefully make me sleepy.

TWENTY-SEVEN

Eddie came over when he got out of school and we were in the garage where he was sort of helping me work on my bike. Even though I went to school Monday and Tuesday, I'd stayed home today because I felt horrible this morning. I think I finally exhausted myself enough that my body switched off my brain and let me sleep uninterrupted Tuesday night. It was clear from the sluggish way I woke up that I needed more, so I mostly snoozed until hunger forced me up for lunch.

Holed up in the garage and working on the bike was another form of therapy. Getting the bike back on the road was a big step in life returning to normal.

I'd spent the afternoon rebuilding everything from the ground up, and it was nearly done. Eddie was cute trying to help. He was science-smart, but he had no idea about tools or how to assemble a bike. The cluelessness was adorable.

"I like that you're not flinching when you move." Eddie sat on the hood of Mom's car. "The day off looks like it was a great idea."

"Yeah, Mom said the same thing." I worked to adjust

the shifting mechanism so it'd be just right. "I still hurt sometimes, especially when I move after being still for a while. At least it's not all pain all the time anymore."

"You scared me, Theo," Eddie whispered. "Not just the accident and the weird kidnapping thing. You've had such a —I don't know. The look in your eyes hasn't been you since I surprised you in Denver. It was like you were waiting for...."

I looked to him from where I squatted next to the bike. With it up on its rack, I saw him through the rear-wheel spokes. His sad expression hurt me. I'd seen many looks on Eddie in the last year, good and bad. I hated that I did this to him.

I laid my tools on the garage floor and went to him, wiping my hands on the towel I pulled from my back pocket.

"I'm okay." I pushed his legs apart so I could get close. I was butted up against the car bumper, but I pulled him to me so I could hug him. "It was a crazy couple of days between the tourney and the accident. I'm glad you were there. You kept me together."

The sadness didn't lift from his eyes, but he put his arms around me.

"I just don't want to lose you. Maybe I'm just being silly."

It was obvious he had more to say. "Spill it."

We stared at each other. It must've been an interesting picture, two people in a stare down while hugging.

"I've seen you get hurt in games many times, this was different, though. Like I said, it was like more happened to you than a car accident."

Was he fishing? I'd given him the rather in-depth story about the accident.

"I don't know," I said. "The past couple of weeks have been crazy. I guess I don't deal well when everything piles up."

"I hope that's all. I'm here for you for sure, but I'd rather not see you like that."

"I'd like that too." I gave him a small smile followed by a kiss.

I untangled myself from him and returned to the bike. He talked while I tested the shifting by spinning the pedals as I clicked the gears.

"So have you picked out what you're wearing to the dance yet?"

"You're kidding, right?"

Who did he think he was talking to?

"Only sort of. I was thinking we'd dress up, look sharp. Like we did that night at the tourney."

"Really? It's not like this is a formal dance."

"No, but I liked dressing up with you, and you know, why not?"

I loved this guy. He was the only one who could get me to fold easily on something I kinda hated.

I glared at him but not really. He just raised his eyebrows and gave me a smile he knew would melt any resistance.

"Fine." I drew out the word in an exasperated way.

"Yes!" He even added a fist pump for emphasis. Crazy guy.

He jumped off the car, grabbed my hand off the bike's shifter, and spun me around. My chest slammed into his, which sent a jolt of pain through me.

He put his arms around me, holding me just above my waist. He swayed to music that only he could hear.

"It's gonna be a great time." He moved me so I'd keep time with him.

This felt nice. If going to a dance meant we could be close like this, though, pressed together and swaying, I'd do that anytime.

I matched my hand placement to his and relaxed into his lead. It was pretty simple—sway and turn. I dropped my head just enough so I could lie against his chest as we moved.

A contented sigh escaped, and he squeezed me just slightly, probably the gentlest hug ever.

"Theo?" I jumped back when Mom called out from the door that led to the kitchen. "I'm sorry. I didn't mean to startle you two."

"It's okay, Mrs. Reese," Eddie said. "Just practicing a little for the dance this weekend."

My face was hot enough it must've been a vibrant shade of red.

"What's up, Mom?" I tried to sound like I wasn't embarrassed out of my mind.

"A young man's here. Cullen? Said he looked for you at school but couldn't find you."

Interesting. I hadn't heard anything since I'd given his info to Mom a few days ago.

"Sure."

Mom pushed the button to raise the garage door. "I told him to wait out there."

As it lifted, Cullen appeared. He looked more at ease than I'd ever seen him.

"Hey, Theo." He entered the garage as Mom retreated inside. "Sorry to just show up, but you weren't at school and I had to thank you."

He wrapped me in a hug, which was completely unexpected. I was glad he was happy, but I hardly knew him well enough for him to have this reaction.

"My dad got arrested yesterday afternoon for computer fraud, and I'm back with my mom as of a few hours ago."

"That's fantastic, man. Glad to hear it."

Eddie looked confused but didn't say anything.

"I don't know how to repay you," he said.

"I didn't do anything." I kept the knowledge I had a secret. "Like I said, there wasn't anything I could do. I guess they just figured it out."

"All I know is, I told you about the problem and it didn't take long for it to disappear."

"Maybe he's just good luck." Eddie came up and wrapped his arm around my waist.

"Maybe. Anyway I just wanted to let you know and thank you for whatever you may have done."

"I'm glad it worked out," I said.

"I'll catch you around school. I'm gonna get going. Mom and I are celebrating."

He looked behind him to a woman waiting in a beat-up blue car. She waved, and I raised my hand in greeting. He jogged off to the car.

"See ya." I watched him go.

That's awesome. TOS must've had someone in the right place who could fix the problem and find the needed evidence against his dad. I hadn't been sure I should've talked about Cullen's problems with Mom and Dad because it felt like TOS had larger issues to deal with, but it was good they helped out random people too.

"That was weird," Eddie said.

"Nah." I went to the rack and pulled the bike off. "It was good. Really good. They needed the help."

I rolled the bike out of the garage before I mounted it.

"You're done?"

"I think so. Only one way to know for sure."

I tested the brakes, and they engaged like I knew they would. It was habit to make sure they worked before I took off. I pedaled very slowly and only picked up speed when I hit the slope in the driveway.

"Helmet!" Eddie called out.

I didn't look back. "I'm not going far at all."

I rolled into the street and picked up enough speed to click through gears. The seat was a little low, but that was an easy adjustment. Leaning over, I got the feel for the handlebars, both in the drop position and the higher one. It was good—or would be after the seat adjustment. I needed to tweak the gearing on the front sprocket, and then it would be perfect. I stood up from the seat and sped up more.

It felt good, the chilly air hitting my face.

I made a U-turn after I was about halfway down the block and cruised back to the driveway.

Eddie wore a frown as I rolled past him and back into the garage.

"Don't you go being stupid, Theodore Reese. We've got a dance to go to and then an anniversary to celebrate. I don't need you getting into an accident on your bike, especially without the helmet."

"I won't." I reracked the bike. "I don't wanna get in trouble with you."

"Damn right you don't."

He hit the button for the garage door, and as it dropped, he peppered my lips with kisses.

TWENTY-EIGHT

I'D BEEN BACK and forth on whether or not to continue with TOS, but I'd decided on a firm yes while I was dancing with Eddie Saturday night.

There was no denying I enjoyed the work. However, I'd be okay not going into the field again. I'd turned the situation over in my head a number of times. While TOS might've been able to fix the chip problem without me, I'd played a key part in bringing that to a close. I couldn't shake the idea that if I hadn't been involved, Dad might not be around anymore.

"I'm glad you're staying." Lorenzo spoke from the screen above my head. "We make a good team. Plus I still need to beat you at *Grand Theft Auto*."

"Yeah," I said in a mocking tone, "that's exactly why you keep me around."

"That was a great analysis of the cloud data." He switched topics away from the fact I owned him in *GTA*. "I couldn't believe how tangled that was. They'd exploited areas we didn't even know about."

"Yeah. It's hard to stop someone from talking if they want to."

A former IT director, Lorenzo's predecessor, had left TOS a few years ago because she wanted to go into private consulting. TOS let her go and created a background so she had good credentials to set up a business. But something had gone wrong in a background check run by a Blackbird-affiliated business and they figured out her cover. TOS couldn't locate this woman now and it assumed she was either deep cover with Blackbird or dead. Agents, including Dad, were working on it.

More than once I thought about Blackbird knowing who I was and that they might come after me. There was nothing I could do about that, and I wasn't going to hide. I could only do what the other exposed agents were—trying to be safe and careful.

Mom and Dad talked about moving, but so far it wasn't clear if we would. Even though Blackbird had visibility on my chip for a few days, it was unknown how far up the chain the info had gone. Everyone from the IT facility was in custody, so they wouldn't talk to anyone anytime soon. We had all the data, and based on the analysis, it didn't look like they'd transmitted out too many details. It seemed like they were waiting to report an overall success, rather than piecemeal statuses.

For my part, I didn't want to move, even if it was just to another house in the same town. This was home.

"I'll have the security recommendations over to you later today to review," Lorenzo said. "I made some tweaks to what you wrote and added some new recommendations from what we've been talking about here."

"Cool. I'll look that over tonight and get it back to you as fast as I can."

We were working quickly to have new protocols in place for all the networked tech to safeguard against future breaches. Realistically there had to be systems in place to update protocols anytime someone left the organization by choice or otherwise. Lorenzo and I had already discussed the issue that my credentials weren't immediately revoked upon my capture. He admitted he'd been too caught up to take those steps. We agreed that couldn't happen again.

We'd been so focused on preventing hacks over the past couple of years, we didn't take into account the more obvious people part of the equation, who could do damage if their knowledge got into the wrong hands.

There was a knock at the door.

"I gotta go. It's time."

"Okay, man. Talk to you later."

Lorenzo's image faded, replaced by one of my hockey player screen backgrounds—this one of the Detroit Red Wings' captain Henrik Zetterberg, who was one good-looking guy.

I went to the door and found Dad and someone else. Based on the old-school bag he carried, he was the doctor who would be rechipping me. It was obvious Dad saw the doctor first because of the small bandage he had.

Nerves fluttered in my stomach. I didn't like getting the last one out, and I wasn't excited about another one going in.

"Come in."

"Winger, this is Neptune," Dad said. "He'll be doing the procedure."

I nodded and met the doctor's hand that he extended.

"It's good to meet you, Winger. I hear we owe you a lot."

I'd gotten this from a few people I'd met since I'd been

back from Denver, and I never knew what to say. "You're welcome" seemed weird. It all seemed weird.

I gave a single nod. It'd become my go-to for this kind of thing, and it still made me uncomfortable.

"I'll leave you to this," Dad said. "I'll be down in the office."

Neptune opened his bag and removed a sheet, which he draped over my bed.

"Please lie down and we'll get to it."

At least this time I knew about the chip.

"I'm going to give you a local anesthetic, which will make your neck numb for the next several hours. We'll give it a few minutes and then get to work."

I nodded because I already knew the drill from getting the last chip out.

Every TOS agent was getting a new chip, which worked differently to keep it masked from the different nodes it connected to as it pinged back to TOS. It was a pretty snazzy upgrade Lorenzo had figured out based on some of the early work I'd done.

"Okay, Winger, you're all set." Neptune had me all sewn up in less than a half hour. "Your neck will feel numb for a few hours. Leave the dressing on at least overnight. If you want to keep the stitches covered, you can change it for a fresh one, but let the wound breathe at least a few hours a day. Plus you can use antiseptic ointment as well to help it heal faster. The stitches should dissolve within three days."

"Sounds good." I already knew the details, but I let him do his doctor thing. "Thank you."

I walked him out of my room and downstairs. He headed for the door. I guess he didn't need to see Dad again.

"Take care, Winger."

"See you next week."

He practically had the door closed before I finished. Whatever.

I went to the office. The door was open, but I knocked on the frame and waited for an acknowledgment, just in case anything was going on I shouldn't see.

"Come on in," Mom said.

It was comforting to find everyone here—Mom, Dad, and John. Everyone had the same bandage I did. Neptune had been busy while he was here.

"It's weird we're all bandaged the same." I dropped myself into one of the chairs in front of Dad's desk. "It's like we're all in the same cult."

"We kinda are," John said, and Dad chuckled. "I'm guessing the new chip for you means you're staying on."

"Yeah. The pros outweigh the cons. Plus there's a lot of work to do on the internal systems now. That's gonna be fun to tackle. So I was wondering...."

Mom and Dad turned focus on me, joining John who already was.

I took a moment. This was kinda big.

"Can I get some field training? Something so I'll have a better idea what to do if something like this happens again."

"Hopefully we won't repeat this," Mom said.

"He's right, though, Katherine," John said. "It wouldn't hurt if he knew some basics. Defensive moves. More of our protocols if situations like this come up again. It's not clear how many in Blackbird know who he is. It'd be good to have him ready. Just in case."

Mom pursed her lips. She wasn't happy. I know she'd hoped I'd hang up TOS. Dad looked conflicted.

"I'm not saying I want to know how to shoot a gun or anything." I shuddered briefly at the idea. "But defense, protocols, and such. I was flying by the seat of my pants in

Denver, and maybe that was part of the success. But the more I know procedure, the better I can improvise."

"I'd be happy to teach him a little, off the record," John said. "But some formal sessions wouldn't hurt either."

"Theo, I love that you want to protect yourself." Dad let go a huge sigh. "At the same time, I hate that you have to think about it."

"Me too." I admitted the obvious.

"Let your mom and me discuss it a little, okay?"

I nodded, and Mom already looked relieved. Probably because she'd have a chance to argue against it.

"I'm gonna head back upstairs and do some homework."

"You around for dinner tonight?" Mom asked.

I thought a moment. "Yeah. No plans. Eddie's got a lab thing going on, so we weren't hanging or anything."

"Family dinner tonight?" Mom looked between me and Dad.

"Thai?" Dad offered.

"Sure," she said.

I liked where this was going.

"John, this includes you too." I'd already assumed it did, but I'm glad Mom told him. "It's been too long since we were all here at the same time."

"I'm in," I said enthusiastically as John nodded his acknowledgment.

She looked at the clock on her computer. "I'll order in about an hour, so we'll eat around seven."

"Perfect. I'll leave my door open so you can just shout up."

She nodded, and they went back to their work as I headed to my room. It was exciting that, at least for this night, my less than normal family was going to do something completely normal.

Thanks for reading *Tracker Hacker!* I hope you enjoyed Theo's first field mission. Keep turning pages because *A Very Winger Christmas* and a preview of *Schooled*, the second *Codename: Winger* book, are still to come.

If you'd like to get exclusive access to a short about how Theo and Eddie met and became boyfriends, you can go to JeffAndWill.com/WingerExtra for details on how to download that story.

A VERY WINGER CHRISTMAS

CODENAME: WINGER #1.5

JEFF ADAMS

A VERY WINGER CHRISTMAS

A CODENAME: WINGER BONUS MISSION

Whitney Houston's "Do You Hear What I Hear?" blasted over the rink speakers as Mitch made a deft move to break us out of the defensive zone. From his position he intercepted a pass and headed toward the neutral zone. I kept opposing D busy, allowing Mitch to pop the puck off the boards so he could pick it up on the other side of the blue line.

I hustled after him with the D I'd grappled with hot on my heels.

Once I got close to Mitch, we made tight passes and zigzagged our way to the offensive zone.

The far-side D ended up in front of us, keeping to the middle lane.

He'd paid attention to Mitch's strategy and made sure to get ahead of us.

Rebik wouldn't give us any space. The problem playing against your teammates was that we all knew each other's game.

"Yo! Yo! Yo!" Spires announced himself, coming in hot

from the bench. One of this season's freshmen, he'd already proven to be a reliable teammate. He sped into the middle of the play as Mitch and I spread out to make things tougher on Rebik since his D partner wasn't with him yet.

Mitch looked between me, Rebik, Spires, and Angles, who was in net. Mitch had a plan. He focused on me but pivoted last second with a pass to Spires, who continued toward the net. Spires barely settled the puck before he shot.

Score!

I got chills between the goal and Whitney soaring into the final verse of the carol. The blend of vocals and music was perfect and exactly the type of music I loved. My parents hooked me on a 1980-something CD called *A Very Special Christmas* long ago, and it became my go-to collection of carols.

For the Christmas Eve game, each player contributed two songs to the playlist. Mine always came from this disc—Whitney and Bob Seger's "Little Drummer Boy."

While I loved all hockey, this pickup game held a special place in my heart. Not only did we play with music, but the positions got mixed up since players went on for whoever came off. This game wasn't just the usual teammates, either; friends and family could play too. Fun ruled all. We also played without most of the pads—we wore helmets and gloves out of necessity.

Why no pads? Christmas sweaters. Those didn't easily fit over pads.

Yes, this had become an ugly sweater party. This year Eddie found me an awesome one featuring *Tron* that had light cycles, identity discs, recognizers, bits, and programs all over it.

He played the role of good boyfriend and didn't question my obsession with the movie even though he didn't understand it. Ever since I'd seen it when I was six or seven, I wanted to be Flynn and get sucked inside a computer. To this day, when I infiltrate a computer network for my work with Tactical Operational Support, I imagine it looks like the *Tron* universe.

My name is Theo Reese, and I might be a nerd.

"Nice shot," I said, clapping Spires on the back. "Way to announce yourself too."

"You guys needed to know I was there, man."

"It sure worked," Mitch said as we headed back to the bench.

We weren't on the bench more than a minute before the Zamboni horn sounded, letting us know the ninety-minute game was over.

"This never lasts long enough," I said to Mitch as we headed to the locker room.

Mitch chuckled. "You say that every year. Is it the music or the sweaters?"

"Both. These are the things that make a perfect Christmas game. And kudos on this year's sweater."

"Right!" He sounded so proud as he grabbed at what he wore and held it out. "Mom outdid herself. I may never get another one because I don't think this can be topped." He'd gotten an actual jersey with a red-and-green pattern featuring trees and snowflakes. "So is your dad making it home for the Reese holiday traditions?"

"The last I heard was that he was on track to make it. Hopefully there are no messages waiting for me that say otherwise."

"Oh good. I still remember how upset he was that Christmas when we were nine."

Back then, I didn't know exactly why he'd missed it, but by the following holiday, I did.

My quirky family of agents didn't always get to be together when we wanted. Birthdays, anniversaries, hockey games, and other events could get missed due to TOS demands. Luckily the agency was mostly chill over the holidays.

We cleaned up, stored our gear quickly, and found Eddie hanging out with Mitch's girlfriend, Iris, in the rink lobby with some of the other friends and family who had either played or watched the game.

Eddie drew me into a hug and gave me a quick kiss.

"Hey," he said as I turned to stand next to him. He kept his arm draped across my shoulders. "You guys should play with a soundtrack more often. It amps up the fun—especially when someone breaks out and sings along." Eddie looked to Mitch.

"How can you not sing along to 'All I Want for Christmas Is You'?" Mitch asked in earnest. "And it's not like I sang the whole song."

If I'd been called out for something like that, I'd have gone several shades of red. Mitch, however, remained unapologetic anytime he busted out a song lyric.

"You were adorable," Iris said, "carrying the puck and doing your best Mariah." She kissed his forehead.

"I was moved." He grinned. "Let's get out of here. I wanna know what my secret Santa got me."

We made our goodbyes, headed to our cars, and made for our favorite diner. Each of us had a gift bag with us as we regathered at the restaurant. This was a newer tradition—at least I hoped it became one, since this was only the second time we'd done it. While Mitch and I have been friends forever, Eddie and Iris had come into the picture last year and the four of us became a tight group.

"Who's got my present?" Mitch asked eagerly as he looked to Eddie and me. Iris didn't have it because she couldn't be his secret Santa, just like Eddie couldn't be mine. *Excited* didn't do justice to Mitch when it came to presents. Ever since the first birthday party I went to for him, when we were four or five, he practically vibrated when it was gift time.

"Calm down," Iris said, pulling him to the host stand. "I know that's difficult. Four, please," she added to the hostess who pulled menus from the stack.

We didn't need those since we could practically recite all the items.

We ordered chicken tenders and nachos rather than our usual big meals because we all had family dinners tonight.

Once sodas arrived we dropped our gift bags in front of the right person. Eddie had Mitch's, Mitch was Eddie's Santa, Iris and I exchanged.

"Yes, you can go first," Iris and I said at the same time to Mitch. We all knew him extremely well and chuckled when he clapped his hands before he peeked inside the bag.

Eddie had stuffed it full of all colors of tissue paper. After Mitch calmly pulled out a couple of handfuls, he got more urgent in removing the barriers to his gift.

Iris laughed, watching her boyfriend continue to put paper on the table even as it fell off onto the floor. "Did you buy *all* the tissue?"

"I wanted him to have enough," Eddie said.

"Oh cool!" Mitch produced a small Zamboni from the bottom of the bag. He rolled it along the table, pushing paper aside, grinning like a little kid.

"It'll go perfect with the little hockey guys you've got on your bookshelf." Eddie looked pleased.

"For sure." He continued to drive it over Iris's arm, causing her to giggle. She truly loved being with such a big kid and his infectious fun. "Thanks, Eddie. Okay, you go."

From his bag, Eddie removed a roll of paper tied with red and green ribbon. He squeaked as he unrolled it.

"What is it?" I asked, leaning over to see. My face heated as I looked at a picture of me. "How did you get that?"

"Dude, this is awesome." Eddie continued to stare at the picture.

"How?" I asked again, super curious.

"I got the idea because you two were ogling that hockey calendar in the bookstore about a month ago."

I remembered it well—hockey players in various poses, and none totally dressed. They were ridiculously hot.

"Anyway," he continued, "I thought Eddie might appreciate a picture of you like that. One day you had the perfect pose—taping your stick, standing in front of your locker in just the pants. I managed to snap a picture, and I merged it with a calendar and, ta-da, an instant hockey hunk wall calendar."

Oh my God! Mitch just called me a hockey hunk. I covered my face before it was the same shade of red as my hair.

"I love it. Look how intense you are, getting the blade taped just right." He nudged me, and I peeked through my fingers to find him looking all happy. If I had to be embarrassed, at least it was for a good cause.

"How are you focusing on the tape?" Iris asked.

"He's embarrassed enough already," Eddie replied. "I don't want to make it worse."

And that made it worse. While he'd seen me shirtless many times, something about the picture made me feel very much on display.

"I can't believe you took pictures in the locker room, or that I missed it."

"I'm glad you like it," Mitch said, ignoring my comment.

"Thanks," Eddie replied, rolling up the picture and tucking it back in the bag. "Iris?"

"You sure? You can go next if you want, Theo."

"Go for it," I said.

I'd used a reasonable amount of colorful paper, left over from what Eddie had bought for Mitch's bag, to hide the box that contained a flash drive on which I'd programmed three new modules for the outdoor Christmas decorations on Iris's house. She loves holiday lights, and Mitch had told me she wanted her dad to buy some new programs, but the ones she wanted were pricey. I studied up on what she wanted and figured out how to do it. Mitch and Iris's mom helped me test it out one afternoon when she wasn't home.

She looked confused as she examined the black plastic rectangle, but when she pulled out the folded paper and read it, her face lit up with a huge smile.

"Oh, Theo!" she said loudly enough to draw looks from nearby tables. "I can't wait to try these out."

"I hope you like them. And if you don't, just let me know what you want changed."

"You guys should come over tomorrow—"

My watch buzzed with Lorenzo's emergency pattern. Dammit.

"—we can check them out."

"That's cool by me. What do you think?" Eddie asked and turned his gaze to me as I tapped a button on the watch to acknowledge.

"Guys—" I sighed, hating what I had to do. "—a client just sent me an emergency message. I've got to see what's up."

"Seriously?" Eddie's brow creased.

"Go," Mitch said. "I can't promise I won't repurpose your gift while you're gone or eat your food." Mitch grinned and took back the bag he'd set in front of me.

Thankfully Mitch kept the tone upbeat. I hoped that'd keep Eddie from getting too pissed off.

"Maybe Eddie should hold on to that while I'm gone," I said as I got out of the booth. I reached for the bag, but Mitch kept it out of reach.

"Nope. Mine until you're back."

"Go," Eddie said. "I'm sure you and I can get it from him later if we have to."

The flash of mischief in Eddie's eyes said we were okay.

I walked away as our food arrived and sat in my car so I could take the call privately.

"Doctor Possible," I said as the call connected. "Winger here."

"Sorry to bother you on Christmas Eve." He sounded stressed.

"I'm afraid we've got a Code Dark that I've been asked to bring you in on. We need to be on a conference call in thirty minutes."

"Can do. That gives me time to get home. What can you tell me?"

"Currently nothing, I'm afraid." He sounded annoyed about that.

"The request comes directly from Raptor, and he provided no additional details to me or Red Hat."

So much for a quiet holiday. This interruption came from the highest levels of TOS.

"Understood. I'll be online in thirty. I need to say some goodbyes and then I'll be on the road."

"Thanks, Winger." Lorenzo disconnected.

Quickly I returned to the table, dropped into the booth, and grabbed a chicken tender.

"I'm sorry, but I gotta go." I stuffed the chicken in my mouth to satisfy my postgame hunger.

Everyone sounded their disappointment, and the earlier goodwill with Eddie went out the window as he fixed me with his trademarked glare of disapproval.

"You need different clients," Iris said. "Ones that know not to interrupt secret Santa." At least she sounded sympathetic.

Mitch handed over the bag. "Open this before you take off."

"Thanks, man." I took the bag that had a bit of weight in the bottom.

Inside sat a puck with the Detroit Red Wings logo emblazoned on it. Mitch often gave me grief about growing up in Boston and being a Red Wings fan, so gifting me a puck was cool.

"Nice. And thanks for not getting me a Bruins one."

I pulled it out to show to everyone, and as I turned it to display the logo, I found the unexpected.

"Dude!"

Henrik Zetterberg's signature cut across the back of the puck in silver ink.

"How'd you get this?"

Eddie leaned over to look as I ran my finger over the autograph.

"An online charity thing last month. I'd been looking at Bruins stuff and then found that."

"We're supposed to have a twenty-dollar limit. This is—"

He shook his head and stopped trying to scoop up some of the beans and chicken from the nacho plate. "Trust me. It wasn't too insane. Besides, if I can't splurge on my best friend...."

"It's awesome." I put my fist out, and he bumped it after he got the nacho into his mouth. "It's going on my desk right next to Eddie's picture."

"I'm okay with that only because it's a puck," Eddie said before kissing my cheek.

I turned and gave him a quick kiss on the lips.

"All right, I gotta go."

"Don't let them keep you from the Reese family traditions," Eddie said with a frustrated edge to his tone. "Some things are more important than work."

I nodded, even though TOS work superseded everything.

"Merry Christmas, guys," I said before I darted away.

"And call me later," I heard Eddie say before I got out of the diner.

"THEO?" Mom called from the living room.

"Yeah." I headed for the stairs since I only had a couple of minutes before the call. Lorenzo had emailed instructions with a link to use, which was odd since it wasn't a TOS secure channel.

She stepped into the hallway, holding a wrapping paper roll.

"You're back early," she said, a tinge of unease in her voice. I'd caught her wrapping something. A lot already sat under our tree, so I wondered what more she could possibly add.

"Don't worry. You've got time to finish. A Code Dark came in." I continued to the stairs.

"Oh." Her tone shifted and she nodded. "I'll leave you to it."

Whatever the issue, she didn't seem to know about it.

"I'll work as fast as I can."

I knew her thoughts were in the same place as mine—we wanted our Christmas if at all possible.

I took the stairs two at a time and grabbed the doorknob long enough for it to read my fingerprints and release the lock. Inside, I slid my backpack off and dropped it to the floor. I removed the puck from my jacket pocket before I got out of it and chucked it on the bed.

At the desk I logged into the TOS network as I put the puck—on its end so the signature faced me—next to the selfie from the summer of Eddie and me on a ferry ride.

I clicked the link on the email from Lorenzo, and my screen went black before the logo for NORAD—the North American Aerospace Defense Command—appeared. I'd done some government work before through TOS, but connecting to NORAD made me nervous and, at the same time, thoughts of *War Games* played through my head.

A single line of text under the logo read: *Stand by for the meeting host.*

In less than a minute, the logo disappeared and the site asked permission to access my webcam and mic, which I granted.

"This is Colonel Robert Winston from NORAD. I'm here with Captain Jessica Marlow and Lieutenant Samantha Cartwright from our IT department."

Two-thirds of my screen showed the colonel as he spoke

at the head of a conference table. The two women flanked him. They were all in uniform and sat inside a dull gray conference room. Four other images ran down the right one-third—Raptor, Lorenzo, Joanna, and me. I didn't usually think about my age in TOS gatherings, but I was decidedly the youngest one here.

"Raptor, who do we have from TOS?" Colonel Winston asked.

He went down the introductions, and since Joanna and Lorenzo each nodded when he called their codenames, I did the same.

"No disrespect, but Winger seems quite young to have the clearances required for this meeting."

"He not only has the proper clearances," Raptor said, "we rely on him to solve problems no one else can. He'll actively work alongside Doctor Possible."

The colonel looked disbelieving. When he finally nodded, I exhaled and stopped clenching my chair's arms.

"Let's get down to business. We lost control of the Santa Tracker website just as it went into Christmas Eve mode as 24 December began at the dateline. All attempts to regain control so far have failed. We're on the clock with a possible international incident occurring if we don't have it back online by 1700."

Someone hacked Santa?

Was he serious?

I'd seen the Santa Tracker on TV. Santa's location mattered when I was a kid. Of course, now I knew my parents used it as a ploy to get me to sleep—but back then, when Santa got near the East Coast, I made no arguments about going to bed.

"To give context on why this is important," Raptor

jumped in, "each year the Santa Tracker contains coded information for agents and organizations around the world."

"Yes, some additional history," Colonel Winston said. "The first time we reported Santa's location, in 1948, it was purely a coded message, but it was picked up by the press as a cute story. In 1956, it became established as a way to disseminate sensitive messages in a very public way. There are other key holidays and events around the world that the intelligence community uses for the same purpose. If we don't transmit the expected information, there could be serious repercussions."

"Have you learned anything about what's impacting the site?" Red Hat asked. It made sense for Joanna to ask the first questions since Lorenzo and I worked for her.

"Captain Marlow will provide that briefing." The colonel nodded once at her.

"The site worked normally from 1 December, when we switched to holiday mode. However, when it became Christmas Eve and the site should've gone into tracking mode, a graphic came up with a red X over a fireplace hearth and the words 'Santa is under maintenance.'" The website, showing what Marlow described, replaced the camera feed. "We've been unable to restore the original site. Efforts to trace the source of the hack have yielded nothing helpful."

"What methods have you tried so far?" I asked.

The feed switched back to the conference room as Marlow and Cartwright elaborated. I scribbled notes and Lorenzo did the same in his window. They hadn't missed anything I would've tried.

"You said you've deployed new versions of the site and they end up hacked within seconds. Any idea how they're finding the new location so fast?" I asked once they'd finished.

"Our theories are that they're either locking on to specific text or images or that they've compromised our master code—we're checking on both options."

I nodded as my mind ground on the problem.

"Can you grant us access to your systems so we can review?" Joanna asked.

"Yes," the colonel said. "I'm transmitting that information to Raptor now. We'll have this channel open so you can collaborate with Marlow and Cartwright."

"Are there others working on this as well?" Lorenzo asked.

"No," the colonel said flatly. "The information on this failure is need-to-know."

"Understood," Raptor said. "I've received the access information, and I'm sending that on to Doctor Possible and Winger. Please keep me informed. Colonel, I'll be in touch."

His screen went dark. Had Raptor hung up on the colonel? There had to be a protocol there that I didn't recognize.

"Doc, Winger, if you need anything, let me know," Joanna said. "I'm limiting my knowledge on this at Raptor's request, but don't hesitate to ping me."

"Understood, Red Hat," Lorenzo said. Her screen went dark.

Somehow I'd missed the colonel leaving the conference room. I guessed since Raptor was gone, he planned to leave the fixing to the four of us that remained.

"How do you want to proceed?" Marlow asked.

Time moved way too fast.

Lorenzo and I worked with the two NORAD officers for nearly three hours, and we were as stumped as they were.

There had to be another way to go.

"Can we deploy to a new server and start with clean server logs?" I asked. "The second the new site's deployed and the takeover happens, there has to be something we've missed. Starting fresh would eliminate the noise."

"We can easily deploy to another cloud server, and you can see for yourself what happens," Marlow said.

"Let's do it," I said. "Doc and I will work on that."

"Give us five minutes," Marlow said, "and we'll have what you need. While you're on that angle, we'll see what happens if we roll back time on the server clock."

"Perfect," I said.

A knock on the door signaled I needed to stop for a moment. I hadn't checked in with Mom, and she'd probably be curious if I'd be able to do dinner or anything else tonight. At this point I had no idea, since I had no meaningful progress to report.

"I'm going on mute for a moment. I've got someone at my door. Doc, if you'll establish a link for you and me to work, I'll join you in a moment."

"Will do, Winger."

I muted the transmission and went to the door. Dad's outstretched arms greeted me, and I stepped into the hug.

"I heard about the Code Dark, but I wanted to say hi and let you know I'm home. You doing okay?"

I stepped back from the embrace. "Yeah, I'm fine. Frustrating problem. Looking forward to getting it sorted out so we can get on with Christmas Eve."

"What you're doing is far more important." I shrugged

and nodded. "Dinner'll be ready in about an hour and a half. We'll bring it up to you if we need to so you can at least eat."

It still seemed crazy that we were investigating a hack on Santa Claus. Weirdest holiday thing ever.

"I'll try to be done staving off an international incident before then."

Which was the point, after all, since dinnertime was quite close to the NORAD deadline.

Dad grinned. "That's my boy."

I loved how he could make this seem so everyday. I'd fielded a couple of texts from Eddie, who'd checked in on me to see if I'd get the family time. He wasn't pleased that I didn't know.

"I'll set my timer for ninety minutes so I can text you and let you know how it's going."

"That'll work. But remember, you don't have to rush for us."

"I know. If anybody gets it, you, Mom, and John do. But I'd rather have our time, especially since John flies out on the red-eye tonight."

We traded fist bumps before he headed down the hallway toward the master bedroom.

"And hey, welcome home. I'm glad you're back."

"Me too." He shot me a smile from over his shoulder.

I retreated into my room and closed the door. He'd been deployed somewhere in Africa from what I knew. While he'd finished his mission two days ago, the routes he took to get home to cover his tracks were complicated.

Back at the computers, Lorenzo worked with Marlow as she prepared to launch a new version of the site.

"I've got the log file open, so I'll monitor what happens," Lorenzo said. "We're also recording everything so we have it for the evidence record as well. Please proceed."

"Here it goes," she said. She typed on her keyboard and in mere seconds indicated the site was ready. On the screen Lorenzo shared, he refreshed the browser. Initially the expected Santa Tracker homepage came up, but in fifteen seconds, the hacked screen took over.

"Just to verify," I asked, "this code came out of your repository?"

"Yes," Marlow said.

"Okay, we'll start analyzing," Lorenzo said. "Winger, I'm sending you a copy of what I captured. Captain, we're going on mute until we have findings."

"We'll do the same," she said.

"I don't understand how this system is left so unsecured compared to the rest of NORAD," I said once Lorenzo and I were on private channel. "If it's so important, why isn't it behind security like other government systems?"

"I've wondered that," Lorenzo said as he typed, his furious *clickety-clack* coming over my earbuds. "Unless that's part of the ruse to make this look unimportant."

We pored over the log files and occasionally the site's code. We'd already tested turning off internet access, and it didn't revert to its normal state. Whatever was happening didn't depend on an ongoing internet connection. We also compared code from NORAD's repository with what was on the server.

"Look at line 367," Lorenzo said. "What do you make of that?"

I scrolled to where he was and saw the difference in a script.

He'd found it.

"It's a code injection. But how?"

"Inside job?" Lorenzo asked. "There's a content management system that updates the content based on time zones—not to mention the secret messages. Could be something there?"

One of the wild cards in our investigation involved how the secret messages got put in place. Marlow wouldn't share that information.

"Any traces showing the injection source?" Lorenzo asked.

"No. Let me see if there's anything else this server can tell us.

Stand by."

I updated the logging routine and refreshed the page to see if any traffic other than mine was present.

There was.

Outgoing traffic from the analytics pixel got a response from something I couldn't identify.

I unmuted the NORAD channel. "Lieutenant, can you deploy the code from the repository into a new environment? There are things in the hacked page that I want to compare to a clean install."

"Of course." She typed on her keyboard as she continued to talk.

"You've discovered something?"

"Maybe. The comparison will let me know for sure or not."

"It's done. I've left you the directory information in the chat window."

"Thank you. We'll keep you posted."

I muted that channel.

"What've you got?" Lorenzo asked.

"There's something fishy in the analytics."

"That would be a hell of a security hole—for a lot of sites."

"For sure." I typed silently for a moment. "Two things I want to try. One second."

I went to the off-line code they'd provided and opened another page on the site. Going over to the hacked version, I put in the URL, and the page displayed immediately.

"See that?" I asked. "The only page impacted is the home page. But with it blocked, you can't access the menu to get anywhere else."

"So the hacked site isn't totally compromised. That seems sloppy."

"I don't get it." My voice dripped with frustration as nearly another half hour passed and we were no closer to solving the mystery of hacked Santa.

"What if you deploy your tracker bots and see where they go?

You've got those honed to detect anything."

"I was thinking the same thing." We grinned at each other, because this might be the break we needed.

I opened up my toolbox, quickly refined one to make it more sensitive to injected code, and deployed a fleet of bots.

"Okay," I said after a few minutes. "I'm ready. Access the site."

He clicked with his mouse.

As expected, Lorenzo's screen showed the hacked page within seconds. My monitor showed tons of information the bots collected, far more than I would've anticipated from a single page load.

"Something's definitely coming from the outside. Check out all this from the single click."

On the little window that displayed Lorenzo, his eyes

darted back and forth almost like he was in REM sleep. He read through lines of data almost as fast as I did.

"Wait, there it is." Lorenzo zoomed rows of data on my screen so I could see what he'd found. "I don't know how they did it, but somehow the analytics script is allowing an injection of code. That's why there's the delay. Once the pixel fires, there's the lag for the malicious code to get in place. Do we have the trace on that?"

"We should."

I pulled up another set of data, and the path was clear. The pixel received information back and overwrote the page remotely. That explained why the script had the slight adjustment. Not only did the hack impact NORAD, but anyone who used this analytics platform could be subject to a similar attack.

"I've got the IP address where the injection is coming from, and I'm locating the source."

"I'm notifying the FBI about this breach so they can alert the analytics manufacturer about this exploit," Lorenzo said. "Before we shut this down, we should make sure we can apprehend the person who did this."

"Agreed. I think we can put a stop to it by blocking the incoming code. Let's talk to Marlow and Cartwright. I think we can test the patch quickly." I unmuted the channel to NORAD. "Captain, I believe we've got the issue."

Lorenzo and I gave the officers a quick rundown.

"My trace on the injection has completed," I said as we finished discussion on what had happened. "The origin of the server sending the injection is in a Caltech computer lab and is controlled by someone living in Pasadena."

"Please send us the address. We'll get some officers dispatched immediately."

"We can send TOS agents for backup as well," Lorenzo said.

"No, we'll take care of the hackers. Jurisdiction falls to Homeland."

"Understood. Winger, I need to update Red Hat and Raptor on our findings and that Captain Marlow is sending in a team. I'll return in a few minutes."

"See you back here in a few minutes, Doc."

"I've set you up with clean code on five different hosts so you can run tests. I also need to make an update to the colonel, so I'll leave you with Cartwright. Let's get this wrapped up," Marlow said.

"Of course, Captain."

———

THE FIXES I built tested out perfectly. The Santa Tracker appeared normally for us, and Cartwright verified that the encoded messages were in place.

Once the testing satisfied Cartwright, she made the new site live to the public because we were so close to the deadline. In her view the risk of the hacker escaping was acceptable.

"All right," Cartwright said just as Lorenzo rejoined, "cross your fingers."

She shared her screen, showing the website. I loaded it on two browsers, and so did Lorenzo.

"Unless the hacker has another way in that we didn't find, we should be good." I said that with as much confidence as I could, knowing full well that a crafty hacker could be difficult to beat. In this case, however, with time ticking on both the NORAD deadline and my family's Christmas, I hoped the end was near.

Captain Marlow came back and resumed her seat. "A team should be at the hacker's location in the next two minutes. They're going in with cameras and comms active, so we'll be able to see and provide support.

What's the situation here?"

While Cartwright updated her, Lorenzo texted me in our chat window: *Who do you think is behind this? It seems like something Blackbird would try—international incident on Christmas.*

I responded: *Exactly. They've been too quiet since Denver and so a holiday disruption wouldn't surprise me.*

"Great work, everyone," Marlow said, satisfied with the status.

For the few minutes the Santa Tracker was back online, it appeared to be functioning normally, no page replacements.

"Analytics are working correctly and traffic levels are rising to where we'd expect them for Christmas Eve. People on social media are already commenting that the site's back."

That concerned me, if only because it would give whoever had done this time to escape with evidence or potentially unleash something worse. But that genie couldn't be rebottled.

"I'm patching in video now from the scene," Marlow said.

The feed from the strike team leader's vest cam took over the screen. At least a half dozen voices sounded off as they charged into an apartment complex. The college students looked shocked at the rush of uniformed people into the central courtyard.

"The source is in apartment two eleven," said one of the team.

All the apartments opened into the courtyard. The leader looked up at the second floor and spotted the number before they took off to the stairs.

The team went silent.

Not surprisingly, the few people outside gave the team a wide berth.

In front of the apartment, the person wearing the camera stepped aside and someone with a battering ram stepped up. It took a single swing to splinter the door and knock it off its hinges.

Shrieks came from inside, and as the camera view swung around, we saw a guy and a girl looking for cover. They wore jeans and T-shirts.

"What's going on?" the guy asked, worry in his voice.

The only electronics visible in the living room were a large TV on the wall and two phones on a coffee table. There were magazines and mail scattered around the table as well and a pizza box on the floor.

"Is there anybody else here?" the leader asked.

"Jess is in her room, I think," the woman said. "What's happened?"

The leader turned to a woman. "Cover them." The woman nodded and turned to the couple, who seemed frozen standing in front of the couch.

Without a word, the team moved down the hall.

Two doors were open, and a quick look revealed a dark bathroom and a messy bedroom with a computer on the desk, running a screensaver.

"Check that," the leader said quietly, and one person stepped out of the group and sat at the desk.

The leader turned back to the opposite door, which was closed. His gun flashed on screen as he reached to the doorknob, which was locked.

Without being asked, the battering-ram carrier came forward and destroyed the door.

Another shriek as the camera focused on a woman at a computer with six monitors in front of her. She was decked out in jeans, a red-and-green sweater, and a Santa hat.

The leader leveled his gun at her. "Back away from the keyboard and put your hands up."

She made a couple of keystrokes before she complied. For someone with a gun aimed at her, her expression was quite belligerent.

"I didn't do anything," she said flatly.

Another team member stepped up to her computer. "She's deleting files," she said as she reached over to cancel the delete.

"Can we recover?" Marlow asked.

"Checking," the officer said.

"Sit on the bed, please, miss," the leader said, waving his gun in the direction of the bed.

The room was immaculate and tidy. Everything was orderly, from the books on the shelves, to nothing on the desk but the computer and lamp. Not even a piece of stray laundry was in view. Not like the room across the hall, or even the living room.

"I don't see a way to recover what she's deleted," the officer at the computer said. "She's using a nonstandard delete protocol."

"This is Winger from TOS. Can you please—"

"One second, Winger. We'll get you patched on comms," Cartwright said. She tapped a few keys. "Okay, go ahead."

"This is Winger from Tactical Operational Support. Can you give me access to the computer? If you'll adjust the settings to allow me past her firewall."

"On it," the officer said as she sat down at the keyboard. "Done," she said in just a few seconds.

I already had the IP so getting in with the firewall down was easy.

"I've got access. Give me a moment."

"You can't just sit down at my desk," Jess said. "Do you even have a warrant?"

"We don't need a warrant since this is a matter of national security."

"There's nothing to find, so I'm just gonna get to sue the government for invasion of privacy," she said, crossing her arms over her chest.

She put on a good front. I suspected we already had enough given the traces we ran, to have the necessary evidence, but I suspected I could find more.

I found her logs and the connection she had open to the Caltech computer lab. She'd run a delete there as well, which I stopped. I found data remnants on the Caltech servers. I suspected their protocols wouldn't allow her custom delete function.

I restored everything on the server. The injection code had the unoriginal name of "Santa Hack." I started a copy of the Caltech server to the TOS cloud so it could be passed to Homeland.

"I found what we need," I said to the group on comms. "The log files from her computer show that she executed a delete on the Caltech server. I recovered those files, and I'm downloading everything for evidence. I'm working to see what I can recover from her personal computer before I copy it over as well. Caltech should be notified that the server should be considered evidence."

"Ma'am," the officer in front of Jess's computer relayed as I reported, "we've got the evidence—"

"It was just a prank," Jess said, going from stern to freaked-out in a split second. "I swear that's all it was. I had to prove myself and, you know, messing with Christmas and the government a little bit seemed like a great way to prove that I have skills."

She did have skills. Not only had she done the hack, she'd done a number on her hard drive's directory structure. The logs hadn't yet been deleted, and that was her downfall since all the evidence of her activity was there.

"What's going to happen?" she asked

"We're taking you into custody," the team leader said.

"My family. I'm supposed to go there tonight."

"After we process you, you'll be able to make a call." The leader spoke in a matter-of-fact tone.

"Lieutenant Blake—" I got the name of the leader for the first time— "please transport the prisoner, and once Winger has the files copied, seize the computer. I'll get back to you with further details on if she'll stay in Pasadena or be moved elsewhere."

"Yes, Captain."

"Winger, Doctor Possible, we thank you very much for your assistance. I think we've got this now. Cartwright, one last check. Is the site good?"

Cartwright tapped keys as she reviewed a screen. "Yes, ma'am. Everything's normal. I'll continue to monitor to make sure everything triggers as needed."

"Very good." Marlow smiled. I was glad she got to break the cool façade she'd worn the past several hours. "Winger, once you get those files to us, you can go enjoy the holiday. You as well, Doctor Possible."

"I'll get you the link to download from our secure server as soon as they're all in place," I said. "I hope you and Lieutenant Cartwright also get to enjoy some of the holiday."

"Thank you," Marlow said before she cut the connection.

I immediately called Lorenzo and provided the secure greeting.

"Well, that was a way to spend Christmas Eve," Lorenzo said. "I don't think I would've ever imagined having to fix the Santa Tracker."

"Right? I kinda thought somebody was pulling a big holiday prank.

Glad we got it done in time, though."

"I guess we literally saved Christmas. Not only did we prevent the whole international incident, but kids won't miss out on Santa's location."

"All in a day's work for TOS IT. You got anything special going on tonight?"

"I gotta head out to my brother's. He and his wife are hosting. My parents left a bit ago."

"Nice room, by the way. Looks like you're in an attic."

"Yeah, this used to be my room—though you'd never know it since my dad converted it to a man cave. At least it provided a good place to get out of earshot while we worked."

"Nice. I love that we're both in our rooms." We shared a laugh.

"I'll let you get going. Have a great Christmas. Hopefully we don't talk again until New Year's... unless it's to spend some time in Azaroth."

"Agreed. Merry Christmas, Winger."

"Merry Christmas, Doc."

I hung up and quickly texted Mom and Dad to tell them I'd join them within the next ten minutes. Before I headed out of my room, I wanted the file copies sent to the captain so this would officially be wrapped. While I waited on the copy, I texted Eddie to let him know I was finished. He quickly responded with two emojis: a smiley face and a Christmas tree.

As soon as I walked out of my room, the aroma from the kitchen hit. I regretted the work had kept me from being able to cook with Mom, Dad, and John, but I'm glad they went ahead.

Traditional Christmas Eve dinner became Belgian waffles, sausage, and maple-filled doughnuts before I was born. Mom had returned super late on Christmas Eve from a mission, and she and Dad went out to a diner. This meal was what they ate.

Rather than going out, we made the waffles, sausage, and whipped cream ourselves and picked up a dozen doughnuts from Dunkin'. None of us wanted to figure out how to make filled donuts since it seemed like we'd end up with a tremendous mess.

As I arrived in the kitchen, Dad took waffles off the iron. They looked awesome in all their golden-brown goodness. Mom worked at the stove with the sausage, which was typically my job.

"What can I do? It looks like everything's almost done."

"You're just in time. One more batch and then we're ready." Dad precisely added batter so it wouldn't spill out the sides when he closed the lid. That proved to be my kryptonite and why I didn't make the waffles, because too much batter ended up on the counter.

"If you want to get the fruit ready and warm the syrup, that'll be perfect," Mom said.

I got the berries from the fridge. The strawberries had

been sliced earlier so they could do their thing in sugar to make good syrup. I rinsed blueberries and blackberries and put them into bowls. The strawberries went into another. We didn't often care if the serving dishes matched, but it was Christmas, so we went more formal.

We'd ordered Vermont maple syrup special. It'd go with the waffles tonight and make a reappearance at breakfast, which would be a feast since we cooked practically every possible breakfast food for Christmas. We'd prepare so much that it would also become lunch.

I poured the syrup into a saucepan and set it on a medium heat.

"I thought I heard you in here," John said as he entered from the dining room. He must've been setting the table. "Are you done for the night?"

"I should be. Lorenzo and I saved the world, or so we were led to believe."

"Not a bad thing to do on Christmas Eve," Mom said, looking over her shoulder and giving me a warm smile.

"I agree. And even better that we finished in time for all this." I gestured around the kitchen. "I'm glad the smell couldn't get through my door, because that would've been torture."

"Don't say that too loud," John said. "You don't want your enemies finding out the way to break you is with sausage and waffles."

John and I chuckled.

"John! Don't say things like that." Mom didn't see the humor.

I went to Mom, put an arm around her, and laid my head against her shoulder while making sure I didn't disrupt her cooking. "It's okay."

"No, it's not. There's nothing funny about it," she said sternly. "You both know better."

"Your mom's right," Dad said. "Some things shouldn't be a joke."

John held his hands up. "You're right, of course. Sorry."

The doorbell rang, which was odd since we weren't expecting anybody. Anyone who knew us would be aware this was family time. It provided a good escape from the kitchen, though, to let the tension evaporate.

"I'll get it," I said. "Keep an eye on the syrup, please."

"On it," John said.

The bell rang again as I quickly rinsed off my hands that had become a little sticky with the berries and syrup. I took the hand towel with me to dry off since whoever it was seemed a little bit impatient. I looked through the peephole and found someone dressed in an Army dress uniform, which was oddly punctuated by a Santa hat.

"Yes? Can I help you?" I asked as I opened the door. The guy holding a red box appeared barely older than I was.

The officer looked at his cell phone and back to me. "Oh good, you're Winger." He showed me the phone screen that had an image of me from the earlier video chat. "That makes this less weird, I guess." He held out the box. "Captain Marlow requested I get this to you as quickly as possible."

I took it and examined it. There was no writing on the package, which was about the size of the box the dozen donuts had come in. It also wasn't heavy, although there was slightly more weight on one of the corners.

"Thank you, sir. Merry Christmas to you and the captain as well."

The officer nodded before returning to his dark sedan in the driveway. I noticed a person in the driver's seat.

I closed the door and headed back to the kitchen, where everyone carried dishes to the table.

"You got a present?" Mom asked as she came over and studied the box.

"What is it?" Dad asked as he passed with a platter of waffles.

"I've no idea." I went to the counter, put the box down, and pulled at the tape that sealed the top down the middle. It wouldn't budge. Mom handed over a knife. I stabbed into the top and ran it down so I could get my hands in to pull the sides open. A red envelope sat on top of a green sweatshirt. A coffee mug nested in a corner.

Mom, Dad, and John gathered around, and given this was from the captain, I wondered if they should see it since there were national security concerns over the work I'd done. Nothing indicated this was secret, though. I opened the envelope, which wasn't sealed, and pulled out a card that had Santa in his sled flying through the air with his reindeer. The card read: *Merry Christmas from everyone at NORAD Santa Tracker HQ.* Marlow and Cartwright had signed the card.

The adults traded looks. They had to know this related to what had occupied me.

I pulled out the sweatshirt and unfurled it to find the same Santa and reindeer that had been on the card and under it a "NORAD Tracks Santa" logo. The same logo had been at the top of the website.

The red-and-green striped coffee mug had the same graphic on both sides. It was a nice thank-you present. And it didn't even betray that I'd done anything directly for them since the card simply wished Merry Christmas.

"So you weren't kidding about saving Christmas?" Mom asked with the closest thing I'd ever seen to her smirking.

I nodded and pulled the sweatshirt over the T-shirt I had on because it was the perfect thing to wear for Christmas Eve. "Let's eat before all this yummy stuff gets cold?"

We took our seats in the dining room. We'd already decorated in here earlier. The green with red trim table runner was down the middle, and the Christmas center-piece of holly and berries along with red and green cylinder candles were in place. A small tree with multicolored lights sat on the sideboard. The living room tree would go up after we ate.

"I didn't think this would be the year that it could be you who'd miss part of Christmas," Mom said. "It's possible you're growing up too fast."

"And I thought *I* was going to miss it," Dad said. "If I'd ended up snowed in in Maine, I would've been... extremely unhappy." I held back a laugh as Dad edited his language.

"I'm just glad it all worked out," I said, filling my plate with food. "It may not go on this way too much longer."

I didn't get sentimental often, but the holidays did it to me. We were an odd family in many ways because of what we did, so times like this were important.

We dug into the food and talked about school, hockey, what John looked forward to with his parents tomorrow, what we hoped to find under the tree, and how fun it would be if we could coordinate a trip to get Christmas magic at Disney World some year.

ONCE WE GOT the kitchen cleaned up, we piled into the living room.

This prelit tree thing turned out to be brilliant. I'd been skeptical when Mom had brought home a new tree. We'd always done fake trees because they were tidier and easier to deal with, but with the lights already in, it seemed like a cop-out. I'd enjoyed making sure the tree had the right balance of light all the way around.

With the lights done, though, it meant I could start my second favorite thing—making sure the beaded garland fell just right. The swoops on each level had to be even, and going up to the next level had to be a gradual rise and not an abrupt jump up.

We all had our tasks. Dad loved managing icicle placement after everything was on, while Mom placed the key ornaments in the right places. There were decorations—like the ones celebrating their first holiday together, my first, as well as the Twelve Days of Christmas ornaments—that had set places. She made sure they got there. John enjoyed doing whatever was needed, but he also snapped candid pictures. Every year he managed to get some priceless images—like Dad icicling Mom from two years ago, or me at age seven covered in tinsel.

We had *A Christmas Story* playing. It became our holiday go-to movie a few years back when we caught it on some channel that played it for twenty-four hours straight. The BB gun incident, getting stuck to the pole, and the way they lost their Christmas dinner were priceless moments that we paused to watch. Mom and I even got Dad a leg-lamp ornament.

As I finished getting the beads just right, Mom, Dad, and John had the ornaments laid out, grouped by color. We always had a color plan, and this year we were trying for a rainbow of color, going from purple at the top to red at the bottom.

Mitch had come over a couple of years ago for tree trimming, and he didn't understand why we didn't just put the ornaments on the tree randomly. He knew I had particular ways I did some things, but he didn't realize that extended to my parents and decorating. I appreciated trees that had an explosion of random ornaments, but I liked how our tree was distinctly us.

"Did you finish your gift for Eddie?" Dad asked. "Aren't you giving that to him tonight?"

"Yep, everything is good to go. As soon as he starts getting ready for bed, I'll get notified and everything will start. I picked up the key and got the alarm code from his mom yesterday. So as long as he's not freaked out that I'm suddenly in his house, it'll all be good." I grinned at them.

I'd figured out the perfect gift for Eddie based on things I'd learned last year during our first Christmas. I hoped he liked it.

"I'm sure he'll love it. A homemade gift is always perfect." Mom looked a little misty-eyed at that thought. I'd been a typical grade school kid, so they'd both received a lot of things I'd made—they looked ridiculous now, but they could still make Mom and Dad reminisce about elementary school. Several of those were going on the tree tonight.

What I'd done for Eddie was about as homemade as it gets for me these days, since I did most of it on the computer.

"Try not to stay out too late tonight," Dad said. "You want to make sure you're asleep before Santa gets here." He winked.

"I should have a pretty good in with Santa, so I'm not

too worried about that." I smirked as I pointed at the sweatshirt. That got me the eyerolls I expected.

We had our tree-trimming system down, and it took exactly as long as the movie to get it done. It looked fantastic—colorful, sparkly, magical.

Once we tidied up, we plopped down on the couch with hot chocolate and popcorn mixed with M&M's and Reese's Pieces. Animated Christmas specials were on tap, starting with Charlie Brown. Instead of going until we fell asleep this year, we were either calling it a night when John had to go to the airport—he had a red-eye to get to his parents in Boise by morning—or when I had to leave for Eddie's.

The chirp from my phone sounding as the fifth special ended brought the night to a close.

"Outstanding evening as always," John said as he stood up.

"Make sure you tell your parents Merry Christmas from us," Mom said.

"And don't forget to take these." Dad got a large bag from behind the tree.

John's mouth formed an O. "Guys, you shouldn't have." He took the bag and didn't look inside, where we had gifts for him and his parents.

"Yeah, we did, because it's not like you haven't left some pretty large things under the tree you didn't think we'd notice," I said. "Hope you have a good trip." I gave him a backslapping hug and then we traded an explosive fist bump.

I gave Mom and Dad quick hugs too.

"Make sure to hug Eddie for us," Mom said as I headed upstairs.

"Will do."

Mom and Dad walked John out, and I went to my room for a quick change and to pick up my backpack that contained everything I needed.

Once I got in the car, I triggered the secret app I'd left on Eddie's phone a couple of days ago. A five-minute countdown began, which would give me a head start before he'd get the message to start the app. It also gave him time to get back to his room. His norm was to put his phone on the charging dock on his nightstand, brush his teeth and whatnot in the bathroom, and then come back and either read or watch TV from the bed. The phone would play sleigh bells every thirty seconds after the five mark to get his attention.

Traffic was light—not surprising given the holiday evening—so I got to his house in seven minutes. His room faced the backyard, so he wouldn't see my car approach. I still parked down the block and across the street just in case he was by a window he shouldn't be.

The lights from his house—they used the old-school large bulbs—lit up the front yard in multicolored splendor. The edges of the house, along with the molding around the windows, the front door, and even the sides running up the roof line, were ablaze. I'd helped Eddie hang those at the beginning of the month, and neither of us appreciated the ladder work that had to be done to hit the peak of the roof. But it was the way his house was always done, and he wanted to do it even though his dad had only wanted to do the front this year.

At the door, I quietly turned the lock and slipped inside, darting quickly to the alarm panel to punch in the code.

Luckily it wasn't like ours that chirped with each button push, because that would have given me away.

The Christmas tree was aglow in the living room.

My watch vibrated to let me know that Eddie had tapped the app and begun the video. It would only be a few minutes before he came downstairs—provided he followed instructions.

As quietly as I could, I laid out the things I brought— Christmas cookies I'd made with Mom yesterday, several containers of frosting in different colors, plastic knives to spread with, cans of icing that could be used for writing or piping, a thermos of hot chocolate made fresh before we started trimming the tree, and the book that would be his present.

I stowed the backpack behind the big recliner that stood adjacent to the tree. I sat down there and waited with the book in my lap. The chair faced the staircase, giving me the perfect view of him coming down.

I fought the urge to keep checking how far along he was. I'd get a notification when he finished. There'd also be a ping if he abandoned the video early. That would certainly be the indication that I'd picked the wrong gift. I had no doubt, though, that this was going to be pretty epic.

Time passed so slowly.

Finally hearing footsteps moving quickly down the stairs made my heart thump in my chest like a bongo drum.

I resisted the urge to meet him because I wanted him to come fully into the living room to see the spread as well as me in the chair.

He looked into the room before he got to the bottom of the stairs. His smile caught the light just right and made him look dazzling as the colors played off his eyes.

From the surprised look, you'd think he'd spotted Santa

Claus. I thought I might explode from seeing all the wonder and love radiating from him.

"Oh my God. Theo…. How did you…? This is like the best…. How are you even…? Come here."

The grin never left his face as he came toward me. I got up, left the book in the chair, and met him for the biggest hug ever. I thought he was going to squish me as he lifted me off my feet. He finally set me down and peppered my forehead and face with so many kisses.

"It's the best Christmas ever. Just amazing." He held me as he talked. "And what's all this?"

"You told me the best part of storytime was getting to frost cookies and have hot chocolate to get ready for Santa. I couldn't leave those out. I know I'm not your grandmother, but I hope this might be the next best thing."

"It's so perfect." A tear escaped from his eye, and I brushed it away with my thumb. "She'd love that someone did all this for me."

Last year we'd talked about Christmas traditions. While I'd laid out all mine, his story was about one that he missed. His grandmother had passed a couple of years ago, and when they'd visited her for the holidays, they had a Christmas Eve routine. They'd read *'Twas The Night Before Christmas* and then frost a special batch of cookies for Santa while they drank hot chocolate.

Eddie remembered it with such a fondness tinged with sadness that I was determined to find a way to recreate it. He showed me pictures from childhood Christmases, and one of them showed him sitting on his grandmother's lap while she read. I'd asked Mrs. Cochrane to show me that picture again a few months ago because I wanted to try to find the exact edition of the book. Since you can buy everything on eBay, I was able to find it.

"This is yours too." I stepped out of the hug and got the book.

"You'll have it to read to your kids one day."

He took the book and stared at the Santa on the cover. A couple more tears fell. "I have no idea how you got this." He flipped through the pages. "It's exactly like the one she had. I saw it in the video, but I had no idea you bought it. I thought it might've come from the library or something. You, by the way, did an amazing job with the reading. I almost watched it again before I came down here, but I didn't want to keep my personal Santa waiting."

Mitch had helped me record the video, and then it was just a matter of editing to show off the pictures from the book as I read. Eddie had talked about loving the drawings, so those had to be in the video.

I stepped up into him and kissed his lips. "Your Santa appreciates that you came right down."

He clenched the book to his chest, much like he'd been hugging me earlier. We stared at each other for a few moments.

I'd had no idea, Eddie being my first boyfriend, how much his looks of love could make me so insanely happy. I hoped I gave him the same back. I didn't think he could look at me like he did if his feelings weren't strong.

"Soooooo," Eddie said, "do you think we've got time to do the cookies before Santa gets here?"

I held down a laugh. Given everything I'd gone through earlier, asking me if we had time before Santa's arrival struck me as hilarious.

"Well, I'm sure he'd understand if we were running late. I hear he makes special dispensation for boyfriends who are in the middle of giving each other presents."

"Oh really?" Eddie asked with a tone that sent shivers

up my spine because it was so mischievous. "Since when do you have the direct line to Santa?"

"Well, you know I can't talk about my clients, but...." That quip I could get away with.

He locked his sparkly eyes on mine for a moment before he busted out a laugh that he very quickly softened. He didn't want to wake his mother.

"You are such a goofball, and I love you for it." He gently put the book on the coffee table, took my hand, and led me around to the couch so we could sit next to each other while we decorated.

"So who do I have to thank for the cookies?" he asked as he helped open the containers.

"Mom and I baked yesterday, and she helped me make the frosting before the game this morning."

"Wow. I know you helped your family cook for the big meals, but I never imagined you making cookies. You must really like me or something." As he said that last bit, he leaned in close, sort of nudged his face into my cheek, and planted a kiss.

"Oh, and I have proof." I pulled my phone from my pocket and showed him the selfies we took along with some that Mom snapped. There were ones of me mixing the dough, rolling it out, of both of us using the cookie cutters, and of me coloring the frosting. "See, I can be a chef."

"More accurately, the pastry chef," he said. "These pictures are everything. You're gonna send me these, right? I need to keep them with all the stuff that relates to this amazing gift. Maybe I can get Mitch to make a calendar out of those too."

I tapped on the phone screen, and in a moment his phone buzzed in the pocket of his sweats. He pulled it out and tapped.

"There, now you've got them." I set my phone on the table in front of us. "I can't believe he made that for you."

"I'm glad he did. I'll have that hot image with me forever."

I groaned.

"What?" He took my hand in his. "You are hot," he said softly.

"Shall we get to frosting?" I said, betrayed by a small squeak in my voice.

"For sure." He took a knife, grabbed a tree, and started spreading frosting. Thank God he let that moment go.

I'd brought two dozen cookies, and Eddie proved to be quite the artist between using the frosting we'd whipped up along with some of the finer tips from the canned frosting. Compared to his, my cookies looked like grade-school drawings.

We frosted cookies and ate some while we drank hot chocolate and traded stories of favorite childhood Christmases.

He said the best gift he ever got was a NERF arm blaster from the *Transformers* movie. Apparently he became quite the terror, shooting at everyone that winter.

He looked at me a little suspect when I told him that my favorite was when I was ten and got the most high-powered PC on the market. That computer eventually led me down the path where I am today, including perpetrating the hack on my parent's phones the next summer.

"We should grab a couple of pictures to mark tonight," Eddie said.

Eddie was a pro at the selfies, in no small part because of his long reach. He snapped a picture of us holding a couple of our cookie creations.

We also took pictures with mugs of cocoa while

standing in front of the tree, and I took one of him hugging the book to his chest. I made sure I had a copy of that one because of how overwhelmingly happy he looked.

The last picture was one of us kissing in front of the tree. I don't know how that one turned out as good as it did because neither of us looked at the camera when he took it. Somehow he held the camera just right to snap it.

This would go down as one of the best Christmases ever. Not only—in the weirdest turn of events ever—did I have a hand saving Christmas, but I'd spent a wonderful evening with my family and then my incredible boyfriend.

I didn't know if it could get any better, but I already looked forward to next year to see if anything could top it.

ACKNOWLEDGEMENTS

Codename: Winger was born at GayRomLit 2014 in Chicago. My husband, Will Knauss, and I were talking with fellow authors Z.A. Maxfield and Clare London about writing careers. As we talked, I started to hatch the idea for the character that would become Theo. Another element from Chicago—someone had a *Kim Possible* ringtone on their phone. I never found out who that was, but my love of that teenage heroine played a role in Theo's creation. My thanks to Will, Zam, Clare, and the unknown ringtone owner for sparking my imagination.

I had a lot of fun writing Theo, and there are some key people to thank for helping me get this book right. Aaron, Brian, Chris, Dawn, Elvis, Laura, Macy, Michael. They provided editorial guidance, feedback and support. Each helped make Theo's first adventure better.

Aaron Anderson is responsible for the cool, mysterious cover design for the series, so a huge thanks to him for giving this series its look.

Kirt Graves is a recent addition to the *Winger* family. I am beyond excited that he wanted to bring Theo's adventures to audio. He voices many of my favorite books and to have him giving life to these stories is amazing and I'm very thankful to him.

A Very Winger Christmas is inspired by my favorite *Kim Possible* episode. "A Very Possible Christmas" features Kim's best friend, Ron, trying to handle a mission solo so Kim doesn't miss out on her family's Christmas traditions. It's a must-watch special each season alongside classics like *A Charlie Brown Christmas*, *How the Grinch Stole Christmas!*, *Rudolph the Red-Nosed Reindeer*, and others.

I've wanted to give Theo a holiday story since I conceived this series and I had a blast writing this short.

Most importantly, thank you for picking up this book. I hope you enjoy this first installment in the *Codename: Winger* series. There's more to come—three more books to be exact. Theo has a lot to do!

I'd love to hear what you think of this story, so feel free to drop me an email at jeff@jeffadamswrites.com to let me know.

MISSION PREVIEW

SCHOOLED

CODENAME: WINGER #2

CHAPTER ONE

THE BELL RINGING for lunch was the best sound ever. My stomach grumbled as I put my economics book and tablet into my backpack and headed for the door. It took a lot of restraint not to push my way through my classmates who were way too slow.

It sounded like there was a monster in my belly. Coach had put the team on a new training regimen when we returned from holiday break two weeks ago. He designed it to improve our stamina for the second half of the hockey season. The side effects were muscle pain, occasional leg cramps if I didn't cool down properly, and an appetite that turned me into a ravenous beast.

In the hall, I moved quickly, weaving around my classmates like I was avoiding defensemen on the ice.

Eddie was right on time, as always, at the intersection of the science and English wings. He shouldered his messenger bag, fell in step next to me, and interlocked his fingers with mine.

"How's my favorite hockey player?" We slowed down just enough for him to kiss me on the cheek. With the swim season under way, he looked forward to lunch as much as I did.

"I'm good now that I'm with my favorite swimmer." I gave his hand an extra squeeze.

"Theo Reese," Mrs. Hollingsworth called from behind. "A moment, please?"

This was not a good time to consult with the computer-science teacher. I'd been in her advanced class for three days when I was a freshman, and we had quickly determined that I already knew her curriculum. We became friends, though, and we often chatted about technology. I enjoyed her spin on the latest and admired that she kept up, even though she taught pretty basic stuff to most of her students.

"Doesn't she know it's lunchtime?" Eddie asked.

"How often do teachers care about that?" I didn't let Eddie go, and we cut across the crowd to get to her. "Hey, Mrs. H," I said when we got to her classroom doorway.

"I know you're on your way to lunch, and I promise I won't keep you long. I wanted to float something by you." She turned from me to Eddie. "Could we speak alone?"

"Go on. I'll catch up to you." I let Eddie's hand go. "Can you get me a chicken sandwich?"

"Sure can. Try not to get lost in a lot of tech talk." He grinned at me. He wasn't wrong; this kind of discussion was my weakness.

He raised his cute eyebrows at me before he dashed off to join the lunch line.

Mrs. H stepped into her room and I followed. "The computer-science club has a competition in two weeks and it involves cyber security. Each team comes to the competition with a file that contains a secure document. In turn, the other teams have to try and crack the encryption. I know security is a specialty of yours, and I wondered if I could persuade you to come in and look at our work, offer advice —" She hesitated for a moment and that was weird. "—and travel with the team to consult on-site."

Wow. This was completely unexpected. I knew the club worked on some advanced projects and competed occasionally, but I didn't know they got into stuff like this. I didn't expect to be invited to participate, and I suspected I could crack their projects in my sleep.

"Doesn't the club usually meet when I'm off campus?" The proposal intrigued me, but I enjoyed afternoons at MIT where I took classes that challenged me. "I'm not sure I could swing that since the semester's just started."

She looked sheepishly at the floor. "I might have gotten clearance from Dr. Shorofsky. He said he'd consider it to be credit toward your lab assignments since it's only a couple of weeks."

"Um. Okay." I didn't know quite what to say. "How'd you even know who to ask?"

"I've got connections." Based on the devious look in her eye, I decided not to ask more. I had my ways to get information and I shouldn't be surprised she did too.

"I can work with the team on what they've developed and point them in the right direction to increase the security. I wouldn't feel right consulting on-site. I'd be a...."

"A ringer, to borrow one of your sports metaphors. Yes, you probably would be." She guided me farther into the classroom. "There's a quarter-million-dollar prize for this competition—half goes to the school, a quarter goes to the club, and the rest splits up among the students to use for college. It will be cutthroat among the teams. Imagine what this program could become with that money, not to mention the cash the individuals would have for their college funds.

The team is doing good work, and I'm not asking you to do any for them. Like you suggested—hack what they create and guide them to make it better. During the competition, you could make sure they're going in the right direction."

"Ah, Mr. Reese, there you are," Coach Daly said.

Why was everyone calling me from behind today? I wanted some lunch and time with my man. But for Coach to look for me now—that wasn't a good sign.

"Mrs. Hollingsworth, do you mind if I borrow him?"

The plea in her eyes surprised me. This was super important to her.

"Of course." She looked to Coach for a moment before her gaze settled on me.

"I'll think about it," I said, which caused her to exhale. Had she seriously held her breath? "I'll come back before I leave today."

"Thank you. I'll share more details then."

She seemed relieved. I had no idea she had such a competitive streak. I'd never been asked to consult for the team before.

Coach gestured for me to follow. The hall didn't have much traffic since nearly everyone was at lunch.

"We're headed to my office," he murmured. "You haven't responded to some urgent texts."

"I turn my phone on when I get to the cafeteria. Mr. Moore is crazy about phones in class, and I don't take chances with detention."

"Maybe you can find a solution so you can be notified and still be stealth?"

Being out of touch for an hour for class or a couple hours for a game had never been an issue, though Tactical Operational Support could need me at some pretty odd hours. Something must've gone wrong.

While we walked, I fired up my phone since Coach couldn't give me details.

"You have your computer with you?"

"Of course."

"Good."

"Details?"

"It's above my clearance. If they've asked me to find you during the school day, it's got to be major."

We moved fast. It wasn't a run, but anyone watching might think we'd taken up power walking. I scrolled through texts from Lorenzo, but none of those offered details. I messaged him back: *Stand by. Getting secured.*

Once we got to Coach's office, I got to work. I pulled out my laptop and booted it up. I grabbed earbuds from my pack, jammed them into my ears and called Lorenzo Davenport, my main contact in TOS IT. I logged in to the TOS network as fast as I could.

"I'll leave you to this." Coach opened one of his desk drawers and pulled out a protein bar that he dropped on the desk. "In case you miss lunch completely."

"Thanks." I pointed at my ears to indicate my call connected. Coach nodded and left the office. "Doctor Possible, Winger here." I used the mandatory TOS greeting. Even after all these years, it never got old using my codename.

"Winger, glad D-Man found you. We've got a critical situation."

"Tell me."

"The mission Keys went on has gone very wrong," Lorenzo said, stress evident in his voice. That rarely happened. "We believe she's dead. That leaves Cocoon as the sole person on a keyboard, and she doesn't have the needed skills. We've got to plug you in and hope you can finish the decryption so she can complete the mission."

This was catastrophic. Claire, or Keys, was TOS's chief cryptologist and security expert. She didn't go into the field often. But, just as I had gone out to stop the hack on TOS's tracker chips, she would've been the best choice to masquerade as part of a hacking duo—especially if the agent had no skills. Knowing she might be gone saddened me. She was a friend and mentor.

"Where do I need to log in?" My voice quivered. I knew no one would judge the emotions, especially Lorenzo.

"Cocoon is on a laptop with the new undetectable network connection. I've already patched you in."

The undetectable network was one of the coolest things we'd deployed recently. It worked over wired and wireless connections in 94.3 percent of the test cases we'd run. It meant we could be on agents' computers almost anywhere without being detected by the host network, even if the computer itself was in use by someone else.

"Cocoon, Doctor Possible here," Lorenzo said. "I've got Winger connected to your laptop and comm channel."

"Don't be foolish like your partner. Finish the job." The male voice was distant but harsh, and I couldn't quite place his accent.

A new window opened on my screen, pushed to me by Lorenzo. I saw the strings of encryption from Cocoon's computer. This was hard-core security, on the level that protected the TOS network and other highly sensitive networks, like the defense department.

"This is complex work, and if I do the wrong thing, they're going to know I'm in here." Cocoon sounded frayed but not out of control. It could be an act for the people in the room with her. I'd never worked with Cocoon before, but other agents often played the part of being distressed to buy time.

"Cocoon, Winger here. I've got control over your computer. In case they're watching, keep typing because my keystrokes will display on your screen."

"Winger, Keys has done a lot of the work." Lorenzo quickly told me what Keys had done. This system was indeed complex if she'd already been working for a couple hours and wasn't in yet. Keys and I challenged each other often, so I knew firsthand the difficulty in designing something she couldn't break.

"Got it. Thanks, Doc."

I scanned the code and deployed some of the programs I'd designed to help me crack systems. I had ideas, based on what Keys had done, but I wasn't sure if I could get through the security if she couldn't.

I focused, worked through what I had in front of me, and used the information my programs provided.

Time seemed to speed by. I stole a look at the clock in the corner of my screen, and I'd already been at this for nearly forty-five minutes. How long would the people with Cocoon wait for this hack?

One of my programs popped up a notification that it found a potential exploit. I strengthened my programs based on things I learned, and it was exciting anytime they discovered a weakness.

"I think I've found something. Cocoon stop typing and just read the screen. I'll let you know when to start again." I worked quickly to read through the code the program had found.

Keys and I played this game often—see who could crack a code puzzle the fastest without running into traps and, possibly, destroying the encrypted information.

"Doc, what are we breaking into here?"

"It's need-to-know. For what it's worth, Keys and I don't know either. Cocoon will confirm when it's open, and I'll deploy malicious code to destroy it once she's clear."

"Understood."

Okay, blindly forward. Not the best way to work, but sometimes necessary.

There were a couple of possible exploits and I went to work on those. I let Cocoon know she should appear to be in deep thought and to resume typing.

I found a continuously changing password. It reset every twenty seconds.

And that was the key. I needed to force it to always use the same password so Cocoon could authenticate and unlock the system.

I looked around the host server to see what routines were actively processing—only 336. I created a quick script to show me what had a processing pattern.

It took less than a minute to find it—a table accessed at twenty-second intervals. The password had to come from there. The table, of course, had its own encryption. The routine that fetched the new password, however, had what I needed. The decryption code was there.

"Think I've got it," I said. "Stand by."

It only took another five minutes and I pulled out an upcoming password and rewrote the system to only use the one I'd picked.

"Okay. I've got the password." I read it out to Cocoon and told her I'd locked the system so she wouldn't have to worry about access.

"Well done, Winger," Lorenzo said.

"Gentlemen, it's done." She sounded confident with the

job complete. Hopefully the people she was with would approve.

"Let me see," said a man's faint voice. "Looks good," the same voice said after a few minutes.

I couldn't see the output. They must be logged in on a different machine.

"I'm downloading a copy for our analysis," Lorenzo quietly said. "Also adding our virus so the information is destroyed on your mark, Cocoon. Winger, you can sign off. Please contact me for a debrief this evening."

Lorenzo was my boss, so I wasn't going to ask further questions. "Understood. Let me know if you need anything else. Winger out."

I hung up, grabbed the protein bar from the desk, unwrapped it, and took a bite before I closed the laptop. I couldn't believe Keys might be dead. I leaned back in Coach's chair and closed my eyes while I chewed on the bar and tried to let the adrenaline drain away. I'd have to come up with a cover for why I didn't meet Eddie for lunch.

Suddenly the office door burst open and slammed shut. Startled, I fumbled getting to my feet.

Shit. A dude all in black, including a ski mask. What the hell? Talk about vintage bad guy. How'd he get in here? This school is secure as a fortress.

"Finally, Winger. We've wanted you for a long time now." The voice was low and menacing.

He rushed me before I could process that he'd used my codename. I assessed my options, and I didn't have many with the desk in front of me and the wall behind. My adrenaline surged. I wasn't going down without a fight.

I jumped up on the desk, sending papers flying to the floor. The guy grabbed at my legs and I kicked him square in the chest, which slammed him into the wall. A couple of framed pictures fell, shattering glass.

I used that moment to jump down and throw a right hook. He blocked the right, but I nailed him in the ribs with my left. His "oof" let me know I'd connected pretty well.

He shoved me back against the desk and I stumbled. His one-two punch struck me below the ribs and under my chin.

Out of nowhere he produced a knife and pinned me against the desk. The dude's eyes through the mask were crazed. I reached behind, grabbed the edge of the laptop, and swung the computer to knock the knife out of the attacker's hand. After getting both hands on the computer, I swung back as he grabbed his injured hand.

"Winger! Pepperoni!" I froze, laptop midair ready to come down. He'd used the secret word. "It's D-Man."

"What the hell, Coach?" I lowered the laptop slowly while he stripped off the mask.

"Remember I told you that you could be tested at any time." He grinned like he'd won a prize.

"You're sending me out of here with a bruised chin." I rubbed where his fist had impacted in an effort to dull the pain. "What'll people think?"

"Maybe you took a puck to the face this morning and the impact left a bruise despite your helmet. You're a hockey player, no one will give it a second thought." He pulled the sweatshirt over his head, revealing the long-sleeve henley he'd been in before. "You did good. Up on the desk to give yourself options was a great choice. Those box jumps you're doing for stamina came in handy. And you want to talk bruises? I'll feel that kick in the chest for days."

Over the holidays Coach Daly and John, who worked with my parents and me on TOS assignments, had taught me some self-defense moves. After what I went through last fall during the tracker system hack, I wanted to know how to take care of myself better in case I ever needed to again.

I leaned against the desk and clutched the laptop while I calmed down. I laughed. It burst out of nowhere and it wouldn't stop.

"Theo?" Coach sounded like he wasn't quite sure what to do with my outburst.

"Come on, it's funny." I gasped for air. "I kicked you into a wall and it was okay. How many students get to do that to a teacher?"

***

Winger's missions continue with *Schooled*
Available in ebook, paperback and audiobook

This excerpt is Copyright © 2018 by Jeff Adams

Jeff Adams has written stories since he was in middle school and became a published author in 2009 when his first short stories were published. He writes both gay romance and LGBTQ+ young adult fiction...and there's usually a hockey player at the center of the story.

Jeff lives in central California with his husband of more than twenty years, Will. Some of his favorite things include the musicals *Rent* and [*title of show*], the Detroit Red Wings and Pittsburgh Penguins hockey teams, and the reality TV competition *So You Think You Can Dance*. He, of course, loves to read, but there isn't enough space to list out his favorite books.

Jeff and Will are also podcasters. The *Big Gay Fiction Podcast* is a weekly show devoted to gay romance as well as pop culture. New episodes come out every Monday at BigGayFictionPodcast.com.

Learn more about Jeff, his books and find his social media links at JeffAdamsWrites.com.